TOM GRAHAM

A Fistful of Knuckles

T0312496

HARPER

HarperCollins*Publishers*
77–85 Fulham Palace Road,
Hammersmith, London W6 8JB

www.harpercollins.co.uk

Published by HarperCollinsPublishers 2013

A Fistful of Knuckles

Cover image produced with the kind permission of John Simm and Philip Glenister.

Tom Graham asserts the moral right to
be identified as the author of this work

A catalogue record for this book
is available from the British Library

ISBN: 978-0-00-753648-1

CHAPTER ONE

WORLD OF SPORT

Sam Tyler stood alone on the high roof of the CID building, the uncaring wind roaring in from across the city and battering him.

That's where I'm going to die, he thought. Right down there.

Inching forward, he peered over.

An eight storey drop. The cold air rushing over me as I fall. Glimpses of sky, of glass, of buildings out there on the horizon, flashing by as I fall – and then the shattering impact as I slam into the concrete.

Sam found himself edging his feet further over the brink, as if the abyss was drawing him into itself.

Thirty-three years from now, I'll run across this rooftop ... and jump from this very spot ... and die, right there ... right down there.

A pair of uniformed coppers strolled casually across the exact spot Sam was looking at, their voices just audible;

'What do you say to a bird with two black eyes?'

'I dunno. What *do* you say to a bird with two black eyes?'

'You shouldn't have to say nuffing, you've told her twice already.'

As the coppers' coarse laughter reached him, Sam leant forward, teetering, almost daring himself to fall. His thoughts were reeling.

The year is 1973, but I remember 2006 ... the future is also the past ... I can recall my own death, leaping from this rooftop, and yet here I am, more alive than I've ever been ...

Sam shut his eyes and tried to clear his mind of the turmoil. He focused on the here and now, on the physical reality of where he was; he felt the bite of the Manchester wind as it cut through his jacket, the sharp sting of the early autumnal cold already hinting at the harsh winter to come, the roar of his blood as it pounded through his ears, the steady beating of his own heart. These things were *real*. The world he was in was *real*. That was all that mattered.

Annie's real too. And she is what matters most of all.

He had stood here before, on this very brink, back

when he'd first arrived in this strange time and place. Looking for a way home, he had believed he would find it here. His plan had been to jump, to jolt himself back into 2006, and escape the alien planet of 1973 upon which he was marooned.

But as he had stood there, nerving himself for the plunge, Annie had suddenly appeared, her hair blowing across her anxious face as she reached out her hand to him.

'*We all feel like jumping sometimes, Sam,*' she had said. '*Only we don't, me and you – coz we're not cowards.*'

'No – we're not,' he said to himself now, bracing his body against the anger of the wind. 'We're many things, but we're not *that*.'

And so, that time around, he had not jumped. He had saved that jump for the future. But it would not be cowardice that would drive him to hurl himself from this precipice, nor would it be despair. He would jump for a reason. He would jump so that he could escape the emptiness of existence in 2006 and return here, to the strange, maddening, exhilarating world of '73. He would jump so he could be with Annie.

I was right to come back here, he told himself. *I belong here. 1973 is my home. No doubts – no regrets – I made the right choice to come back.*

If he had made the right choice to come back here,

why did he feel, deep inside, that there would be no happily ever after for him and Annie? Why did he fear that what lay ahead was not life but darkness and death – and maybe something worse than death?

He knew the source of his fear. It came from *her*, the blank-faced brat who had floated out of his TV screen whispering words of doom and despair ever since he had pitched up here. The Test Card Girl, that incessant gremlin from the deep pit of his subconscious, would not let him go. She haunted him, taunted him, forever wheedling him to give up and die.

'You have no future,' she told him, over and over. *'You have nothing to look forward to but misery and hopelessness and oblivion ...'*

Sam felt himself slowly falling forwards, giving himself up to the lure of the drop. At once, he pulled himself back, stumbling away from the edge, his heart racing. He drew in huge lungfuls of cold air and forced his tumultuous thoughts to calm down.

'Everything's going to be all right,' he told himself, looking out across the grey Manchester cityscape spread out all around him. 'Everything's going to work out fine ...'

Movement caught his eye. Three dark specks were travelling slowly and steadily across the autumnal skyline, passing over the city towards him. It was a trio of light aircraft, flying in formation, trailing behind them banners printed with bright red letters. Sam peered and squinted, trying to make out the word on the first banner.

'*World* ...'

He shielded his eyes and tried to decipher the second banner.

'*Of* ...'

World of – what? Leather? Opportunity? Adventures?

Before the third plane's banner came into view, a man suddenly began speaking in a cheery and familiar voice directly behind Sam's back.

'Hello, and a very warm welcome to *World of Sport.*'

Sam spun round. The rooftop had transformed into a TV studio, with typewriters clacking and reporters bustling; behind a desk sat a man smiling warmly beneath his moustache – a man whose face and voice were straight out of Sam's memories of childhood Saturdays.

Dickie Davies shuffled the sheaf of papers on his desk and announced brightly: 'And in a full line up this afternoon we've got exclusive live coverage from CID A-Division, including all the latest shoddy police practice, professional incompetence and casual sexism from regulars Ray Carling and Chris Skelton – plenty of action there – plus we'll be bringing you the highlights of the week's heavy-drinking, chain smoking, and nig-nog baiting from DCI Gene Hunt, so make sure you stay tuned for all that.'

Dickie Davies now raised his eyes to stare directly at Sam, the good-natured light going out of them.

'But right now we're going over live to the rooftop of Manchester CID where Detective Inspector Sam Tyler is once again trying to convince himself that he has any sort of a future with Annie Cartwright. Of course, the two of them have about as much chance of being happy together as Evel Knievel has of clearing a jump without breaking every bone in his back … and deep down Tyler knows it. But until he stops kidding himself and starts facing up to the awful reality of the situation, then I'm going to have to keep on popping up like this and having words with him.'

Dickie stood up from behind his desk, and as he did his moustache vanished, his body shrank, his suit became a black dress, and his face morphed in the small, round, pale face of a twelve year old girl, with a big teardrop painted on each cheek.

'Awful things are going to happen,' the Test Card Girl said sadly. 'You should never have come back here.'

The TV sports' studio melted away. There was just Sam and the Test Card Girl, high up atop CID, the city of Manchester spread out all about them and the grey sky reeling over their heads.

Sam clenched his fists and said: 'You don't scare me anymore. I know what you are. I know what you're playing at.'

'I'm just telling you the truth, Sam …'

'Oh no you're not. You're trying to mess with my head. But you're *nothing*! You're not even real!'

'But I'm very real, Sam. And so is the horrible fate that's in store for you and Annie.'

'I'm done listening to you. You're just a bad dream. Go back to where you came from.'

The Test Card Girl listened mournfully, shaking her head with infinite sadness. She hugged her little teddy bear doll, rocking it – and then, quite suddenly, she hurled it over the edge of the roof.

'And there it goes,' she said. 'Better off out of it. Better off dead than facing what you and Annie have to face …'

'You're wasting your time,' Sam said. 'You won't make me give up. You won't make me despair.'

'It's not looking good, Sam. It's all going to end in tears. *Your* tears. For ever. And ever. And *ever.*'

'I'm not listening.'

'Shall I tell you what's going to happen?'

'Get out of my head!'

'Don't you want to know the truth, Sam? Don't you want to know what *I* know … about Annie?'

'I said *get out*!'

'She has a past, Sam. Like *you* have a past. But it's a very different sort of story from yours, Sam. Shall I tell you about it? Shall I? Shall I, Sam? Shall I?'

'*Damn you, get out of my head!*' Sam bellowed, and at that moment the air was ripped apart by a deafening roar. Dark shadows swept across him; glancing up, he saw the trio of planes shriek overhead, recklessly low, their banners streaming behind them – but now the lettering had changed. It read: *Terry Barnard's Fairground.*

When he looked back down, the rooftop was empty. He was alone again. The planes dragged their advertisement for the fairground away across the rooftops of Manchester. The wind cut through him like a knife. Looking down, he saw that his hands were shaking.

'Don't let her get to you,' he gently told himself. 'The little bitch isn't real. She's just messing with your mind.'

Suddenly, the door to the roof flew open and an over-excited Chris Skelton burst out.

'You see that, Boss!' he cried, pointing at the planes as they veered away. 'Pretty nifty, eh? You reckon we could get one of them for CID? Eyes in the sky! Do they come with guns on? Now *that's* the future of policing, Boss. You think they'd train me up?'

He grinned at Sam, the huge, round-ended collars of his blue nylon shirt flapping and fretting like cherub wings in the harsh Manchester wind. But as he read Sam's expression, his grin faltered.

'Hey, boss, you all right?'

'I'm fine,' said Sam, sticking his hands in his pockets and clenching them into fists to stop them shaking. 'I just ... needed a few minutes alone to think about stuff.'

'No time for thinking, Boss. The guv's yelling for you. We got a shout.'

From far below, the Cortina's horn brayed angrily for

Sam to move his arse – *pronto*. The Guv was impatient. There was a big, bad city out there that needed its sheriff.

'Dead body in a bedsit in Greeton Street,' Chris said. 'A big bloke, beaten to a pulp, 'pparently. Very nasty. Sounds like a good 'un.'

The Cortina honked again, more threateningly. Only Gene Hunt could be so expressive with a car horn. This time, Sam obeyed his guv's summons; he moved his arse – *pronto*.

The big bloke in the bedsit in Greeton Street had indeed been beaten to a pulp. And just as Chris had predicted, it *was* very nasty. DCI Gene Hunt stepped into the room carefully, so as not to get congealing blood on his off-white leather loafers. He moved about the room in his camel hair coat, his tie knotted loosely beneath the raw, aftershave-inflamed turkey flesh of his throat. Sam followed him. The bedsit's fat, string-vested landlord watched from the open doorway.

'What's his name again?' Gene asked, looking down at the dead man.

The landlord said: 'Denzil Obi. A darkie name. He were one of them half-castes. You know, half-coloured, half-normal. Mongrel type.'

'Mixed race,' Sam corrected him. 'Please – it's not "half-caste", it's not "mongrel" – it's mixed race.'

'Don't make no difference now,' observed the landlord.

'Can you take him with you, lads? I want to let the room as soon as possible, like.'

'Meat wagon's on the way,' said Gene.

'Do you boys clean up too? I mean, look at them carpets.'

'I'll Brasso your flamin' knick-knacks on me way out an' all. What state was the front door in when you found him? Had it been forced?'

'No. I had to use my key. I came up because Denzil was behind on the rent, which weren't like him. He were regular, you know. A good lad, for a coon.'

'Please!' Sam insisted irritably, speaking over his shoulder as he looked around the flat. 'Can we knock it off with the BNP language.'

Gene shot a glance at the landlord: 'No, I don't know what the flamin' chuff he's on about either.'

The landlord scratched at the hairy dome of his stomach through the holes in his string vest. 'I was just sayin' that Denzil were okay, that's all. He didn't deserve this.'

Sam looked at the front door; it was fitted with three sturdy bolts and a spyhole for seeing who was on the other side of it.

'Security conscious,' said Sam.

He stepped carefully across the blood-splattered floor and examined the window.

'No sign of this being forced either, Guv. Looks like Denzil opened the door and let his killer walk right in.'

What little furniture was in the room lay overturned.

12

Clothes and possessions were strewn about the floor. There were bloodstains on the bed and up the walls. There were even splatters of red across the ceiling.

'He didn't go quietly,' said Sam. 'Must have been a hell of a fight.'

'And this lad looks like he could handle himself,' said Gene, indicating Obi's muscular arms and torso. 'Body builder, was he?'

'Boxer,' said the landlord.

'Who beats a boxer to death?' asked Sam, shaking his head.

'Another boxer?' shrugged the landlord.

'Or a whole gang of 'em,' put in Gene.

Sam looked about the room: 'Not much room in here for a lynch mob, guv. Barely enough room for the body.'

'You saying this place is *small*?' piped up the landlord, looking defensive. 'It's *cosy*. People like it.'

'Any of your other cosy tenants hear anything?' asked Gene. 'This whole building must have been shaking like a fun house at the fair when this boy got walloped.'

'No other tenants, not here. Downstairs is empty.'

'What about the flat above this one?'

'Just a couple of layabouts up there, but they've buggered off to India or something. Students.'

'Pity,' said Gene, flexing his hands and making his leather driving gloves creak. 'I'm in the mood for questioning students.'

Sam peered down at what remained of Denzil Obi. He had been beaten into anonymity, his nose and eyes reduced to swollen puddings of battered flesh. His mouth had been battered into a misshapen, toothless hole. He was barely even recognizable as a human being. The only identifying mark Sam could make out was the large spider tattooed on the dead man's neck, its spiky legs reaching up towards the remains of Denzil's ear.

Suddenly, something else caught Sam's attention – something inside of Denzil's slack, gaping mouth. He leant closer.

'You're getting unpleasantly intimate with the victim, Tyler,' Gene said gruffly. 'Your little woman not keeping you satisfied?'

'Guv, there's something in the back of his throat.'

'His pelvis, probably, given the pasting he's had.'

'No, Guv, it looks like something metallic.'

'His fillings?'

Sam peered closer, trying to see without touching the body. Gene loomed over him.

'Well? What is it?'

'I can't quite see, Guv. Whatever it is, it's gone down his throat.'

'Don't be squeamish, Sammy-boy. Have a rummage.'

'I can't do that,' Sam protested.

Gene loomed closer: 'Think of it like a first date – stick your fingers in and see what you can find.'

'For God's sake, Guv, I'm not qualified to conduct an autopsy!'

'You don't need ten years in medical school to fish out a ball bearing, Sam. Dive in, he won't bloody bite.'

'Guv, this is a crime scene, and we're going to act professionally, and we're not going to start mucking about with the body, and we're not going to-'

Gene ripped off his driving glove, elbowed Sam aside, and thrust his hand into Obi's mouth. After a spot of blind fumbling, he produced something and held it up with bloodied fingers. It was a bullet.

'Blimey ...' murmured the landlord. 'Is that what did him in?'

'If it is, then Denzil Obi choked to death,' said Gene. 'This round hasn't been fired.'

Sam squinted closely at the bullet. It was indeed perfectly intact.

'Somebody shoved it down his throat,' he said.

'Either that or the coon got peckish,' said Gene. And then, with enough sarcasm to sink a battleship: 'Sorry, Tyler. *Mixed. Race.*'

The coroner peeled off his latex gloves, dropped them into a pedal bin, and belched like a walrus.

'Beg pardon. I had whelks,' he said, patting his flabby chest and growling out more gas.

This put into Sam's mind the ghastly image of the fat

coroner's digestive system clogged with semi-digested seafood. He felt his own stomach heave uncomfortably. How the hell could the coroner talk like that, here of all places? Damn it all, they were at a morgue not a restaurant!

Unmoved and unconcerned, Gene Hunt lounged against a wall, his arms folded, his manner casual: 'So Doc, what's the story with Rocky Marciano? Anything for us to go on?'

'Denzil Obi's been dead about two or three days,' said the coroner. 'He suffered a prolonged and powerful attack, almost exclusively to the face and head. Massive fractures to the parietal and zygomatic regions.'

'That bit and that bit,' translated Gene for Sam's benefit, pointing to the side of his head and then his cheek.

'Nice to see you're picking up the lingo, Inspector,' said the coroner, impressed.

'I'm not just looks and charm,' growled Gene. 'So what was the weapon used? Iron bar was it? Baseball bat?'

'Interestingly, no. The nature of the skull fractures are inconclusive, but the contusions to the face and head bear very clear imprints of a human fist. Punch marks, gentlemen.'

'Well that makes sense,' put in Sam. 'Denzil Obi was a boxer. Are you sure these weren't old bruises?'

The coroner smiled condescendingly and said: 'I flatter myself, young man, that I can tell an old contusion from a cause of death. Denzil Obi was punched – repeatedly, and with impressive force,' he fought to suppress another deep, whelky belch, 'until he died from cerebral haemorrhaging.'

'But … whoever did this must have hands the size of anvils!' Sam said.

Again, the coroner shook his head: 'Quite the opposite. A broad fist wouldn't inflict quite this degree of concentrated damage; the force of the blows would be more widely dissipated. The man who killed Obi had *small* hands – small, with strongly condensed bone structure, rock solid, packed tight. I measured the bruises; the man who inflicted them has fists slightly less than three inches across the knuckles – about the same length as your index finger, Inspector Tyler. Every punch would have been like an intensely focused hammer blow.'

'One bloke, you reckon?' asked Gene. 'Just one bloke to overpower Obi and beat him to death?'

'It's perfectly feasible,' said the coroner. 'I could find no evidence that the victim was restrained in any way during the attack, and all the injuries he sustained are consistent with an attack from a single assailant. One man attacked him. One man killed him.'

Gene pulled a sceptical, pouting expression, but the coroner smiled and went on. 'A single blow, powerful enough and delivered in the right place, could leave even a professional boxer reeling. If the victim was dazed and semi-conscious, his assailant could rain blows on him unresisted. In this case, though, Obi didn't go quietly. He fought back – at least for a while. His hands were freshly cut and bruised. The struggle may have lasted some minutes.' He grunted up a noisy bubble of stinking air. 'Like the struggle between me and these whelks. Excuse me, gentlemen – if I don't get some liver salts down me *I'm* going to be the next one on the slab.'

'But what about the bullet?' asked Sam as the coroner pushed past him.

'Shoved down his throat *after* he died,' the coroner called back as he strode away down the corridor. 'A tantalizing mystery for you sleuths to puzzle over.'

And then, with one last resounding belch, he was gone, leaving Sam and Gene alone.

'Denzil was a boxer,' said Sam. 'Whoever killed him was a boxer too – somebody who knows what they're doing with their fists.'

'Most likely,' said Gene. 'A boxer with a grudge – and very small hands.'

Without warning, Gene reached out and roughly grabbed Sam's hand.

'Guv, what the hell are you doing?!'

'The length of your index finger,' he said,' growled Gene, peering at Sam's finger. 'It's gonna be like Cinderella

18

and the glass slipper; whoever owns the fist that matches your pink little manicured digit, he's our man.'

'I'm not playing Prince Charming for *you*, Guv! You're not using *my* finger as a measuring stick for murderers!'

'I thought you'd always wanted to give me the finger, Sammy-boy.'

'Give over!'

Sam wrenched himself free from Gene's powerful grasp.

'Let's at least *try* and behave like professional coppers, Guv,' he said. 'Denzil knew his killer. That would explain why he let him into the flat. They quarrelled – fought – after a few minutes, Denzil was overpowered, and the killer pummelled him to death. But why stick a bullet down his throat afterwards?'

Gene shrugged: 'Symbolic. *I* dunno. We'll ask the killer when we nick him.'

'And how are we going to do that, guv? Where are we going to start?'

'Somewhere conducive to contemplation, where the mighty Gene Hunt noggin can work its magic.'

'And where's that, guv?' asked Sam.

Gene looked at him flatly and said: 'Where'd you think, dumb-dumb? And *you'll* be the one getting them in.'

The Railway Arms was quiet at this time of day. The atmosphere seemed poised, ready for the crush of drinkers, the clamour of manly voices, the braying of blokey laughter that would fill the place come evening time. The familiar pumps gleamed along the bar, promising Watney's, Flowers and Courage on draught. The ashtrays sat clean and expectant, like baby birds awaiting feeding. The floor was not yet sticky underfoot with spilt beer. And Nelson, resplendent in his flowing dreadlocks and a gaudy shirt depicting the sun setting over a Caribbean island, seemed nicely mellowed, perhaps conserving his energies for the bustle and bullshit of the evening crowd.

'*Very* thirtsy coppers today,' he observed, glancing at his watch as Gene strode in through the door, Sam in his wake. 'What's the reason for dis early visit? Are we celebrating victories or drownin' our woes?'

'One of your lot just got whacked,' announced Gene, leaning against the bar and sparking up a fag. 'We need a moment to cogitate on the clues. Two pints of best, and make it snappy.'

'What you mean, one o' *my* lot?' asked Nelson as he pulled the pints.

'A black,' said Gene, speaking around the cigarette clamped between his lips. Sam literally cringed. Gene glanced at him, 'All right then, a 'mixed race black'. 'Appy now, Tyler? Whatever you call him, he was mashed to smithereens like a blood pudding under a steamroller.'

20

'Is dat so?' said Nelson, raising his eyebrows but playing it very cool. 'Terrible. It's a terrible world we're livin' in.'

'It is,' put in Sam. 'There's terrible things that get done. *And* said. Nelson, I apologise on behalf of my DCI. He isn't really a pig-ignorant National Front scumbag racist, he just sounds like one.'

'Who you calling an NF scumbag?' retorted Gene. 'I'm colour blind, me. I know all the words to the Melting Pot Song. *Gonna get a white bloke, stick him in a black bloke …*'

'That really is enough, Gene!' Sam silenced him, and he meant it.

But Nelson was laughing: 'Blue Mink! Now I tink I got that stashed away some place.'

'You see?' growled Gene, gulping down a mouthful of beer and giving himself a froth moustache. 'Nelson knows what's racialist and what ain't. The trouble with you, Tyler – well, apart from all the *other* troubles with you – is that you think screaming like a nancy with a stinging dick at what normal blokes say makes you some sort of saint. Well it don't. It just makes you a mouthy get with no sense of what's what.'

'It's a little thing called political correctness, Guv. It's all to do with treating diversity with respect.'

'"Diversity with respect"!' sneered Gene, downing another frothy draught. 'Kid gloves is for butlers and snooker refs, Tyler. You can't wear 'em in the street. Or on the beat. Now knock it off and let the mighty Genie noggin' get to work. I got a killer to catch.'

Gene carried his pint and smouldering fag over to corner table and ensconced himself.

Sam shook his head and turned to Nelson: 'I'm sorry you have to hear talk like that.'

'Oh, forget it, friend!' Nelson beamed at him, his showy Jamaican accent vanishing and being replaced with the broad tones of Burnley. 'Water off a duck's back. Your boss, he don't mean no harm. He's just repeating what he's learnt.'

'It's not right, the way he talks. Where I come from, Nelson, it's all very different.'

'Yup,' said Nelson. 'And where *I* come from too.'

CHAPTER TWO

STELLA'S GYM

'Have you been drinking with the guv again?' asked Annie, looking up at Sam from her desk at CID. 'Sam, it's barely lunchtime!'

'I only had the one, to keep him company,' said Sam. 'Why, can you smell beer on me?'

'That, and about a million fags.'

They glanced across at Gene who was back in his office, chewing on a biro while casting his eyes over the racing pages. He'd found no inspiration in the pub; perhaps he hoped he'd find it among the runners and riders.

'You're looking tired, Annie,' said Sam, drawing up a chair beside her. 'Is everything alright?'

'Working here? It's one big summer holiday.' She

smiled, but then her smile faltered. 'Actually, I've been a bit down.'

'Why? It wasn't Ray again with that awful plastic thing?'

'No, Sam, it wasn't Ray and that awful plastic thing.'

'I've warned him, Annie, I'll have him disciplined if he keeps bringing that in.'

'It's nothing like that,' said Annie. 'It's my own fault. I've been letting a case get to me, taking it personally.'

She opened a file on her desk and revealed a photograph of a slim, frail-looking girl staring blankly at the camera. Her eyes were almost completely closed by fat, shiny bruises; her top lip was swollen. Beneath this battered mask Annie had carefully written the victim's name: *Tracy Porter.*

'A&E called me in a couple of days ago to speak to her,' Annie said. 'Her boyfriend's the one who did it – and it's not the first time, neither – but she's too frightened to go on record. I've been trying to persuade her, but she's saying she walked into a door.'

Sam nodded. It was an old story. How many more beatings would young Tracy Porter endure before she ended up on the same mortuary slab as Denzil Obi? How many Denzils and Tracys would come and go through just this CID department alone – battered, bullied, and beyond help?

Sam closed the file. He had seen enough smashed and brutalised faces for one day.

'I know it's not easy, Annie, but you've got to keep a professional distance with stuff like this.'

'Normally I do. I don't know what it is about this girl that's gotten to me. I think it's the frustration, the way she's protecting that bastard who did it to her. I can't get through to her, Sam. *Just name him,* I say. *I'll help you – but you've got help me first.* But it's no good. Sometimes I want to shake her, it makes me so mad.'

'Looks like she's been shaken enough already,' said Sam.

'Exactly. So then I feel guilty that *I* want to get rough with her an' all. She's hardly the brightest star in the sky, but she still doesn't deserve what she's getting.'

'It can sound heartless to say it, Annie, but once you've done all you can you really do have to walk away. That's the job. You have your life, she has hers.'

'If you can call what she's got 'a life', trailing around with Terry Barnard's fairground, living in a crappy caravan, getting smacked about by that thug of a boyfriend. She doesn't know how to look after herself, or else she's just given up. I had to literally twist her arm to make a check-up appointment with the hospital, just to make sure everything's healing up okay. I think the only reason she agreed to go is because I promised to meet here there.'

'You think she'll show?'

Annie shrugged: 'If she does, I'm going to have one last crack at getting her to give evidence.'

'Don't get your hopes up too high, Annie. We're just coppers. We all get frustrated. *I* do. Chris does. Even Ray and Gene, they take it personally sometimes. But none of us can save the world. We can do our best, and we can do our job, but we can't do the impossible.'

'Speak for yourself,' Ray Carling said, looming suddenly over them. 'The impossible's my forte. I can give you the number of a few birds who'll testify to that.'

'Ray, please, would you give us some space?' said Sam, forcing himself to keep his cool.

'Not until you've answered a question for me, Boss,' Ray replied.

'Okay. What's your question?'

'What do you say to a bird with two black eyes?'

Instantly, Annie stiffened and looked away. Sam wearily rubbed his forehead.

'Ray, you have picked the single worst *possible* moment to start telling that joke. And besides, I've heard it. And it wasn't funny the first time.'

'Only trying to raise a smile,' said Ray, stuffing a strip of Juicy Fruit into his mouth. 'Perhaps I'll bring that plastic thing back in again. That gets a few laffs.'

'No you *won't* bring that plastic thing back in again, Ray! I've bloody warned you!'

'Suit yourself, you tight-arsed get,' shrugged Ray. 'We all need to get through as best we can. Go off our rockers, otherwise. At least Chrissy-wissy's got a sense of humour round here. *He* likes that plastic thing.'

Chris's head popped up from behind a mountain of paperwork weighed down with an overflowing ashtray.

'I *love* that plastic thing!' he said eagerly. 'Have you brought it in again?!'

Ray sauntered over to him: "Fraid not. Orders from the laffin' gnome over there. But I got a question for you, Chris. What do you say to a bird with two black eyes?'

Ignoring him, Sam turned back to Annie.

'Sorry about that,' he said. 'It's just Ray being Ray.'

Annie smiled at him and said: 'Thanks, Sam – you know – for not being like all the rest.'

Across the office, Ray reached the cruel punch line and Chris brayed with laughter.

Keeping his back to them both, Sam leant closer to Annie and dropped his voice: 'Listen, maybe I can cheer you up by taking you out for dinner some time?'

'You asking me out on a date, *Boss?*'

'As your superior officer I suppose I could *order* you out on a date with me.'

'How romantic. Where have you got in mind? The canteen downstairs?'

'I think we can go a little more upmarket than that. You choose the restaurant. Anywhere you like, Annie. Don't worry about the expense. Manchester is your oyster!'

Sam stopped suddenly. Oysters. They made him think of whelks. And whelks made him think of the fat-bellied coroner belching and grunting in the morgue.

'Anywhere you like, Annie, but – please – not seafood.'

'Why not?'

'I've sort of … gone off it recently. Well? Am I tempting you?'

Annie swivelled playfully in her chair and said: 'I don't know. You've taken me by surprise, young man.'

'Not the first time you've said that, I'll bet.'

'I'll have a think about it and get back to you,' she said, making a show of moving folders and files around on her desk. 'I'm busy. But if you're lucky I might be able to squeeze you in somewhere.'

'And not the first time you've said *that*, I'll bet.'

'You *are* as bad as the rest of 'em!' Annie cried at him, blushing.

'*I'm* the king of the bad 'uns round here!' Gene suddenly intoned from the doorway of his office. 'Tyler! Stop fiddling with DI Bristols and start acting like a copper with a job to do. Raymondo! Christopher! I'm bored of reading the paper and I don't feel like a taking a dump just yet; catch me a killer so I can play pat-a-cake with him in the interview room 'til it's home time.'

'Got a possible start for you, Guv,' said Ray, waving a piece of paper. 'I've been digging up what I can about this half-darkie lad what got whacked.'

'Mixed race,' Sam corrected him, knowing nobody was interested. 'It's so simple: it's *mixed race*.'

'Looks like he was a local boy,' Ray went on. 'In and out of trouble as a kid, got himself nicked a couple of times – thieving, spot of aggro here and there, nothing serious. Worked around and about as a bouncer, did a spot of lugging down the warehouses. Then he started picking up a living as a bare-knuckle boxer at illegal fights.'

'*Is* there a living in that?' asked Sam.

'If you know what you're doing, Boss, aye, 'course there is,' said Ray. 'There's a lot of money slopping around in that game. But most of them lads are trying to go legit now – like Denzil Obi. It's safer being a pro. Life in the boxing underworld can be pretty rough.'

'Inside the ring and out of it,' said Gene, nodding to himself. 'So – our boy Denzil was looking to go straight, make an honest living at last. But somewhere along the way he'd piddled on somebody's chips – and aforesaid somebody caught up with him, popped round his flat and aired his grievances. Come on, Ray, get me some names – who were Obi's acquaintances? Did he have a trainer? Sparring partners? Boxing buddies?'

'I don't know about none of that – but this was found at his flat,' said Ray, and he passed a laminated card to Gene.

Gene peered at it and read out loud: '*Stella's Gym. Denzil 'The Black Widow' Obi. Full membership.*'

'The Black Widow!' grinned Chris. 'That's wicked, that!'

'Stella's Gym ...' Gene mused. 'Don't know it. Got an address for it, Raymond?'

'It's on the back of the card, Guv.'

'Excellent. Ray, you stay here with 'wicked' Chris Skelton and carry on digging up everything you can about Obi. Go through the arrest files, see what dodgy underworld boxers we've got on the records. And find out who's in town – boxers, brawlers, shady fight promoters, anyone Obi might have come into contact with. And as for *you*, Sugar Ray Tyler-'

'Yes, Guv?'

'Grab your shorts and skipping rope. We're popping down the gym.'

'Can this really be the right place?' asked Sam as he and Gene clambered out of the Cortina and approached the entrance of a gloomy, filthy alleyway.

Gene sniffed the air with contempt: 'Much like the aroma in your flat, Sammy. I can see why you try to cover it up with that druggy pong.'

'They're not drugs, they're joss sticks,' replied Sam. 'How many times do I have to explain that, Guv?'

'No amount of explaining's going to make your gaff stink any less like a dope-smoking pansy-boy's boudoir. Now then; lead on, Samuel, and boot any dog-eggs out the way. I don't want to get my loafers soiled.'

'Heaven forbid you should soil your loafers,' said Sam, and gingerly he stepped into the alley, picking his way through the heaps of reeking garbage. 'This place is worse than a pigsty! Doesn't seem like a good location for a gym.'

'Get over it,' Gene growled as he loomed menacingly after Sam. 'Real men ain't frit by a spot of dirt.'

'It seems they are if they're wearing their best loafers, Guv.'

'*Second* best, you prannet. First best's for the ladies.'

They reached a set of filthy doors, above which hung the remains of a sign. The few letters still attached to it said: ST LLA'S YM

'This must be it,' said Sam.

He pushed open the doors and revealed a gloomy passageway beyond, with a set of stairs leading down into even deeper darkness. For a moment, a sharp, icy sensation passed through Sam's blood. He sensed something – something he could not define. For a moment, he could not bring himself to descend that bleak staircase and enter the darkness at its foot.

But why? What am I afraid is down there?

But it wasn't the descent into Stella's Gym that froze his blood with fear. It was that deeper descent into the even greater darkness of the subconscious that terrified him. Because he had glimpsed into that pit of his own psyche before, not least when he had been pistol-whipped unconscious in the compound of the Red Hand Faction and found himself lost in a black, nightmarish void.

Something stared back at me from that void ... something with inhuman eyes, an inhuman face ... a devil ... a devil in the dark! I saw it ... and whatever it is, it saw me. It knows me. And it's coming for me. Slowly, but surely, it's coming for me ... and then ... and then ...

But at that moment Gene shoved roughly past him and strode confidently into the murky hallway.

'Keep up, Sam, we haven't got all day.'

Forcing his nameless fears aside, Sam followed Gene down the steps and through another set of doors.

They found themselves at once in Stella's Gym. It was a stark, windowless, concrete cavern lit by overhead strip lights. It felt more like an underground car park than a gymnasium. Between the hard concrete floor and the hard concrete ceiling stood rows of hard concrete columns plastered with photos of slab-faced boxers and naked women. Moving between the columns were an assortment of huge, sweating men pounding away at punch bags, heaving weights, dancing over skipping ropes. The air was thick with the mingled stench of body odour, embrocation and stale, wet towels.

One again, an overpowering sense of dread swept across Sam. His heart was pounding. He leant against a concrete pillar, afraid he might pass out, and in horror he saw amid the pinned-up photographs a face he knew at once; staring out at him was the Test Card Girl – a faded, dog-eared, black and white snapshot pinned up between pictures Henry Cooper and Raquel Welch.

'Don't you want to know the truth, Sam? Don't you want to know what I know … about Annie?'

Sam's head swam. He braced himself, forced himself not to faint. The girl's mocking voice echoed through his mind, stirring up the terrible sickness that threatened to overwhelm him.

'She has a past, Sam. Shall I tell you about it? Shall I? Shall I, Sam? Shall I?'

In sudden anger he snatched the photo of the Test Card Girl. But all at once he found himself holding nothing more than a tatty newspaper cutting of Joe Bugner poised for action.

To hell with your mind games, you little brat! You won't get inside my head! You're not real! You're nothing!

Sam crumpled the photo into a ball and fell into step with Gene. Together they moved forward, making for a roped-off boxing ring where two men lunged and clashed under the under the noisy guidance of a short, pug-nosed Irishman.

'Hey you!' Gene barked.

The Irish trainer fell silent, turned, and looked Sam and Gene over. His flat, ugly face was not friendly, and neither was the atmosphere in the gym.

'You addressing *me?*' the trainer asked in his spiky Belfast accent.

'I most certainly am, Paddy.'

'The name's Dermot.'

'I don't care what you call yourself, you gobby spud. Zip your trap and pay attention. And that goes for *all* of you!'

All the men had stopped working out and were staring at the unwelcome visitors, clocking at once that they had a couple of coppers amongst them – Sam's leather jacket and Gene's voluminous camel hair coat were as much giveaways in this place as bobby's helmets and badges.

The atmosphere tightened. Sam set his face, determined not to show that he was intimidated. But Gene, who thrived on machismo like a rosebush thrives on quality shit, hooked his thumbs into his belt, thrust out his chest, and squinted slowly round at the men who surrounded them.

Please, guv – don't antagonise them, Sam silently willed him. *Keep it cool, keep it calm … no need to wind anyone up …*

'Right, you faggots,' Gene declared. 'Stop eyeing up each other's arses and pay attention. I'll keep it simple so as not to confuse you. My name's Detective Chief Inspector Hunt, CID, A-Division – you know, the police. And this here's my retard nephew tagging along on work experience.'

Sam kept his face fixed, maintaining what professional dignity he could.

Dermot, the pug-nosed trainer, leant casually on the ropes of the boxing ring and said: 'And what can we be doin' for you fellas, then? Lookin' to put a spot of muscle on yourselves, are ya?'

Gene fixed him with a look and said; 'Denzil Obi, the Mixed Race Widow.'

'What about him?' said Dermot. 'Denzil's not here.'

'No,' said Gene. 'No, he's not. He's gone to that big, stinky gym in the sky.'

A ripple of tension ran through the men. Dermot straightened up, his face serious. 'What you talkin' about?'

'Denzil Obi was found dead in his flat this morning,' said Sam. 'Beaten to a pulp.'

'So it's a not social call but a murder enquiry,' Gene declared. 'Any of you monkeys feel like having a chat? Eh? Anyone here know enough words to tell us anything?'

Silent faces stared back at them.

'One at a time, lads, no need to rush,' growled Gene.

Sam looked from one to the other, and it was then that he noticed a lean, wiry man – more sleek and well-toned than bulked-up and brawny – who was sporting a spider tattoo on the base of his neck, almost identical to Denzil's. For a fleeting moment, Sam and the man with the tattoo made eye contact – and then the man looked nervously away.

At that moment, Gene spotted the man with the tattoo, and at once strode towards him.

'Oi! What about you? Eh? Knew Denzil, did you? *Eh?* Speak up, lad! Or would you rather chat about this under the lights down at the cop shop?'

'Hey, constable, you lay off Spider!' Dermot protested.

'I don't like spiders – I squash 'em,' said Gene. 'Or pull their legs off and flush 'em down the plug hole. But only if they ignore me – you get my drift? Eh? Spider?'

Spider gave Gene a glowering look. He tightened his fists. Gene tightened *his*.

'I said lay off 'im!' Dermot cried. He ducked under the rope and waddled aggressively towards Gene on his short, stocky legs.

'Look, out, Sam,' said Gene, looking down at Dermot. 'Looks like I've upset the Lollypop Guild.'

Dermot planted himself protectively in front of Spider: 'Let him be, constable. Him and Denzil were buddies – that ain't no secret. Real close.'

'Best friends?' asked Sam.

'Like brothers,' said Dermot.

'Faggots, were they? Nancy boys? Like to dip your wick in the ol' chocolate pot, eh Spider?'

'Officer, you're out of line!' the Irishmen cried. 'You're *well* out of line!'

'What you gonna do about it?' asked Gene, leaning down so that his face was level with Dermot's. 'You gonna get Sleepy and Bashful to give me a going over?'

'Guv, please,' said Sam quietly, trying to calm the

situation. The atmosphere was tense beyond belief. The men in the gym seemed ready to rush them.

Maybe the machismo in the air's gotten to him, San thought. *Maybe he can't help himself.*

Spider stared furiously at Gene for a few moments, his eyes red and watery, and then he turned and stormed away.

'Let the fella grieve in peace,' Dermot said. 'Spider's a good lad. Like I told you – him and Denzil, they were like brothers the pair of 'em. Think of his feelings. Let him shed a few tears. Then he'll talk to you.'

'He'll talk to me *now*,' growled Gene. 'You might be the leprechaun's bollocks in this shite-hole, Murphy, but when it comes to a murder enquiry you're less to me than a puddle of pissed-out Guinness.'

'I'm warnin' you …' muttered Dermot at the back of his throat.

'Get back to Santa's gotto, there's rockin' 'orses need wrapping,' said Gene, and he pushed past the little Irish men to go after Spider. But at once Dermot planted himself directly in Gene's way, blocking him – and as he did, the other men in the room pushed forward to back him up. Sam braced himself. The anger in the room was like an electric charge. Hands were clenched. Muscles tensed. Eyes narrowed. The whole gym seemed to thrum and vibrate with a deep, pulsing, masculine energy, like the prelude to a storm or the first ominous rumblings of an earthquake. The thrill of imminent violence filled the room.

Sam froze.

Dermot prepared to throw a punch.

The boxers got ready to join him.

Gene puffed himself up.

It was then that they heard the gasp of a woman a few yards away to their right. It was an almost sexual sound. The lemony aroma of *Charlie* cut through the fug of sweaty men like the reek of powerful pheromones. Sam and Gene glanced across and saw bleached blonde hair, scarlet lipstick caked across wrinkled lips, a tight-fitting, zebra-patterned leather skirt, fishnet stockings encasing muscular legs, white stilettos. The balls-to-the-wall old bird who stared so frankly at the men in the gym raised her left hand to her painted mouth and teased a red lacquered nail between twin sets of nicotine-darkened teeth; as she did so, her right hand ran down her solidly curved body, from zebra-striped breasts to leather-clad crotch, in a single fluid movement of barely suppressed animal arousal.

'Hands in your pockets, boys, your five-tissue fantasy's arrived,' Gene observed.

CHAPTER THREE

SLAPPER

'I'm Stella, and this is my gym,' said the woman in the zebra-striped top, lounging back in her chair and planting her stilettoed feet on her desk. 'This place is mine. *Mine.* You come into Stella's Gym with questions, *I'm* the one you speak to first. Got that?'

Sam didn't know whether things would have kicked off had Stella not arrived the moment she did. But whatever the score, her sudden appearance had defused the situation. All eyes had turned to her as she stood there, running her hands over her own body and chewing her glistening bottom lip. Sam's first thought was that she was somebody's drunk and unpleasantly randy aunt, but whoever she was she radiated some sort of authority over the men in the gym. They respected her. Gene had sensed this too; instinctively, he'd turned his attention from the wretched Spider and the plucky Irishman defending him, and instead focused solely on this high-heeled, peroxided Amazon.

Beckoning Gene and Sam with a red-clawed finger, she had brought them through a door that led from the gymnasium area into her private office. It was lined with framed photographs of big men, boxers every one of them: some were groomed and suited; some sleek and oiled and posing in the gym; others sweating in the ring during a fight; not a few gushing blood and hardly able to see through swollen eyes – one or two lying sparko and splattered on the canvas, defeated and senseless.

'Didn't expect to find a bird running this gaff,' said Gene, casting his glance around the office.

'Thought the name might've given it away,' Stella said, not looking up from filing her talons. 'I was born into boxing. My dad, his dad, his dad before him. It's in my blood. It's my life.'

'You should've been born a bloke,' said Gene.

'So should you, Detective Chief Inspector whatever you said your name was.'

'The name's Hunt. Gene Hunt.'

'And I'm Detective Inspector Sam Ty-'

Gene silenced him with a curt wave of the hand, like Sam was cramping his style on a date. Which perhaps, in a way, he was. Gene's eyes were fixed directly on

Stella's – and hers were now fixed on his. They were locked onto each other, oblivious to the rest of the world, like lovers. Sam fell silent and gave the two of them their space; it seemed wrong to intrude.

'Denzil Obi's got himself killed,' Gene growled. 'You know who I'm talking about.'

'Of course I do. Denzil was one of my boys. I'm sorry to hear he's come a cropper. Still, it happens.'

'Does it?'

'In this game, aye, it does. Boxing's a tough world.'

'What do you know about Denzil?'

'This and that. Depends who's asking.'

'The Law, that's who's asking, now answer the bloody question.'

'That's no way to address a lady in her office.'

'And that's no way to treat a police officer on a murder enquiry,' Gene said. 'You're starting to sound to me like somebody who knows more than they're letting on.'

'Little me?' replied Stella, and she turned her attention back to filing her nails. 'I don't know nuthin' … leastways, not about that sort of thing.'

'Who killed Denzil Obi? Any ideas?'

'None.'

'Make a guess.'

'I can't.'

'Pick a name out the bloody hat.'

'Constable, I don't know *anything*.'

'Bollocks.'

'Not a thing.'

'Double bollocks.'

'It's not my job to nick villains, Mr DCI Gene Hunt. *You're* the policemen.'

'You better believe it. And as a policeman I can take you straight into custody and put the right royal squeeze on you, sugar. The *right* royal squeeze.'

Stella dropped the nail file onto the desk, moistened her red lips with her tongue, and looked up at Gene through her long fake lashes. 'So. If I don't cooperate, will you haul me down the station in handcuffs?'

'Before you can say 'post-menopausal slag', you bet I will, toots.'

Stella took her feet down from the desk, stood up, and planted her hands on her leather-clad hips.

'Right then,' she said. 'I'm not co-operating.'

'Then I'll have to start getting rough.'

'Then get rough.'

Gene glowered at her: 'I'm not bluffing.'

'Neither am I,' said Stella, her voice now a husky whisper. '*Neither am I.*'

Gene moved closer, his face hard, his eyes harder. Stella pointed her breasts at him and lifted her chin defiantly. Sam could hear them both breathing noisily.

And then, it all happened. Whether it was Gene who made the first move or of it was Stella, Sam didn't see.

All he knew was that there was a rapid flurry of movement, thrown fists, slaps, kicks, and a sudden torrent of things swept from the desk as Stella was thrown roughly over it and handcuffed.

'Don't just stand there gawping, Tyler!' Gene barked as he held Stella down, pressing her with all his weight to subdue her struggling. 'Help me getting this wildcat into the motor!'

'We can't take her out through the gym, Guv, not in cuffs! The boys out there will rip us to pieces!'

Gene thought about this, even as he renewed his grasp on his thrashing captive.

'You got a point,' he said, and hauled Stella upright, clamping one arm round her throat. 'We'll just have to move this mucky mare the way they do with pianos.'

'Guv …?'

'The window, Tyler. Get it open.'

Sam hesitated. Surely this wasn't right? Was there no better way than this?

Gene suddenly roared: 'Not next week, dopey nuts! Right *now!*'

And catching the excited gleam in Stella's eyes, Sam realized that for all her thrashing and struggling, Stella herself would have no objections to such rough handling.

Don't think about it, Sam. Just do it. Let's just get this bloody thing over and done with!

By means that could only be described as undignified, they got Stella to the Cortina. Gene bunged her into the back seat like she was a sack of old taters. At once, she struggled to come back at him, teeth bared, eyes flashing fiercely. Having both her hands securely cuffed behind her back didn't daunt her for one moment from taking them both on simultaneously.

'Get in the back and sit on it!' Gene ordered, shoving Sam onto her. 'Keep it under control until we get to the station.'

Sam find himself sprawled across Stella, fighting blindly with her, trying to grab some part of her so he could hold her still.

'Get this weedy boy off me!' she cried, thrusting her knee into his stomach. 'Get the guv'nor back here!'

'The guv'nor is driving!' growled Gene, planting himself behind the wheel and furiously revving the engine. He stamped on the gas and the Cortina lurched forward.

Sam grappled horribly with Stella as she hissed insults at him and demanded the personal attentions of the guv. But when she realised Gene was not going to relinquish his role and skipper of the Cortina, she fell into a sulk. It gave Sam precious time to get his breath back.

But the moment they reached the station, it all kicked off again. Gene wrenched on the handbrake like he meant to snap the handle and stormed round the back, grabbing Sam with both hands and hurling him out of the way.

Sam fell against the hard pavement and saw Stella going crazy, aiming for Gene's eyes with two-footed rabbit kicks from her stilettos. But Gene got hold of her waist, dragged her out, and flung him over his shoulder, marching off with her like a Viking bringing home a plundered wench.

They burst into the CID room, Gene red-faced and striding, Stella thrashing and screaming abuse, Sam panting and trying to keep up. Chris's eyes bugged halfway out of his head at the sight; Ray's mouth dropped open so that his chewing gum fell into his typewriter; Annie sprung up from her seat, looking confused, not sure if what she was witnessing was an actual arrest or some sort of blokey prank.

'I got me some cheesecake,' Gene declared to his team as he lumbered by, slapping Stella's arse so powerfully that the sound of it echoed round the office like a gunshot.

'Call that a slap?!' Stella yelled at him as he carried her away down the corridor. 'Harder! *Harder, you fairy!*'

Gene booted open the door of the Lost & Found Room and disappeared inside. Sam paused, exchanging silent looks with his open-mouthed colleagues.

'It's like a caveman's wedding,' he said. 'Back to work, everyone. Me and the guv have got it all under control. Everything's fine.'

Nobody believed that any more than Sam himself did. Nervously, he turned and followed Gene into the Lost & Found room.

Her hands cuffed behind her back, Stella sat, panting and sweating, on a wooden chair, surrounded by abandoned bicycles, unclaimed briefcases, and all the rest of Manchester's unwanted bric-a-brac that had found its way here over the years. Sam tried to keep his attention away from the way Stella was sitting; like a low-rent, fag-stained Sharon Stone, she had her legs open just that bit too far. Her blonde hair had tumbled over one eye. Her breasts rose and fell heavily beneath the zebra-patterned fabric of her top; she was Moll Flanders meets Bet Lynch on a bad day.

Gene fished out a packet of Embassy No.6's from his jacket pocket.

'You crumpled my fags, you fruitcake,' he accused her, carefully removing a wonky fag from the packet. 'That, toots, is crossing the bloody line.'

He lit up and drew on the nicotine like it was the elixir of life itself.

'Right,' said Sam at last. 'Let's all calm down. I don't think any of us have got the energy for any more messing about.'

'Speak for yourself, young 'un,' said Stella, her eyes fixed on Gene. Her lipstick was smeared across one cheek, her Dusty Springfield mascara was all over her face, and yet, dishevelled as she was, there was still a fierce fire burning in her eyes and in her blood. 'You brought me here to pump me with questions. Well then – get pumping.'

Sam sighed and said calmly: 'Stella, there's no need for all this. All we want from you is information about-'

'Not you, girly-bollocks,' Stella interrupted, still staring at Gene. '*Him*. The *real* man. The guv'nor.'

Gene lounged against the wall, the fag smouldering in his gob, and silently narrowed his eyes at her.

'You want to pump me?' Stella glared. 'Then pump me. Like only you know how.'

For several highly charged seconds, Gene fixed her with his stare. The air was thick with the mingled aromas of Gene's *Brut* and Stella's *Charlie*. Once again, Sam felt he was intruding on a private moment between these two – a ghastly, stomach-churning private moment he would rather not witness. It was like being in a seedy backstreet club. It was worse than the coroner with the whelks.

Gene exhausted his cigarette and heeled it into the floor. Then, very much taking his time, he began to pace slowly up and down behind Stella's back.

'Denzil Obi,' he said, his voice low, his manner controlled. 'I'd appreciate it if you'd tell me what you know about him.'

'He were a nice enough lad,' said Stella. 'In his way.'

'Meaning?'

'He didn't have a good start in life. Had to make his way as best he could.'

'Bit of a Jack-the-lad, was he?'

Stella shrugged. Gene paced.

'He had ambitions to become a boxer,' Gene said. 'What can you tell me about that?'

'He weren't a bad welterweight. Nifty. Bit of a rough diamond, but with work he could have gone places.'

'It's not the places he could have gone that interest me but the places he came from. The Black Widow had a seedy past, didn't he. Illegal fights. Bare-knuckle bouts. He must have rubbed shoulders with some right horrible bastards.'

'Most like,' said Stella.

'And pissed a few of 'em off in the process.'

'Perhaps.'

'Any ideas who?'

'Nope.'

''Course you do.'

'I'm legit, Mr DCI. I know nothing about the underworld.'

'Pull the other one, luv, it lights up and plays Leo Sayer.'

'I don't associate with villains,' protested Stella. 'Not willingly, anyway. I'm straight.'

'Straight? *Straight?!*' Gene grasped her by the hair and twister he head round. 'You're as kinky as a bloody corkscrew, and in more ways than one. Names! I want bloody names! Denzil Obi got on the wrong side of someone – who was it? Give me a name!'

'Make me.'

'I said give me a name!

'And I said *make me*!'

'*Give me a name! Give me a name*!' And now Gene began to punctuate his words with a series of slaps. 'Give!' – *Slap*! – 'Me!' – *Slap*! – 'A' – *Slap*! – 'Blood!' – *Slap*! – 'Ee name!' – *Slap, slap*!

Sam's instinct was to intervene, but he restrained himself. Nobody would thank him for stepping in, least of all Stella. What was going on between these two was something too murky, too unsavoury for Sam to get involved with. He was better off out of it. He didn't want to be soiled.

Gene yanked Stella's face closer to his own and hissed into it: 'Big fellas getting handy – that's what gets your juices bubbling, isn't it. That's why you run that seedy gym. Watching blokes beating eight buckets of shite out of each other turns you right on, don't it!'

'Oh yes!' The words came out of her as a gasp.

'And getting on the receiving end of it tweaks your dial even more!'

'Oh *yes* ...!'

'You dirty randy kinky scrubber,' Gene snarled, and he hauled her up from the chair. One of her white stilettos went skittering across the floor. He gripped her by the shoulders and shook her; Stella's head lolled about wildly, her hair falling all over her face, her manacled hands clenching and flexing behind her back.

'You want the rough stuff? Eh?' he barked.

'As rough as you can make it, Guv'nor.'

'Careful what you wish for … you might just get it.'

Stella was panting hard, pushing her heaving breasts into Gene's barrel chest: 'You're … You're …'

'Speak up, petal!'

'You're getting close to making me … making me …' She was breathing so hard she could barely get the words out. '… Making me talk.'

Gene span her round and yanked her arms up awkwardly behind her. She let out a cry – a cry of ecstatic pain.

'Talk!' Gene ordered. 'Talk, you pervy slag. Or would you rather I turn you over to my colleague DI Tyler? *He* won't treat you tough like this. Oh no. He'll be soft and gentle. *Very* gentle.'

'No!' Stella cried.

'He won't lay so much as a finger on you. He'll be patient, keeping his temper, treating you like a *lady*, with *respect*.'

'No, please!'

'Hour after hour of it! Cups of tea. Polite questioning. Playing it by the book. Never losing his rag – not once. Being *nice*!'

'*Please!* Don't leave me alone with him!'

'You don't want the Tyler treatment? Then get talking!'

'Denzil and Spider!' Stella panted, struggling to speak

through the delicious pain. 'They grew up together. Spider used to stick up for Denzil when the other kids picked on him and called him a coon and all that. They got them tattoos done together, to show they were like ... you know, blood brothers. They didn't have no family, not really – just each other.'

'Very touching,' said Gene. 'But this a murder enquiry, not *This Is Your Life*. I want to know who'd have a grudge against Denzil!'

'Denzil and Spider got into the word of illegal bare knuckle fights when they were still just kids,' Stella went on. 'It was all they could do to survive. Between them, they went up against some right hard bastards ... big-money fighters, real legends ...'

'Names! Names!'

'Too many to mention!'

'*Give me names*!'

'Lenny Gorman, Bartley Shaw, Patsy O'Riordan out of Kilburn. I could name a dozen others. Big men ... real men ... *hard* men ...' Her eyes glittered at the thought. 'Any one of them could have had a grudge against Denzil.'

'Why? Why would they have a grudge against Denzil?'

'It's what the underworld's like,' said Stella. 'Fights that get fixed, fellas making off with winnings what aren't theirs, blokes paid to bust other bloke's hands. It's the way it is. Betrayal and revenge. Denzil and Spider got involved in some pretty scummy business to earn themselves a crust. They were no different from anyone else in that world. Or in *your* world, Mr DCI Gene beautiful beautiful Hunt!'

'Knock off the flattery and stick to the facts!' snorted Gene, rewarding her compliment with a cuff round the ear that sent one of her dangly earrings flying off to join her missing stiletto.

'They had a past, that's no secret,' Stella went on. 'But they were good lads at heart. They were just trying to survive in a world that didn't give a stuff about 'em. And now boxing's changing, offering a chance for boys like them to go legit, turn pro. They saw a chance to have a *real* life, a proper life, all above board and legal. That's why they wound up at my gym. I got 'em training under Dermot. He was Denzil and Spider's mentor. I told 'em, I said *work hard, lads, do what Dermot tells you, and I'll I see you meet all the right people, get real chances to make a go of it*. But it looks like Denzil's past caught up with him.'

'And if someone's settling an old score with Denzil, then odds on that they'll want to settle it with Spider too.'

'Most like,' said Stella. 'If I knew who it was, I'd tell you. I'd let you rough me up some more first, but I'd tell you.'

'Aye, I think you would at that,' said Gene, nodding to himself. 'One more thing before we adjourn for scones and tea. We found a bullet in Denzil's gob, unfired, shoved down after he died. What's that all about?'

'A sign,' said Stella. 'No, not a sign ... more like a rebuke.'

'A rebuke?'

'Them boxers in the underworld – they're bastards, but like all bastards they've got a code of honour. The only weapons they fight with are their fists. Anyone using guns or knives or baseball bats, they're seen as ... as disrespectful. Cowards. Not real men.'

'So,' mused Gene, his eyes narrowing. 'At some point in his sordid past, Denzil Obi – and probably Spider along with him – got paid to give some bloke a straightener. And they used a weapon to do it, maybe a gun. And the bloke they walloped has either got a very aggrieved relative, or else he didn't snuff it and is now feeling perky enough to go looking for revenge.'

'And he carried out that revenge with his bare hands,' put in Sam at last. 'Denzil was punched to death. No weapon.'

'Just a bullet down his wind pipe as if to say *guns are for poofters*,' said Gene. 'Very poetic.'

'I've told you everything I know,' said Stella. 'You'll have to speak to Spider if you want more – but I don't think he'll talk to you.'

'No. He didn't *seem* very chatty,' said Gene. 'Where can we find him when he's not at the gym?'

'You'll be able to slap his home address out of me, I promise you.'

'Appreciated,' said Gene, releasing her from his powerful grip. 'Well, Angela, you've been very helpful in our enquiries. Thank you for your time and cooperation. You can put your shoe and earring back on now. I'll leave one of my colleagues, Detective Sergeant Carling, to get that address from you. He's the chap with the moustache, you might have glimpsed him on the way in here. You'll like him. He's pretty handy.'

'But not a patch on you, I bet,' said Stella, looking languidly up at him.

'Few men are, luv. Few men are.'

And Gene, who was indeed some kind of a gentleman, offered her a post-interview cigarette.

CHAPTER FOUR

GET HER TO THE GREEK

Night was settling over Manchester, and the boys from CID had repaired to the fag-stained snug of the Railway Arms. After his session with Stella in the Lost & Found Room, Gene had worked up a majestic thirst; Ray, too, had earned himself a drink, having been obliged to slap Spider's address out of her; and even Chris needed a stiff one, his innocent young eyes still goggling at the sights he had witnessed. Given all the giving and receiving of pleasure through violence going on in CID today, Sam half expected to hear the strains of *Blue Velvet* playing on the pub stereo – but no, it was just Steely Dan singing *Do It Again*.

'It's dem tursty coppers again!' grinned Nelson from behind the bar. He turned up his West Indian accent to

10 for their benefit. 'Is it de beer or de music or mah bee-*oo*tiful face dat keeps bringing you back in here?'

'Beer, music, then face, Nelson, in that order,' said Sam. 'Don't be offended.'

'If you were four hot ladies sayin' dat, *den* I'd be ahffended! What can I be gettin' you boys?'

'Four pints of best. God knows, we've earned them today.'

'Makin' dis city safer for de lahks of me – you surely *have* earned 'em!' Nelson beamed. He was really putting on his routine tonight. As he pulled the pints, he shot a glance at Gene: 'Hey Mister DCI, you lookin' lahk de cat what licked up *aaall* de cream!'

'The guv's in luv,' smirked Ray. 'He met the girl of his dreams today.'

'There is a line, Raymond,' intoned Gene. 'I'd hate to see you cross it.'

'She's more your age than mine, Guv,' Ray said, winking at Sam. 'Hey Chris, if you don't mind the guv's leftovers maybe you'd like a go on her.'

'Stella?! Give over, I'm no granny-sniffer!' protested Chris.

'She'd make a man of you.'

'She'd make *mincemeat* of me!' Chris cried. 'I'm not into all that kinky stuff anyway.'

Ray sniggered. Gene looked sceptical. Chris got defensive.

'I'm not!' he insisted. 'If you're thinking of them magazines, I told you, I was looking after them for a mate. *You're* the one who keeps bringing that plastic thing in, Ray!'

'Oh please, not the plastic thing,' groaned Sam, handing pints across. 'I don't want to think about the plastic thing.'

'No plastic things, no kinky wrinklies, not here, not tonight,' ordained Gene, and they all lifted their pint glasses. 'Leave the filth of the world on the doorstep, lads. Let's keep the Railway Arms hallowed ground.'

'Amen to dat!' put in Nelson.

Enveloped in the thick, cancerous atmosphere of the pub, Sam, Gene, Chris and Ray raised their rich, golden pints and drew deeply on them.

As Sam wiped away his froth moustache, Nelson leant close to him, dropped his exaggerated accent, and said in a low voice: 'Only four of you this evening, Sam?'

'I'm meeting Annie later, somewhere else,' Sam whispered back.

'Nelson's little establishment not good enough for the likes of you two, eh?'

'We're having dinner together.'

'You can get dinner here,' Nelson grinned. 'Two bowls of Smash and a selection of fish fingers.' And turning on his accent again he added; 'Birdseye's finest! On de house! Wit mah compliments!'

57

Sam laughed and toasted him with his pint glass.

'So,' declared Gene, indicating to Nelson to get another round on the go, 'pie and chips with DI Jugs more appealing than drinks with the boys is it, Samuel?'

'It's not the pie and chips he's looking forward to,' said Ray, and Chris sniggered like a schoolboy.

'Actually, we're going Greek, so it's more likely to be calamari and stuffed vine leaves,' said Sam with dignity, '*if* any of you lot know what they are.'

'I know what stuffing vine leaves is all about,' smirked Chris. 'It was in them magazines I was looking after for me mate.'

'Is that why the pages were stuck together?' asked Ray.

'I spilt me calamari,' said Chris.

'More than once,' said Ray.

'This is like having a drink with the fourth form,' sighed Sam, and put down his pint glass. 'I'd love to hang about and listen to this cracking banter all night, but the table's booked and Annie will be waiting. So, gentlemen, if you will excuse me?'

Chris opened his mouth to say something daft, but Gene cut in gruffly: 'No more hilarious gags from you, Christopher. I'm very fond of this shirt, I'd hate to ruin it by splitting my sides.' And he glowered so menacingly that Chris hid behind his pint glass. Gene went on; 'Before you leave us, Sam, I've got some shop talk for you – for all three of you. Whoever killed Denzil Obi is a dangerous man – an *extremely* dangerous man – and right now, while we're stood here, he's running around as loose as a whore's drawers. It's likely he'll go after Spider whatever-his-name-is. It's also likely Spider won't want us around – he'll be more interested in avenging his beloved blood brother. So – we're going to keep an eye on Spider and see if the killer reveals himself by coming for him. But that doesn't mean we can just sit about on our arses. I want to get to this murdering bastard before any more blood's spilt on my manor, is that understood?'

Sam, Ray and Chris spoke as one: 'Yes, Guv.'

'The man we're after is a boxer – a boxer with small hands,' said Gene.

'How small's small, guv?' asked Ray.

Gene grabbed Sam's hand and forced his finger straight.

'Our measuring stick,' Gene said. 'The width of the killer's knuckles match the length of Sam Tyler's pokey-finger.'

'What bit of the boss can we use if we can't get to his finger?' asked Ray, grinning at Sam. 'You see, *my* finger's too big. *Way* too big.'

Chris tried his own finger against Sam's and was delighted to find that they matched exactly – 'Look at that! Peas in a pod!' – but then Sam forced his hand free from Gene's grasp.

'This is my last word on the matter for tonight, gentlemen,' said Gene. 'Tomorrow, I want leads – I want information – I want the name of the killer and where we can find him and what he likes on his chips – everything. Understood?'

'Yes, Guv.'

'Very well. Sam, your dopey bit of crumpet'll be gagging for her ouzo by now – bugger off and entertain her.'

'Will do, Guv,' said Sam. 'I'll see everyone first thing in the morning, then.'

And as he made for the door, he heard Gene drain his pint, slam his empty glass down, and say: 'Right, let's talk about birds and football and motors.'

Sam stepped out into the deep, dark Manchester night, pulling his jacket around him tighter to fend off the cold. Away in the distance, across a bleak expanse of open ground, he saw coloured lights whirling and flashing, heard a cacophony of screaming and amplified voices and raucous music. For a moment, he felt a sudden sting of fear, as if he had glimpsed the outskirts of Hell.

Don't be such an idiot, Sam, he told himself at once. *It's just the fairground.*

Tony Barnard's Fair. He recalled standing high up on the rooftop of CID and seeing the planes trailing their banners across the sky. And then, in the next instant, he recalled *her* – the Test Card Girl – goading him, mocking him.

'*Don't you want to know the truth, Sam? Don't you want to know what I know … about Annie?*'

Round and round she went, buzzing through the inside of his head like a trapped wasp, tormenting him with vague doubts and unnameable fears, poisoning his feelings for Annie.

Resolutely, he marched along the street, his back to the noise and colour of the fairground.

There is no dark secret about Annie. It's all lies. It's just some crap from deep in the subconscious rising to the surface. A waking nightmare. It's nothing. It's less than nothing.

Less than nothing. But could he be so sure? If the Test Card Girl was less than nothing, why did the mere sight of her freeze the blood in his veins? Why did he even now, just thinking of her, feel as if the shadow of death had fallen across him? Why, only moments before, had he glimpsed the far off lights of the fairground and thought – of all things – of hell?

He stopped. He listened. The city had fallen silent. Unnaturally silent. Nothing moved except for his heart, which he now found was pounding furiously.

And then, up ahead, he saw her – the Girl – bathed in the unearthly orange glow of a sodium streetlamp. She was standing motionless, watching him, dressed in her little black dress, her face pale, her eyes filled with the pretence of sadness. She hugged her bandaged doll, then, mockingly, slipped away into a dark alleyway.

Sam rushed after her, tore down the alley, and burst out into the street at the far end. The shops were shut up and dark. The street lights were all out. The whole street sat in an unnatural, smothering gloom.

And there, just visible as a pale shape in the darkness, was the Test Card Girl standing motionless, staring back at him.

'Why are you doing this?!' Sam bellowed at her. His muffled, echoless voice was swallowed by the filthy blackness. 'What the hell are you trying to tell me?! *Why don't you just come straight out with it?!*'

He began striding towards the Girl, his shoulders back, his jaw firmly set. Just as the darkness smothered his voice, so it seemed to cling to his body and limbs like treacle, slowing him, dragging him back, entombing him. He forced his way forward.

'I know this isn't real!'

He could barely move, so heavily did the cloying darkness weigh down on him.

'No more mind games, you little brat! Spit it out. Get it off your chest. Then bugger off out of my head forever and leave me in peace!'

The Test Card Girl moved not a muscle. Her pale face glowed dimly.

'My place is with Annie! And her place is with me! And when I chose to come back here, to this time, to 1973, I did the right thing! And there's nothing you

62

can do or say that'll make me change my mind!'

He tried to reach her, but now he was being forced to his knees by the invisible pressure that bore down on him. He fought against it, but it was too great for him. It felt like he was being engulfed by a great avalanche of damp soil, crushing his body, filling his mouth, choking his lungs.

It's like being buried alive ...

And then, quite suddenly, everything changed. The waking nightmare vanished. The deserted high street was now bustling with people and traffic. He could see the lights of late-night newsagents and off-licenses, the illuminated windows of restaurants and chip shops, the brightly illuminated front of a cinema showing *Jesus Christ Superstar*. The Test Card Girl was nowhere to be seen. Manchester was just Manchester again. And there, standing outside Eleni's Greek taverna, was Annie, stamping her feet to keep warm as she waited for him. In that moment, she seemed like an emblem for Life itself. Sam pushed from his mind the horrible memory of suffocation and death – he pulled his jacket straight and ran a hand through his hair – and then he strode forwards, resolute, uncowed, undefeated by the worst nightmares the Test Card Girl could throw at him.

Tonight isn't for that little brat with the dolly in her arms. Tonight is for me ... Me and Annie.

When Annie turned her head and caught sight of him,

her sudden smile swept all horrors and fears before it, like a steel plough through snow.

Eleni's Taverna was authentically Greek only in as much as it had moussaka on the menu and the theme from *Zorba* playing on an endless loop in the background. There were empty bottles of sangria hanging on the walls and a pair of castanets dangling from beneath a sombrero, all of which suggested a very confused concept of Greek life and culture. But for all that, the food was passable and the atmosphere was warm and Annie was happy and relaxed there, and that was all Sam cared about.

'I don't think our waiter's really Greek,' he confided, pouring Annie a refill of wine.

'He *sounds* Greek,' said Annie.

'Sort of. In a strange way. But only with customers. I heard him in the kitchen shouting at the chef. He sounded like Bobby Charlton.'

'They've got a model of some old buildings,' said Annie, indicating some tourist tat sitting in an alcove.

'Annie, it's a model of the Colosseum,' said Sam. And then he added: 'You know, we should go and see it. Together.'

'But we can see it right now, Sam, it's just over there.'

'No, no, I mean the real thing. In Rome.'

But she was smiling at him, teasing him.

'I'll take you to Rome,' Sam declared. 'How does that sound?'

'It's a long way, Sam. And expensive!'

Sam opened his mouth to say they could easily pop over for a weekend – and then reminded himself that here in 1973, flying visits to Rome were out of the league for humble DI's like himself to afford.

'I'll get you there one day,' Sam promised.

'First Greece, then Italy,' Annie said, raising her eyebrows. 'You must have ants in your pants.'

'I lead a jetset playboy lifestyle. Play your cards right and you could be part of it.'

'A chance to live the dream, eh? How can I refuse?'

Live the dream. Is that all Sam was doing – living a dream, a fantasy? It was the thought that had been haunting him for so long, that none of this existed outside of his own head.

It exists, he told himself. *It's real. It's more real than life in 2006, anyway. Stop thinking about all that. Don't let the doubts gnaw away at you like this.*

He was determined to rid his mind of all the poison planted there by the Test Card Girl. When he was with Annie, the world made more sense. It seemed right and natural to be sitting with her in a restaurant – even in *this* place – sharing a bottle of wine and just joking around. His place was with Annie. He knew that, deep inside, without reservation. And he was *damned* if he was going to let anyone or anything destroy that feeling. To hell with the Test Card Girl and her song-and-dance routines; they were nothing – wisps of smoke rising from his subconscious – bad dreams to be woken up from and forgotten.

And yet. And yet.

'Tell me about your past, Annie,' he said, topping up her wine glass.

'My past?!' exclaimed Annie. 'Oh, it's one big riot of glamorous people and exotic locations.'

'I don't know anything about your family, your parents …'

Annie rolled her eyes. 'I haven't come here to talk about all *them*!'

'I'm interested. What are your mum and dad like? Have you got brothers or sisters?'

'You're starting to sound like an immigration officer.'

'I just want to know,' said Sam. 'How were things at university when you did psychology? Did you have lots of friends? And lots of *boy*friends? And what was it like when you started in the police, before I showed up?'

But Annie just smiled and waved all that away. Why? Why wouldn't she engage with him about her past? Was she genuinely not interested? Was she hiding something? Or was there some other reason?

Suddenly, their waiter – who went by the name of Stavros – paused at their table.

'Is-a every-a-thing-a all-a-right-a?' he enquired.

'Si, grazie mille,' said Sam.

'Ah, you-a speak-a da Greek-a!' Stavros beamed.

'I'm fluent,' said Sam, fixing him with a look.

'Ah! Good! Good!' grinned Stavros, his face locking into a strange rictus. 'Moltos bonnos, monsieuro. Avanti, avanti.'

And with that he vanished back into the kitchens, sharpish.

'I take it all back,' said Sam. 'He's 100% Greek. Absolutely.'

'I haven't been out like this for ages,' said Annie. 'I know it's a silly place, but it's doing me the world of good. Work's been getting me down.'

'Are you still trying to get that girl to speak to you?'

'Tracy Porter? No. No, she's refusing to name her boyfriend as the bloke who beat her up. She's discharged herself from hospital and gone back to him. So that's that. Case closed … until she turns up in A&E again, beaten to a pulp once more. And then I suppose we'll go through the same song and dance all over again.'

'Like I said before, you can only do what you can do. But Annie, I didn't come here with you to talk about work. I wanted to talk about *us*.'

'Of course, Sam. Sorry. My head's been so full of that stuff.'

'I know. No need to apologize.' He smiled at her, and she smiled back. 'Do you remember, Annie, a little while ago – I told you I had a strange feeling of needing to be somewhere important ... but I didn't know where or why. Do you remember that?'

'I remember it,' said Annie. 'Of course I do. I told you then that I felt the same thing.'

'And do you *still* have that feeling?'

'Sometimes. And you?'

'Often,' said Sam. 'Most days, in fact. It won't go away.'

'What does it mean, Sam? Are we going slowly bonkers together?'

'I don't think so. And if we are ... well, I can't think of anyone I'd rather end up sharing a padded cell with than you.'

'How very romantic,' said Annie.

'I'm not sure that came out quite right. Anyway, it doesn't matter, because I'm pretty sure we're not going mad.' He tried to push out of his mind memories of coming here to the restaurant – mad memories of the Test Card Girl and the hallucinatory worlds she kept dragging Sam into. 'Do you believe in Fate, Annie?'

'I don't know. It's not something I think about. Why? Do you think it's Fate that's making us feel the way we do?'

'That's how it feels.' He looked for the right words and completely failed to find them. 'Oh, I don't know. I can't express it.'

'Can I tell you something, Sam?' Annie asked, dropping her voice.

'Something confidential?'

'Yes. It's about that girl who got beaten up – Tracy Porter – but it's about me too.'

'Go on.'

Annie thought for a moment, then said: 'There was something about her that kept playing on my mind. I lost sleep over it. I thought it was just one of those things … you know, pressures of the job … but now I'm not so sure.' She paused, looking for the words, then went on slowly: 'I can't express it any better than you can, Sam, but … it's like … it's like when I looked at Tracy, I felt I was somehow seeing *myself* … or … a version of myself. No, that's not quite it. It's … it's like …'

'It's like you needed to save Tracy Porter in order to save yourself,' said Sam.

'Maybe. Something like that,' said Annie, looking intently at him from across the table. 'But … it doesn't make any sense. Save myself from *what*?'

'The million-dollar question. I feel the same. And I ask myself the same question, Annie: *what is it that's out there that I'm so afraid of*?'

'Because there *is* something out there … isn't there, Sam.'

Sam nodded, and said: 'God knows what, but yes, I think there is.'

Instinctively, they reached for each other across the table. Their fingers interlaced.

'Whatever it is out there that's so frightening,' said Annie, 'it's not the likes of Patsy O'Riordan. It's something … something very different.'

'Patsy O'Riordan?'

'That's Tracy's boyfriend,' said Annie. 'That's the thug who works at Barnard's Fairground. He's the one who beats her up.'

'Patsy O'Riordan …' muttered Sam to himself. He knew that name. Dammit, he'd heard it somewhere before. But where? When?

'I'm not frightened of men like Patsy,' Annie went on. 'They're just cavemen. What's *really* scary is something else, something I can't put my finger on.'

'Patsy O'Riordan … Patsy O'Riordan …' Sam was whispering to himself.

'Sam? Are you listening to me?'

The image of Stella in her stilettos and zebra-striped top, handcuffed in the Lost & Found room with Gene slapping her about appeared in Sam's mind.

'*Denzil and Spider went up against some right hard bastards*,' Stella was saying.

'*Names! Names!*' Gene was insisting, smacking her head back and forth. '*Give me names!*'

'*Lenny Gorman, Bartley Shaw, Patsy O'Riordan out of Kilburn. Big men … real men … hard men …*'

'Patsy O'Riordan once fought Denzil Obi!' Sam said, his mind working fast. 'Patsy arrives in town with the fairground ... and at the same time Denzil Obi winds up dead. That's it! That's our lead! That's our first real lead!'

Instinctively, Sam let go of Annie's hand and he began searching his pockets for his mobile. He would ring the guv's office, leave a message on his machine for him to pick up first thing in the morning and ...

But then he stopped searching for his mobile and recalled where he was. Some old habits died very hard.

'Annie – you said you were meeting Tracy when she comes for her hospital appointment, right? Let me come too. Let me speak to her. Maybe she'll speak to me, or at the very least start to trust me. I can use her to get closer to Patsy O'Riordan. What do you think, Annie? Do you think that would work?'

He looked across at Annie and saw at once that the intense mood between them had been broken. *He* had broken it. Not even the theme from *Zorba* being played for the millionth time could bring it back.

'This job, eh, Sam?' said Annie.

It was cold and very dark when they left the snug of the taverna. Sam offered to walk Annie home, but she said it was better to get a cab.

'You're not off with me are you?' Sam asked. 'When you mentioned the name Patsy O'Riordan a light came on in my head. I suddenly saw a connection.' He shrugged. 'You know how it was when you're working on a case. Sometimes your brain just won't switch off.'

'I know what it's like,' Annie said. 'And no, I'm not off with you. It was a lovely evening – almost like being in Greece for real.'

'Um. Maybe.'

'And I won't be offended if you ask me out again sometime.'

'Would you be offended if I did *this*?'

He leant forward and kissed her on the mouth.

'Well?' he asked. 'Was that … offensive?'

'Not sure,' said Annie. 'Try it again.'

He did.

'Jury's still out,' said Annie. 'One more. Just to make my mind up.'

'If you absolutely insist.'

As they kissed for a third time, they were interrupted by howls and wolf-whistles from across the road. They looked round, half expecting to see Gene and Ray and Chris – but no, this time it was just a group of lads, tanked-up and overexcited, rolling back from the fairground.

'We never seem to get a moment,' said Sam.

'Well, at least you can look forward to the red hot date I've invited *you* on.' And when Sam looked at her blankly she pinched his cheek playfully and added: 'Tomorrow. At the hozzie. Meeting with Tracy. *Remember*?'

He hooked his arm around Annie's and walked her in the direction of a taxi rank. Away in the darkness, they saw the spinning lights of Terry Barnard's Fairground. The screams and heavily amplified music rolled through the night and became a filthy mush of sound like something rumbling up out of a nightmare. Momentarily, Sam glimpsed a figure standing silhouetted by the coloured lights. Tall, straight-shouldered, motionless. Was he watching them?

Don't get paranoid, Sam.

An array of red and blue light bulbs burst into life around the helter-skelter, illuminating the motionless figure's neat, crisp suit. It was curiously old fashioned, even for 1973. The angular cut, without lapels or collar, recalled the sort of suit that was fashionable back in the sixties.

What did they call it? A 'Nehru suit', was it?

The coloured lights played across the man's body, but strangely his head and face remained in shadow, featureless, anonymous, obscured.

A gang of excited kids raced past, and as they tore off, whooping and laughing, the figure was gone. That sudden absence was even more unsettling than the sight of the man himself. Protectively, Sam tugged Annie closer to him.

You have nothing to fear but fear itself, he told himself.

And for that moment at least, with Annie nestled against him, he believed it.

CHAPTER FIVE

TRACY

Side by side, Sam and Annie strode into the hospital foyer. The place was bustling. Nurses clipped by primly in their white pinafore dresses and boxy paper hats. Doctors in chalk-stripe suits and lab coats strode confidently along clutching bundles of X-rays. Porters wheeled huge beds in and out of the even huger lift doors, or pushed grim-faced patients this way and that in squeaking wheelchairs.

Annie glanced at her watch: 'We're early. Tracy's follow-up appointment is at 10.45.'

'You think she'll show?'

Annie shrugged: 'I got the feeling she was just starting to trust me, and that might be enough to motivate her to come. But who knows?'

'Then I guess we just have to wait,' said Sam.

'No, not there,' said Annie. 'Too close to the doorway. She'll be really jumpy, Sam. She won't be able to deal with walking through that doorway *and* seeing two coppers at the same time, especially since she doesn't know you. She'll need space, and she'll need to deal with everything very slowly, one step at a time.'

'That,' said Sam approvingly, 'is called "intelligent policing".'

'It's just common sense, you dope. There's no need to try and flatter me at *every* turn, Sam, I'm not about to go off you.'

Sam laughed and, with exaggerated chivalry, indicated with a sweep of the arm for the lady to go first. Annie led the way along a short corridor which bustled with nurses and porters and hobbling patients. She stopped at a discreet bench tucked away beneath a notice informing of the dangers of whooping cough and a stop-smoking poster depicting a small girl being made to breathe in her father's cigarette smoke. The legend IF YOU LOVE HER, DON'T KILL HER were emblazoned above the image.

'This bench is so narrow we're going to have to squash against each other,' said Sam. 'Up close.'

'What a nightmare. We'll just have to endure it.'

'I suppose we will.'

They squeezed themselves, flank to flank, onto the

bench. Sam felt Annie nestle tighter against him. He nestled back.

'Do you think she'll show up?' Sam asked.

Annie shrugged. 'Your guess is as good as mine.'

'But what do your instincts tell you?'

'They tell me ...' For a moment, she chewed her lip and thought. Then she looked at Sam intently, with a strange expression behind her eyes. 'I don't know what my instincts are telling me, Sam. I ... *feel* something ... something about Tracy, and this whole case, but ...' She searched in vain for the right words, but gave up. 'Oh, I don't know.'

'*Try* and explain,' Sam prompted her gently. He took her hand. 'Try, Annie. I might understand more than you think.'

He felt her fingers close around his.

'Well,' she said, her voice very low, her manner hesitant. 'You know how I said this case was getting me down? The thing is, I've been worrying about it all the time. I've even been dreaming about it.'

'That's one of the hazards of this job.'

'Oh, I know that. But this is different.' She broke off, lost in her own thoughts, and then, choosing her words carefully, she spoke with great deliberation. 'I'll tell you. These feelings I've been getting, Sam ... these fears ... I've been having them for a while, just sort of vaguely floating about in the back of my head. I sort of ignored them. But then it all changed when the nurses here called me in to see Tracy Porter. She was fresh in – she'd just been beaten up. I got here and I ... I sensed it even before I walked into the room where she was lying.'

'What, Annie? What did you sense?'

'That something was wrong. I mean, *really* wrong. You know that feeling you get when the phone suddenly rings at like three in the morning? You know how your heart jumps into your mouth, coz you know, you just *know*, it's going to be something awful? Well, what I got was a feeling just like that. Even before I reached the ward they'd put her in, my heart was going, Sam, it was really going, and my palms were all damp, and it was like I was bracing myself for ... for jumping out of a plane, or something. And what for? I mean, what the hell for?'

She checked Sam's expression to see if he was following what she was getting at. Sam said nothing, merely held eye contact and gave her hand an encouraging squeeze.

Annie took a breath, and carried on. 'So, anyway. I tried to keep my mind on the job, and I walked in the room, and there was Tracy on the bed, her face swollen and her eyes half shut with the bruises. You remember the photo. Now the thing is, Sam, I've seen worse stuff than this before. Hundreds of times. So have you. We all have, it's what coppers deal with every day. But it was really upsetting me – and I mean *really* upsetting me. I got frightened, like I was the next one line to get battered like that.'

'You felt vulnerable?' Sam asked.

'Yes! Helpless. And really scared, like I wanted to look over my shoulder all the time. Why would I feel that way, Sam? Why would it affect me like that?'

Sam sighed and fidgeted awkwardly. What could he say? How could he tell her that somewhere out there, something was approaching through darkness – something evil, something inhuman – something that knew Annie's name, just as it knew Sam's, and that all its power and malice was bent towards them? How could he tell her that he had glimpsed this thing, this Devil in the Dark? How could he say that it was through him, through his subconscious, that it was reaching out to her?

'You said you've been having dreams,' he said. 'Can you tell me about those?'

Annie laughed nervously: 'Shouldn't I be lying down on a couch for that, with you sitting next to me taking notes?'

Sam smiled: 'I'm not a shrink, Annie, but I reckon I might understand what you're saying better than anyone. Now – tell me – what have you been dreaming?'

'It's all confused, you know, the way dreams are. At first I did my best to forget them, because I'd wake up scared, like the way you did when you had nightmares as a kid. But then, when I kept having them, I tried to remember so I could understand. They're always muddled,

Sam – images all on top of each other, like trying to watch BBC1, BBC2 *and* ITV all at the same time.'

'Just wait for cable ...' muttered Sam under his breath.

'All I remember of them are single moments. An image. A sensation. I know enough psychology to know if there's any meaning in a dream it's hidden away in the details.'

'And what details did you remember, Annie?'

Closing her eyes, recalling the ghastly images of her nightmares, Annie said softly: 'Sometimes I dream of things rotting. There are maggots crawling about. And sometimes I dream of ...' Her eyebrows furrowed. '... Sometimes I dream of a man ... A man in a suit ... A Nehru suit, like they used to wear in the 60s ...'

Sam almost jolted.

'A Nehru suit?' he whispered. 'No collar, no lapels ...'

'That's the one. In the dream, the man always wears a Nehru suit. Expensive, sharp ... I can't see his face, but I'm frightened of him because ...'

Sam felt his mouth go dry. He swallowed hard and asked: 'Why? Why are you frightened of him?'

'I don't know.' She furrowed her brow. 'It's like ... It's like he's ... Sometimes I feel it's like he's my-'

Quite suddenly, Annie gave a little gasp and sat suddenly upright. Her hand went to her chest, as if she were feeling her own heartbeat.

'She's here,' she whispered. 'It's that feeling like before ...'

Sam glanced down the corridor at the hospital foyer and spotted a frail young woman, little more than a girl, moving uncertainly amid the to-ing and fro-ing of the medical staff and patients. She was wearing faded denims with a polka-dot patch unhandily stitched over one knee. Her thick-soled, high-heeled sandals made her totter slightly, as if she had not yet learnt to walk in them, and the shapeless, man-sized lumberjack shirt she had on somehow only emphasized her fragility by sitting so bulkily on her.

'Is that her?' he asked.

Annie nodded.

As the girl drew closer, one unsteady step after another, the bruising around her eyes and mouth became more apparent. She had attempted to disguise it by letting her mousy hair fall down across her face, and by donning a googly pair of plastic sunglasses with thick, pink frames – but her efforts were in vain. She could have worn a paper bag over her head and somehow you would have intimated that the face beneath it was battered and traumatized. Tracy Porter gave off the air of being a victim the way a business tycoon gives off the air of mountainous wealth.

'Are you up to speaking to her?' Sam asked, putting his hand on Annie's arm. 'You're feeling okay?'

'My heart's going again, like before. But I'm okay, Sam.'

'Annie ... this dream you were talking about ... The man in the Nehru suit ...'

'Oh, for goodness sake, Sam, later. Let me go and have a word with Tracy, just me and her. If she's not too jumpy, I'll bring her over, yeah?'

Annie got to her feet, fixed her expression into one of openness, adopted unthreatening body language, and headed down the corridor towards Tracy. The girl flinched and glanced over her shoulder at the main doorway, as if she was ready to bolt back out. Not that she could *bolt* exactly, not in those blocky sandals. Perhaps teeter away at speed until she twisted her ankle.

Sam couldn't hear what Annie said to her – no doubt words of friendliness and concern in order to win the girl's trust just that little bit more. Tracy raised her hands to her face to cover the injuries, but Annie took the girl's hands in her own and held them, making physical contact, bridging the gulf between her and this terrified, wounded creature.

And then, without warning, the Test Card Girl spoke, right behind Sam's head. 'They're the same man, Sam.'

Sam leapt up like he'd received an electric shock, and span round. There was nobody there – just the now empty bench, and above it the anti-smoking poster, with its image of a small girl breathing in the smoke issuing from her father's cigarette. Sam peered closer at the poster. Did he know that girl? Was it *her*, the brat from the test card?

Tentatively, Sam reached out his hand towards the poster. He hesitated, his fingers half an inch from its surface, suddenly unwilling ... and then he forced himself to do it. His hand pressed against nothing more than a glossy sheet of printed paper.

'What did you mean?' he asked, speaking out loud, staring hard at the girl in the photograph. '*Who's* the same man? The man I saw at the fair last night and the one in Annie's nightmares? Is that what you meant? Tell me! Tell me what you meant!'

The girl in the poster did not move. And now he looked harder at her, she was certainly not the Test Card Girl. Nothing like her.

Nothing like her ... at least, not now. But what about a moment ago? Did that poster change behind my back? Had she been there, smiling down at me, inches away ...?

The thought gave him the creeps.

IF YOU LOVE HER, DON'T KILL HER the poster warned him,

Sam shook his head to clear it, trying to rid himself of paranoia.

'You know what I meant, Sam,' said a small girl in a wheelchair as a porter trundled her along.

Sam jumped and span round. The Test Card Girl was sitting in the wheelchair, pale-faced and gently smiling.

'And when she said she got frightened, and wanted to

look over her shoulder ... when she said she felt she was the next one in line ... she was right, Sam.'

'No ...' Sam said. Or rather, he silently mouthed the word, because no sound would come.

'She *is* the next one in line.'

'No.'

'And it's going be worse than just a beating, Sam. Much worse. Believe me.'

Sam flattened himself against the wall.

The porter looked at him with slow, dull eyes. 'You all right, mate?'

'What did you mean by that?' Sam hissed at her, his fists clenching. 'Tell me what the hell you meant!'

'Just tryin' to 'elp,' shrugged the porter. 'Bloody weirdo.'

And with that, he went on his way, pushing the wheelchair off along the corridor. The Test Card Girl craned round in her seat to keep her smiling face fixed on Sam until she disappeared round a corner.

'This is him,' he heard Annie saying. 'DI Tyler. He's really kind. A really kind man.'

He turned, and there she was, gently coaxing Tracy towards him.

They didn't see me jump out of my skin just then. Thank God!

'Tracy!' he said, trying to sound perfectly natural and unflustered. He summoned up as friendly a smile as he could manage. 'Call me Sam. Pleasure to meet you. I was hoping that, before you have your check-up with the doctor, you could spare us the time for a quick chat?'

Sam's CID badge bought them access to a dreary little room decorated with nothing more than an eye chart and an empty cork board. Tracy shuffled in, nervous and uncertain, wobbling on her built-up sandals. She refused to take off her sunglasses and seemed permanently on the verge of rushing out.

Annie did what she could to put her at her ease. She settled Tracy in a plastic chair and pulled up a seat beside her. Sam sat across from them, not too close – he didn't want to seem overbearing – but not so far away as to appear remote. He had a clear view of Tracy's blackened, swollen face. Whether she was pretty or plain was impossible to see; all he could make out were discoloured swellings, stitched cuts, and the blank-eyed stare of those enormous sunglasses.

Patsy must have leathered into her like he was pummelling a punch bag. She's lucky she didn't end up in the morgue. How many beatings does this poor girl endure from one week to the next? Is this how she lives her life? Is this, for her, business as usual?

He recalled the Test Card Girl's taunting words about Annie: 'She *is* the next one in line. And it's going be worse than just a beating, Sam. Much worse.'

I'll never let you end up like this, Annie. I swear it now. I'll die before I see you smashed to pieces.

It was no time for thoughts like this. He had an interview to conduct. Sam cleared his mind, focused, and concentrated on Tracy.

How to begin? He decided his opening gambit should be informal, breezy, low key. 'So. Tracy. You're not a local lass, are you?'

'London,' said Tracy. 'Kilburn. Like Pats.'

'If you don't mind me asking, how did you meet Patsy? Are you a fight fan?'

'Me and some mates went to the fair. Pats was there, and I caught his eye.'

Sam nodded and smiled: 'And so he asked you out?'

'And we 'ad full blown nookie on the first date, is that what you want to 'ear is it?'

'Tracy, I'm just trying to establish a context for-'

'You wanna know where he stuck it and 'ow many times?'

Despite her battered body, there was still a spark of fire in this young woman. Was she being protective towards Patsy? Or was her sudden aggression the result of years of misery and abuse? Whatever was going on in her poor, brutalized mind, Sam knew he had to tread very carefully.

'I have no intention of prying into your private life,' said Sam, pitching his voice to sound as unthreatening as possible. 'I'm interested to know more about Patsy O'Riordan. What can you tell me about him?'

Tracy bristled defensively. 'Before you start on me, mate, I walked into a door.'

'I understand.'

'You'd better, mate, coz if you start anyfink else like, I'm right out that door, you reading me?'

'All I'm doing is asking about Patsy.'

'Yeah, right, the way coppers are always "just asking"!'

Was he playing this wrong? Was he doing nothing but hitting all of Tracy's anger-buttons? Sam flashed a glance at Annie; she looked back with an expression that said *it's okay, just keep talking to her.*

Trusting Annie's judgment, Sam went on: 'So, you and Patsy met at the fair. When was that, do you remember?'

'A few years back.'

'Are you happy together? Are you planning on getting married?'

'Yeah.'

Sam waited for her to elaborate. After a few silent moments, he prompted her: 'Is that "yeah, you're happy together" or "yeah you're planning on getting married"? Or was it "yeah" to both?'

Tracy turned stiffTracely to Annie, holding up her hands in a *what the bloody 'ell's this fella on about* shrug. Annie smiled at her and patted her hand.

Diplomatically, Sam summoned up a self-deprecating

laugh: 'Let me ask you about something else. I'm involved in an investigation concerning a man called Denzil Obi. Does that name mean anything to you?'

Tracy shrugged and shook her head.

'You've never heard of him before?'

'Am I supposed to have 'eard of 'im?'

'Mr Obi was a boxer,' said Sam.

Tracy adjusted her sunglasses. Was it a nervous gesture? Sam decided to wait and see what she said next, unprompted.

It took a few moments, but at last she spoke: '*Was* a boxer?'

Sam nodded.

Tracy fiddled with her glasses again: 'I don't like the sound of this.'

'What do you mean, Tracy?'

'This boxer, he's gotta be dead, right, which is why you're askin' abaht 'im. Which means you're looking for somebody to send down.'

Sam kept his voice soft but clear. 'Mr Obi *is* dead, yes. But we're not looking for "somebody to send down", Tracy, we're looking for the person who killed him. No fit-ups, no fall-guys. We want the man who killed him. Now – the only reason I'm asking you about Denzil Obi is that I've been told he used to know Patsy. They've gone up against each other in the ring.'

'Maybe. I dunno. I never go to the fights.'

'Violence not your scene?'

The moment he'd said it, Sam could have bitten his tongue off. It sounded provocative, sarcastic, even mocking.

But Tracy took the statement at face value and replied: 'I don't like seein' Patsy gettin' walloped ... though it's always the other fella what comes off the worst. Besides, Pats don't like me going out.'

'Going out? You mean, to fights?'

'It's right for 'im to know where I am,' said Tracy, and again she sounded defensive, as if Sam were criticizing her domestic arrangements. 'Fights are for blokes. Birds like me should be at 'ome waitin', keeping the place in order and that. Don't you 'ave a missus?'

'Me? No, not a ... not a "missus" as such, no. There *is* somebody but, we're ... well, we're not ...'

'There ya go then, you don't know what it's like, do ya! But *I* do. A bloke's missus has her place, and that's the way it is and that's what's right.' She sat back in her seat and once again readjusted her sunglasses. 'You'll find that out for yourself one day, young man.'

She's a slave, Sam thought. *That's what these bruises are all about. What did she do to provoke them? Wash up a plate and leave a trace of food on it? Speak out of turn? Not have the dinner on the table when Patsy got in?*

Without warning, Tracy scraped back her chair and got to her feet.

'I've 'ad enough of this.'

'Please stay another couple of minutes,' said Sam. 'I promise, I have just two or three more questions I'd like to ask and then that's it, I'm all done.'

'No. You're all done *now,* mate. I ain't got nuffing to say that's no use to you. I walked into a door, and Patsy earns an honest crust down at the fair. He's a good man. He looks after me. I love him.' Tracy's hard London accent twisted that word, stretched it, contorted it: *I laahve 'im.* 'I laahve my Pats, and if some bloke's snuffed it, that ain't nuffing to do wiv him and it ain't nuffing to do wiv me, so there's your lot.'

She tottered on her high shoes to the door, pushing hopelessly at the handle for a few seconds until she realized that the door opened *inwards,* and then turned her blackened face towards Sam. He saw himself reflected, twice over, in the dark lenses of her sunglasses.

'Coppers,' she sneered. There was real venom in her voice.

And with that, she was gone.

Sam and Annie sat in silence, looking at each other. Annie raised a hand and laid it against her chest.

'It's beating fit to bust,' she said. 'Why? Why does that girl affect me like that, Sam?'

Sam tried to say something comforting, but no words came. What the hell did *he* know? All he could do was put his arms around her in a mute, hopeless display of protection. And to himself, he repeated his vow:

I'll never let you end up like that girl, Annie. Nobody will lay a finger on you. I'll die first. If that's what it takes, I'll die to save you.

CHAPTER SIX

TOFFEE APPLES

CID, A-division. The strip lights were glaring, and the air was already thick with the heady aroma of Embassy No. 6 and *Brut*.

Gene Hunt had marshalled his troops. Chewing on a slim panatella, he planted himself squarely in front of Sam and Annie, Chris and Ray, appraising them sceptically with narrowed eyes. He carefully removed the cigar from his lips, shamelessly adjusted the lay of his testicles, and began to speak.

'Right, playmates. The case of the Black Widow appears, at last, to be making progress. Thanks to the razor-sharp intellect of Sam Tyler we have a lead!'

'Actually, Guv,' put in Sam, 'it was something Annie said that suggested the-'

'Patsy O'Riordan,' said Gene, cutting across him. 'That's our suspect. The delightful and fragrant Stella from *Stella's Gym* mentioned his name in passing, and it seems that he's currently on our books for knocking the living daylights out of his bird. He's a boxer – just like Denzil. He's involved in the world of illegal bare knuckle fights – just like Denzil. He works for Barnard's Fairground – which, by a staggering coincidence, rolled into town two days before Denzil Obi got fatally thwacked. There's a strong possibility that he is a character from Denzil's past with a score to settle. So, summing it all up – we have a victim, a possible suspect, a hint of a motive, and the beginnings of a case. Put 'em all together and what do you get?'

Silence. Gene scowled.

'*Policework*! That's what you get!' he barked, gusting cigar smoke from his nostrils. 'I know it's first thing in the morning but we can at least *pretend* to be awake, can't we?'

As one, his team replied: 'Yes, Guv.'

'Yes, Guv,' Gene echoed back to them. 'Right then. Policework. Let's start fitting all the bits and pieces together until they make some sort of sense, shall we? Let's get the ball rolling with something we know for sure: Denzil Obi was punched to death by a single assailant – an assailant with unusually small fists.'

'No bigger than this!' put in Chris, proudly holding up his finger to demonstrate.

'No bigger than that,' continued Gene. 'Three inches across the knuckles. We know this from the wounds on Obi's body. If we can match the size of Patsy O'Riordan's fists to the size of them wounds, we're a big step closer to establishing him as the killer.'

'More than a big step, I reckon,' said Ray. 'We'd have him by the short 'n' curlies.'

Sam shook his head. 'Not necessarily. Matching the size of O'Riordan's hands to the wounds on Denzil Obi's body is a good link, but it's not something we can guarantee will stand up in court. There's lawyers who'll blow evidence like that out of the water.'

'Balls to the lawyers!' scoffed Ray.

'No, Ray, not *balls to the lawyers*,' Sam protested. 'It's going into court with an attitude like that that leads to cases falling apart. We need a solid motive, we need as much hard evidence as we can get, we need witness statements, we need …'

Ray was making yackety-yack gestures with his hand.

Sam hardened his voice: 'Ray, this isn't the bloody playground. We're police officers. And a man is *dead*. If we want to nail Obi's killer, we need to play this by the book, build up a real case, cover all our bases.'

'Hate to say it but Tyler's right,' said Gene. 'We've all seen cases chucked out on a poxy technicality. It's not a nice feeling. And I want a nice feeling, you hear what I'm saying? I want that nice, warm feeling in the pit of my bollocks that comes with a rock solid conviction and a right brutal bastard going away for life. And *this* is why.'

He held up the photograph from Annie's file that showed Tracy Porter's battered face. Chris winced. Ray slowly shook his head in disgust.

'That's how he treats his missus,' said Gene. '*She's* too frightened to speak up – so we'll be speaking up on her behalf. We're going to nail this he-man – we're going to nail him right to the flamin' wall. We are going to put a case together tighter than a tadpole's fanny.'

'Right behind you in this, Guv,' said Chris.

Ray glanced at Sam, then at Gene, and at last said: 'Me too, Guv.'

'One big 'appy family, then,' intoned Gene. 'Right. First up, we need to pin down O'Riordan's location.'

'That's not too difficult,' said Annie. 'He's at Terry Barnard's Fairground. The fair won't move on until after the weekend.'

'Okay, so he's at the fair – but *where* at the fair?' said Gene. 'Selling tickets? Driving the ghost train? Cleaning the puke out of the waltzers? We need to track him down, so tonight we'll go out there and find him. And once we've found him, we'll get a good look at his fists to make sure they fit.'

'Get a look at his fists?' asked Chris. 'How?'

'I don't give a penguin's frozen pecker *how*, Christopher – be creative – use your bloody initiative – just find a way of making damn sure that his fists ain't no bigger than three inches, understand?'

'No, Guv, I don't,' Chris frowned. 'Why don't we just pull Patsy in and measure his fists here at the station?'

'Because Patsy O'Riordan is a gyppo,' Gene said, leaning forward and spelling it out for him. 'A Pikey. A rambling ne'er-do-well.'

'What the guv's saying is he's a traveller, Chris,' clarified Sam, but nobody was listening.

'If Patsy gets wind we're looking to collar him, he's free to disappear back into the wild blue yonder,' Gene went on. 'So I don't want him nicked, collared, or so much as spooked until we've got evidence enough to charge him. Do you understand *now*, Christopher?'

'Yes, Guv.'

'Super-duper. We all understand what we've got to do then? Locate the suspect, establish a link to the victim, and bit by bit put together a case so watertight Ironside would shit his chair trying to contest it.'

'How are we going to do that, Guv?' asked Sam. 'How are we going to shore up this case? Any ideas?'

Gene raised himself to his full height, exhaled a plume of panatella smoke, and narrowed his eyes: 'I've *always* got ideas, Samuel.'

'Such as?'

'Though the wheels of the Gene Jeanie might grind slowly they grind exceeding chuffin' small.'

After a bemused pause, Ray said: 'Do what, Guv?'

'I think that was the guv's way of saying he's working on it,' said Sam. 'First things first, then. Let's identify and locate Patsy O'Riordan and see if we can somehow get a chance to measure his fists. Should be interesting.'

'If this O'Riordan feller works at the fair,' piped up Chris, 'then does that mean we all get to go? You know, to the fair and that?'

'It does indeed, Chris,' said Gene.

Chris's face lit up.

Gene went on: 'When it gets dark, we'll mingle with the regular punters. Keep a low profile. Act natural. Don't draw attention to yourselves.'

'Guv,' Chris asked eagerly, 'can we, like, go on the rides and that? I mean, you know, to look natural.'

'You can take a slash in the hall of bleedin' mirrors for all I care, Christopher, just as long as we pin down O'Riordan and get a the measure of his fists.'

Gene slammed down the photograph of Tracy Porter's lumpen, brutalized face. Next to it, he slapped a forensic photo of what remained of Denzil Obi.

'Keep these images in mind,' he growled. '*That's* what we're doing this for. *That's* what this case is all about. We're putting a stop to *this*.'

Everybody looked silently at the ghastly photographs – even Chris, who was getting desperately excited at the prospect of going to the fair.

'We know the victims, Guv, but what about O'Riordan himself?' said Ray. 'How will we recognize him? What's he look like?'

'Therein lies the fun and games,' said Gene. 'We don't have a picture or even a description, so we'll have to use our innate animal cunning to track him down. That's what we get paid our pennies for. One way or another, he'll be around that fairground, and that means, gentlemen and lady, *we – will – find him.* Understood?'

'Yes, Guv.'

'I didn't catch that.'

'*Yes, Guv!*'

'Splendid! Right then. I'll see you all tonight at Terry Barnard's. Dress warmly. Treat yourselves to a toffee apple. And don't buy the donuts – I've seen how they make the holes.'

It was night, and Terry Barnard's Fairground appeared as a crazy chaos of lights and music whirling frantically in the darkness. Sam and Annie arrived together, meeting up on the edge of the open ground where the fair had established itself.

'When was the last time you went to the fair?' Annie asked.

'When I was so-high,' said Sam.

'Brings back memories, doesn't it.'

Sam shrugged. He should have felt nostalgia, but the

swirling, coloured lights and the blaring music unsettled him. The screams of excited youngsters on the roller-coaster made him think of hell. He shook his head to free it from such stupid thoughts.

'Come on,' he said, taking Annie's hand. 'I know we're supposed to be working, but let's think of this as a sort of 'second date' – what do you say?'

Her answer was to plant a kiss on Sam's cheek. Nothing spectacular, almost sisterly – but it worked wonders. Once again, for all his fears and nameless terrors, Annie had it in her to bring the warmth and sunshine back into Sam's soul. He tightened his grip on her hand and together they trudged across the muddy ground towards the fair.

The place was alive with colour and music and people and noise. Kids bundled up in duffel coats and snorkel parkas where cramming onto the ghost train, whooshing down the helter-skelter, getting pinned to the walls of the spinning centrifuge cage. A precarious rollercoaster rattled unsteadily overhead. Beneath a sagging tarpaulin, Sam spotted rows of arcade games – old style one-armed bandits, metal claws that gripped but then dropped cheap toys, table football, glass cases containing masses of moving ten-pence pieces that forever threatened to tumble out for the player to gather up but which defied gravity and refused to fall.

Further on, the waltzer was hurtling round and around, carrying its cargo of screamers and shriekers.

'Any sign of Chris on that thing?' asked Sam, peering at the faces as they flashed by. 'I bet you a tenner he's a waltzer man.'

'Then that's a tenner you owe me,' said Annie, and she pointed. Chris was sitting astride a painted horse on a sedate and slow-moving carousel, swinging his legs gleefully and shoving his face into a huge cloud of pink candyfloss.

'Macho man!' Annie called out to him as he went by.

Shocked at being discovered, Chris looked up sharply, candyfloss sticking to his nose and eyebrows.

'I'm on reconnaissance!' he protested as his painted horse carried him away.

Sam laughed – and then his laughter froze as he caught sight of the Test Card Girl riding along the carousel just behind Chris. She turned her pale face towards him as she bobbed gracefully by.

'Come on,' said Sam, tugging Annie's hand and leading her away. 'Let's find this thug O'Riordan.'

They threaded their way through the bustling crowds. Sam expected to see the Test Card Girl again at any moment – taking money at the ticket office for the ghost train, selling toffee apples, going round and round on the centrifuge, perhaps skipping by with a cluster of jet black helium balloons in her hand – but he saw no sign of her now. Perhaps he had just imagined her riding on the carousel.

No. I didn't imagine her. She was there – popping up like a recurring nightmare yet again … Damn it, will I never be rid of her?

Sparks flashed and crackled overhead. Sam flinched – then relaxed. It was just the electric current feeding the dodgems.

'Hey,' smiled Annie, nudging Sam's arm. 'No prizes for guessing who's on the bumper cars.'

Gene was cramming himself into one of the cars. Across from him, Ray was doing the same.

'In their heads, they're about twelve,' said Annie.

'That's being generous,' said Sam.

Dads were settling into the cars with their kids, and granddads were settling in with their grandkids.

'I hope Ray and the guv don't get too aggressive,' said Annie. 'It's for families.'

'It's only the dodgems, Annie. How aggressive can they possibly get?'

The ride's compere hollered over the speaker system: '*Three! Two! One! And awaaaaaay they goooo!*' Instantly, Gene's car sprang forward, broadsiding a young couple with surprising force. Ray slammed his car into the back of one carrying an old man and his nervous grandson, barking abuse when the old man told him to *take it easy, son.*

'I think the guv's taking it a bit serious,' said Annie, as they watched Gene swerve and ram, utilizing his police driving skills to devastating effect. A child screamed, a father raised his voice in angry protest, and Gene silenced them both with a succession of ferocious head-on collisions. A kid in a bobble hat lost his nerve, leapt from his car and fled the ride altogether, weeping openly.

'I feel I should intervene,' said Sam. And at that moment, on the other side of the dodgems, he glimpsed a spider tattoo moving past in the coloured lights. 'Annie! Look!'

'What? Where?'

'I saw him, Annie – it was Spider, the fella from the gym. What's he doing here?'

'Maybe he likes fairgrounds.'

'Or maybe he's more interested in finding Patsy O'Riordan.'

'And what would Spider want with him?'

'Only one way to find out.'

They were pushing their way through the crowds, trying to find Spider. Sam barged his way through a mob of teenagers – '*Oi! Watch it mate!*' – and glared frantically about. Suddenly, he saw Spider – and Spider saw him. They made eye contact, stared at each other for a moment – and then Spider bolted. Sam raced after him, shoving and shouldering his way through the crush. Spider ducked and weaved a few yards ahead of him.

'There he is!' Sam called to Annie ... but Annie was nowhere to be seen, separated from him and swallowed up by the crowd.

Sam pressed on, following Spider out of the crowd and under the rickety framework of the rollercoaster itself. Above them was a crazy latticework of scaffold pipes and rough planks. Stray beams of coloured light filtered in, dappling them in a shifting haze of red and orange and blue and yellow.

'Spider! Wait up! It's okay, I only want to …'

Suddenly, Spider span round, his eyes blazing, his face fierce. Up went his fists, one tucked beneath his chin, the other circling the air just in front of his face. A livid red light fell across him from the flashing fairground bulbs; just for a moment, he seemed to be spattered in blood.

Sam took a step back, his hands raised palms outward.

'Whoa there, Spider. Easy. I just want to speak to you …'

Spider stayed exactly as he was, poised to fight. The only thing that changed was the colour of the light that dappled him. It went from blood red to electric blue, then to a flickering lemon yellow, then to a slowly pulsing pale green.

'You remember me?' said Sam, keeping very still, determined not to provoke him into lashing out with those lethal fists of his. 'I came to the gym. My DCI behaved like a dick, but I'm different. All I want is to talk to you. Please – Spider – put your fists down.'

The framework of scaffolding about them lurched and

rattled. Overhead, the rollercoaster thundered by on its tracks, screaming and whooping as it went. The structure shook, the planks creaked, the feeble-looking blocks and wedges upon which the whole edifice stood groaned and shifted.

'Jesus, this place is a death trap!' Sam muttered, flinching as if he expected it all to come crashing down on top of them. 'Spider – please – let's talk, but not here, yeah?'

'Ain't nothing to talk about,' Spider grunted at him through gritted teeth. He kept his boxer's fists in place. 'You want to nick me? Then go ahead and try.'

'Spider, I told you, I just want to talk. I'm a police officer pursuing a murder – you're a close personal acquaintance of the victim – it's hardly surprising that I'm going to want to talk to you, is it! Now please – put your fists down.'

Sam waited, giving Spider the time and space to make up his own mind what to do next. The rollercoaster rocketed overhead once again, rattling every scaffold tube and straining every plank.

Slowly, Spider relaxed his pose.

'Thank you!' sighed Sam. 'Now come on. Let's get out of here before this shit-heap comes down around our ears. I'll buy you a toffee apple somewhere and we can talk.'

'No. You want to talk, we talk here.'

'I'd really prefer we went for that toffee apple, Spider. It doesn't feel very safe here.'

'You don't *feel safe*?!' spat Spider, sneering. 'Is that what you're used to feeling, is it? *Safe?!* Safe and ruddy sound, is that what you're used to?'

'We spoke to Stella from the gym,' said Sam. 'She told us things have been tough for you.'

'Not so tough as they've been for Denzil lately,' Spider growled back.

'That's why I'm here. I want to find out who killed him.'

'And so you came straight after *me*.'

Spider's hands were at his sides now, but as he walked slowly towards Sam he gave off an aura of menace and violence even more overbearing than when he had raised his fists. Stray shafts of coloured light fell across the spider tattoo on his neck, bathing it in all the hues of the rainbow. Sam forced himself not to give ground. The insane lights filtering through from above shifted and changed, spraying them both with shimmering specks of restless purple.

'Knock it off, Spider,' Sam said, sounding tougher than he felt. 'I just need to talk. I'm not accusing you of anything.'

'I don't care *what* you think,' breathed Spider, positioning himself directly in front of Sam, eyeball to eyeball, almost nose to nose. 'This business, it ain't nothing to do with you.'

'Grow up, Spider.' Sam maintained eye contact. He refused to be intimidated, not by Spider's overbearing presence, not by the awful spider tattoo across his throat, not even by the rickety rollercoaster that went crashing by once more, setting everything creaking and rattling. 'Why'd you come to the fairground tonight, eh? Who were you looking for?'

'No one.'

'You were looking for Patsy O'Riordan, weren't you.'

'I said I weren't looking for no one.'

'You think Patsy killed Denzil. Don't you. And that's why you came here.'

'How am I going to persuade you to keep your nose out of this business, eh?'

Menacingly, Spider raised a fist slowly and laid it against Sam's chin. The span of his knuckles was huge, more like a sledgehammer than a human fist. Far, far bigger than the three-inch knuckle span of the man who beat Denzil Obi to death in his grotty little bedsit.

'Denzil Obi was beaten to death,' said Sam. 'His assailant had small hands. Much smaller than yours, Spider.'

'That won't stop you pinning it on *me*, though, will it?'

'I'm not here to pin anything on anyone. I'm here to find the man who killed Denzil Obi. And I think, Spider, that makes two of us.'

Without warning, Spider shoved Sam away. Stumbling

backward, Sam fell against a set of spindly scaffold tubes. He could feel these slender metal rods thrumming dangerously with the fierce, wild energy of the rollercoaster they bore.

Spider lashed out, but instead of aiming at Sam, he drove his right fist into the scaffold supports. Then he did the same with his left fist.

'Spider! Jesus! For God's sake!'

Slam! Slam! Spider powered his huge fists, one after the other, into the feeble framework that held everything up.

Sam grabbed at him, trying to pull this madman away before he got them, and the screaming thrill-seekers tearing by overhead, all killed.

But Spider turned fiercely on him, his eyes blazing: 'What's the matter? Not *feeling safe*? Eh? You frightened them poles are going to give out? You frightened of what might come down on your head any second?' For a moment, his words were drowned by the clamour and roar of the rollercoaster. He grabbed Sam by the lapels of his jacket. 'Now you know how it feels!'

Spider's throat was working convulsively, working the legs of the spider tattoo, giving the ink an illusion of life. He seemed on the verge of tears.

This man is having some sort of breakdown, Sam thought. *All he's ever known is violence and the threat of violence and a hand-to-mouth career made out of violence. And with Denzil dead, he's lost his only friend*

in the whole world. No – it's more than that. He's lost
his only connection with humanity. He's completely alone.
He has nothing. Nothing – except revenge.

'I won't lie to you, Spider. Right now I'm scared.'

Spider sneered at him.

But Sam added: 'I'm scared you're going to do something really stupid. I'm scared you're going to go gunning
for Patsy O'Riordan, and that you're going to force us,
Spider, *force* us to arrest you for it. Damn it, Spider, I
want Denzil's murderer behind bars, not you! Think,
Spider! You want justice for Denzil? Then work *with* us!
Together, we can nail the killer. We can nail him, Spider,
so he goes down for thirty years to life. *That's* justice
– not you running around like a one-man lynch mob.
Help us, Spider. Help *me*.'

The next thing Sam knew, he was being thrown roughly
aside. Spider bolted back out into the crowd. By the time
Sam found his feet and set off after him, he was gone.

'Sam! There you are!'

It was Annie, running him to, panting.

'Did Spider go racing by you just then, Annie?'

'If he did, I missed him. Sam, are you all right?'

'You didn't see where he went? Damn it, we've lost him!'

'We've lost *him*, Sam – but look who we've found
instead.'

She indicated ahead of them at a crudely painted sign
suspended above the crowd. It read:

**YOUR CHANCE TO FACE
THE LEGENDARY BARE-KNUCKLE FIGHTER
* * * PATSY 'HAMMER HANDS' O'RIORDAN * * *
LAST ONE ROUND, WIN TEN POUND!!!
ARE YOU MAN ENOUGH????**

An eager crowd of young men jostled around the make-shift boxing ring, keen to impress their mates and girl-friends, trying to nerve themselves to take on the challenge and face Patsy 'Hammer Hands' O'Riordan. Sam and Annie joined the crush, straining to catch sight of Patsy himself. At first, there was no sign of him – the ring was empty – but then, to a great cheer from the crowd, a rather scrawny young man leapt up, stripped off his shirt, and began strutting about, posturing and posing.

'Is that him?' asked Annie. 'It's not what I'd imagined.'

But it wasn't him. Patsy appeared moments later, ducking under the ropes, stepping into the ring, and rising himself up to full height. He presented himself arrogantly to the crowd.

'Chuffin' Nora ...' murmured the shirtless young man in the ring.

'Flamin' 'eck ...' breathed Annie.

'My God ...' whispered Sam.

Everybody stared.

CHAPTER SEVEN

LORD OF THE RING

The first thing Sam saw was a monstrous, demonic face with glowing red eyes and slavering, bestial jaws streaming with fire and blood. This image of hell covered Patsy's chest, tattooed into the latticework of scar-tissue that was his flesh. There were nicks and knocks, slashes and slits, grazes and gashes and great, gouged trenches, telling the story of a lifetime of pain and violence and blood and thuggery. Across his stomach sat three ghastly indentations – Sam knew at once that they were old bullet wounds – and these had been elaborately decorated with a trinity of tattooed women; naked, buxom, horned and horny, these she-devils caressed the wounds, pressed themselves sexily against them, made demonic love to them. Patsy had turned these old battle scars into proud trophies

– more than that, he had turned them into depraved objects of lust. He was proud of his injuries. They were symbols of his manhood. They were a turn-on.

My God ... thought Sam, his blood running cold. I've seen that tattooed devil face before! I've seen it swimming up like a shark out of the darkest waters of my psyche.

Patsy raised his arms and turned slowly, letting the crowd feast its eyes. The tattoos, like the scars, covered almost every inch of him – devils, skulls, snarling animals, naked women with bat's wings and forked tails. A tattooed dagger pierced his left cheek and emerged, dripping blood, from his right. Around his neck was a tattooed noose. His bald head, shiny and hard as a bullet, was inked to give the illusion that his skull was cracked and fractured like shattered glass. Cunningly, his right ear had been tattooed to make it look as if it were ripped off entirely – until Sam realized that it was ripped off entirely, leaving nothing but a ragged, fleshy hole in the side of Patsy's head. Patsy O'Riordan's body was a walking monument to violence, lust and scar tissue.

So this is the demon I've seen leering at me from the dark. But why? Why have I dreamed this terrible man?

Sam recalled the photograph of Tracy Porter from Annie's file. That slim, frail, hollow-cheeked girl was this ogre's girlfriend. His girlfriend – and his punch bag. Looking at Patsy now, Sam thought that Tracy had got off lightly only to end up in A&E; a beating from Patsy could quite easily put her in the morgue. Why did she stay with such a creature? Was it fear that held her prisoner? Or did she – and this seemed inconceivable – did she actually love this man?

God knows. But one thing's for sure: if anyone could beat a man like Denzil Obi to death, it's Patsy O'Riordan.

Having shown himself to the crowd, Patsy turned to the boy who had offered himself as a challenger. They looked like creatures of different species; Patsy towered over the boy, his battered, ink-stained skin rippling, his eyes blazing more fearsomely than those of the devil-face on his chest.

'What's ya name, son?' Patsy asked in a deep, low voice.

The boy in the ring quailed, took a step back, forced himself not to flee.

'... Stu.'

'And you reckon you can go one round wiv me, Stu?'

No, thought Sam. And he sensed that the crowd were thinking the very same thing. And so was Stu.

But still the boy said: 'Yeah, I reckon.'

He had jumped into the ring, he had accepted the challenge. His mates were watching. There was no backing down now.

Patsy nodded slowly and raised his fists. A tattooed scroll unfurling along his massive forearm read: abandon hope. Stu lifted two trembling fists in return.

'O'Riordan's a caveman!' whispered Annie in Sam's ear.

'I don't think he's even evolved that far,' Sam whispered back. 'He's going to batter that kid into next week!'

'Didn't that boy think twice before jumping up there?'

Sam shrugged. Whatever it was that compelled men like those in the ring to seek out violence for the sake of it, he didn't understand it.

'Can you make out Patsy's hands?' he asked Annie. 'How small are they? Three inches across the knuckles?'

'Hard to say. They're not huge, but ...'

'How can we get close enough to find out?'

Before Annie could answer, a bell clanged. The round was on. The crowd roared as Stu lunged forward and threw a succession of rapid punches. He fought wildly, blindly, without style – an amateur brawler. His knuckles smacked against Patsy's face. Patsy made no attempt to dodge, duck, or defend himself. He didn't react. He didn't even blink.

Stu threw everything he had at Patsy, jumped back to give himself a breather, then hammered in again. The crowd went ballistic. But still, Patsy just stood there, his fists raised and unmoving, his eyes open and unblinking. It was like watching a young man fighting a statue.

Suddenly, Sam caught a familiar face amid the crush of onlookers. It was Chris. He had managed to worm his way right up to the side of the ring and was trying to gauge the width of Patsy's knuckles from a distance. He kept holding out his finger, trying to estimate how it compared to Patsy's fists. He looked frankly ridiculous.

'Chris, don't be a bloody idiot ...' Sam muttered.

But in the next moment, there was a sudden shift in the ring. Stu was rushing forward, throwing fast, blind punches, but this time Patsy sprang into life. With breathtaking speed he fired out his left fist, then his right, in quick succession, like pistons. Bash-bash! The first blow flung the boy's head sharply to the side, the second lifted him clear off his feet. He landed flat on his back and lay motionless. A single tooth bounced to a stop on the canvas a few feet from him.

Patsy turned away and rolled his shoulders. It wasn't a victory – it had been a warm-up session, nothing more – a little light sparring to wake up his muscles. He glowered about at the yelling crowd, searching for a more worthy opponent.

Stu's mates clambered into the ring, but not to fight. They grabbed Stu's senseless body and started dragging it away. As they did, Chris dived into the ring and pawed at Stu's face, trying to measure his finger against the swelling bruises on the boy's cheek and jaw.

For God's sake, Chris, don't draw attention to yourself! Sam willed him silently.

But it was too late.

Patsy had spotted Chris and was striding towards him.

As Stu's mates hauled their fallen friend out of the ring, Chris tried to crawl away with them, but all at once he found his way blocked by a massive, tattooed leg. Chris's nose bumped against Patsy's kneecap; he slowly raised his eyes, looked up at Patsy's thigh, his boxing shorts, the decorated bullet holes across his stomach, the devil face leering from his chest, until finally he made eye contact with Patsy himself.

Very meekly, Chris said: 'We could be friends.'

Sam felt Annie tug at his arm.

'Let's get him out of there,' she urged.

'We mustn't draw attention to ourselves,' Sam replied, stopping her from rushing forward. 'We're supposed to be undercover.'

'Sam, that monster'll kill him!'

'Chris isn't up there to fight. He'll jump out of the ring and run a mile, you'll see.'

Sam watched as Patsy grasped Chris by the shoulders and lifted him to his feet.

'My next opponent, is it?' Patsy growled.

'Who? Me?' said Chris. And with exaggerated nonchalance he said: 'Nah, I'm just some little fella.'

'Ain'tcha man enough?'

'For what?'

'To face Hammer Hands O'Riordan.'

An encouraging cheer went up from the crowd. Chris looked anxiously about, then seemed to take courage from the onlookers' support. He shrugged Patsy's hands away from his shoulder, straightened his knitted tank top, and said: 'I can look after meself.'

'Oh, Christ ...' muttered Sam.

'Last one round, win ten pound,' said Patsy. 'Fink you can manage that?'

'I wouldn't say no to ten quid,' said Chris, cockily. 'But ... you know, I'm doing okay. I don't need a tenner. And I'd hate to cause you an injury.'

Sam covered his face with his hands. Was Chris fearless? Was he suicidal? Or was he just a berk?

Patsy brought his ugly, tattooed face close to Chris's and sniffed him, first one side, then the other, like a lion. Chris took a nervous step back. Patsy turned to the crowd, raised his voice and cried out: 'He's agreed to fight!'

A roar went up. Chris's face went white.

'I never agreed to nuffing,' he whined, and he appealed to the baying mob for support. 'I'm good for a tenner, I don't need the money!'

But the crowd had taken up the chant now. Fight – fight – fight – fight!

'We've got to stop this!' said Sam, and he pushed forward, but the press of bodies was so tight now that he couldn't get through.

'Chris! Chris!' called Annie, but her voice was swallowed up by the noise.

Fight – fight – fight – fight!

'Get ya stuff off, boy,' Patsy said, looming over Chris. 'Strip down, to the waist.'

'I can't, I got a wheezy cough,' pleaded Chris.

Patsy began to pose and posture again, displaying his battered, scarred, tattooed physique from every angle. Chris swallowed in a dry throat.

Fight – fight – fight – fight!

'I tell you what,' stammered Chris. 'No need for fisti-cuffs. Give us an Indian burn and we'll call it quits.'

Patsy raised his fists and adopted the stance of a boxer. Chris looked frantically about like a cornered animal.

'Can't we talk about this?'

Fight – fight – fight – fight!

'We can do a deal, how's that? You can't say no to a deal!'

Fight – fight – fight – fight!

Chris leant forward to whisper something in Patsy's ear, but found himself confronted by a gaping, fleshy hole. He pulled a horrified face and moved round to Patsy's *other* ear; cupping his mouth, he whispered into it.

Patsy listened, paused, then turned to the crowd.

'Thirty quid!' Patsy declared. 'Thirty quid he's just offered me!'

The crowd went mental, booing and whistling and hurling abuse.

116

Patsy turned his terrible, fiery eyes back towards Chris and said: 'Is that all your life's worth to ya, young 'un?'

Chris seemed on the verge of tears. He whispered again.

'We're up to fifty!' Patsy relayed to the crowd.

Coward! Wanker! Fight – fight – fight, you spasmo –fight!

Chris fell to his knees.

'I'll pay you a thousand!'

He flapped at Patsy with his hands, a wretched supplicant before a barbarous, pitiless god.

'A million! *Two* million! You can have me fags an' all!'

Sam could see Chris's mouth working away, but now his words were drowned by the furious mob. Even so, it was obvious that Chris was pleading. He grabbed one of Patsy's hands and kissed it pathetically, like he was meeting the pope.

Degraded by this miserable creature's presence, Patsy pushed him away, and Chris tumbled backwards out of the ring. The crowd jostled him, drubbed him, insulted him, shoved him, until at last he broke free and went stumbling off, disappearing from view behind a noisy generator that was feeding power to the rides. Sam and Annie caught up with him and found him shakily trying to light a cigarette.

'Chris, what the hell did you think you were doing?'

Sam yelled at him. 'You could have blown our cover back there, do you realize that?'

Chris gripped his lighter with both hands to keep it steady.

'Sorry, Boss.'

A fart of terror escaped from his arse.

'Sorry, Boss.'

He belched like a walrus, seemed about to be sick, managed to swallow down his rising gorge.

'Sorry, Boss.'

Despite his anger, Sam had to feel sorry for him. His mood softened.

'Well, at least you got out of there in one piece,' he said.

Annie rubbed his arm – then pulled her hand away from his soggy clothing.

'I was sweating cobs!' Chris said.

'Feels like it,' grimaced Annie, wiping her hand with a Kleenex. 'What did you think you were playing at, Chris?'

'I was trying to measure the size of his hands.'

'Well, full marks for the Dunkirk spirit, Chris,' said Sam, 'but next time, try not go about your policework like such a tit, okay? You risked the whole operation.'

'*And* your own neck!' put in Annie.

'Yeah, but I got a result,' said Chris. 'Didn't you see what I did?'

'Yes, we saw. You laid eggs like a chicken and begged for your life.'

'Ah! That's how I *wanted* it to look! But that was all part of my cunning plan, Boss.'

'Chris – that weren't a plan – that was sheer screaming panic.'

But Chris shook his head knowingly and said: 'You thought I was kissing his hands to ask for mercy. But I weren't. *I was measuring them.* That's what we came here for, weren't it, boss? I felt his hands to see the size of 'em. And you know how wide they were across the knuckles? From here to here.'

He pointed to one side of his mouth then the other. And to demonstrate further, he laid his finger across his lips longways.

'Three inches, near as dammit,' he said. 'Patsy O'Riordan's knuckles are three inches across.'

'Three inches?' said Sam. 'Are you absolutely certain?'

'I'd swear to it, boss. In court. Patsy O'Riordan – he's your man. And *I* just proved it.'

Sam and Annie exchanged a look – then Sam patted Chris's shoulder.

'You're a bullshitter, Chris – but it looks like you've confirmed our killer.'

But Chris shrugged Sam's hand away, looked down his nose at him, and said with pride: 'Careful who you're calling a bullshitter, boss. You're talking to the bloke who's gone a whole round with Patsy 'Hammer Hands' O'Riordan.'

The demonic face inked onto Patsy O'Riordan's chest once again haunted Sam's dreams that night. He awoke early, bathed in sweat, his blankets balled at the end of the bed. Padding to the bathroom, he splashed cold water onto his face and tried to recall the details of his dream, but all he could now remember were muddled, hazy images – the demon face looming out of the darkness; pounding fists; Annie being struck and falling into a deep, dark void; Sam blundering, lost and alone, through a nightmare labyrinth that went on forever.

'Forget it!' Sam whispered to himself. 'These dreams don't mean anything. They don't. They *don't!*'

His heart told him otherwise, but he forced himself to ignore it.

CHAPTER EIGHT

A FRIGHTENED MAN

Arriving early at CID, Sam found Gene was the only one to beat him in.

'Up with the lark, Guv?' he said, stepping into Gene's office.

'Didn't sleep, Tyler. Things on my mind.'

'I thought you might have worn yourself out on the dodgems last night. You were certainly going for it.'

'Merely demonstrating the art of good driving,' Gene growled back. 'The Nureyev of the highway. They should have looked and learned, not had me banned.'

'They banned you from the dodgems?!'

'Wipe that smirk off your gormless face, Tyler. Them fairground pikeys besmirched my honour.'

'You can't blame 'em, Guv, you *were* getting a bit leery.'

'*I was bumping! That's why they're called bloody bumper cars!*' yelled Gene.

'They're *dodgems*, Guv. You're supposed to *dodge*.'

Gene glared at Sam for a few seconds, then settled himself again. 'Anyway. Forget it. We're not here for that. What matters is the Denzil Obi case.'

'Well, thanks to Chris we've got a possible match between Patsy O'Riordan's fists and the wounds on Obi's body.'

'Which is good enough for *me*, Sam, but you know as well as I do that standing Chris up in court to say that he reckons O'Riordan's the killer because he *kissed his hands and thinks they might be the right size* isn't exactly going to secure us a conviction.'

'Spider was at the fair last night, guv. I managed to catch up with him.'

'And what did he say?'

'Not a lot. He was very threatening. I thought he was going to smash my face in.'

'Frit you, did he?'

'No, Guv, he didn't 'frit' me.'

'Bet he did. Bet you pooped some.'

'Guv, I attempted to engage to elicit information in the pursuance of this homicide enquiry,' Sam said, ignoring the pouting, eyelid fluttering, limp-wristed posture Gene adopted to mock him. 'He was in a bad way, emotionally. Very highly strung, on the verge of some sort of breakdown I'd reckon. Denzil's death has really hit him hard.'

Gene shrugged: 'Either that or he's play-acting.'

'He wasn't play-acting, Guv. I think Denzil was all he's ever had in life. And when he lost Denzil, he lost *everything*.'

Leaning back in his chair, Gene thought for a moment, then asked: 'Faggots, you reckon?'

'What does it matter? God, Gene, two men *can* be close, you know!'

'Well, depends what you mean by "close", don't it, Tyler. There's close and there's close. I mean, there's mates, right – and there's *'best'* mates – and then there's *'arseholes in the bogs'* mates, which ain't right.'

Sam massaged his temples for a moment, told his temper not to rise, and said: 'Let's just keep our minds on what's important here. Spider was at the fair last night –the same fair that Patsy O'Riordan works at. Both men are connected to Denzil, and Patsy is now our chief suspect. So, if we're right, and Patsy killed Denzil, then it's a fair guess to say that he might very well be after Spider too.'

Gene nodded thoughtfully. 'I've been thinking about that. You remember there were three locks on Denzil Obi's door.'

'Yes. And a spyhole too.'

'And a spyhole …'

Gene trailed off, lost in thought. After a few moments, he said: 'Denzil was a frightened man. Three locks and a spyhole – *that's* frightened. And yet he opened the door for the man who killed him.'

'Looks that way, guv.'

'If it was Patsy O'Riordan standing there, why the hell would he let him in? There was bad blood between them. He *knew* that Patsy had a grudge against him – a deadly grudge – a *killer* grudge – and still he opened the door and let him in. Why? *Why*?'

Sam shrugged: 'Maybe Spider can answer that.'

'I'll *bet* he can.'

'What do you mean, guv?'

'You're a copper, Tyler – figure it out.'

Sam frowned, not following Gene's thinking. He imagined the scene moments before Denzil was attacked: there was Denzil, in his flat – a knock at the door – Denzil instantly wary and suspicious – he goes to the door and checks the spyhole – he sees a face he knows – a face he trusts – a face he is willing to open the door to ...

'*Spider!*' said Sam.

He imagined Denzil seeing Spider's face through the spyhole – the door opening – and then, looming out of nowhere, Patsy O'Riordan appears, his compact, rock-like fists slamming into Denzil's face with terrifying force.

'No,' said Sam, shaking his head. 'It's impossible. I

124

saw Spider's fists last night at the fair, guv. They were well more than three inches across.'

'Measure them, did you?'

'I didn't need to, Guv, I had one *this close,* right in my face.'

'How close is "this close", Tyler?' Gene loomed towards Sam and thrust his own fist right against his face. His hard knuckles pushed against Sam's nose. 'Is "this close" *this* close?'

'More or less,' said Sam, backing off.

'Well there you go! *Any* fist is going to look like a big 'un *that* close. And I'll bet you were dropping bricks in your freshly ironed Y-fronts an' all. Sorry, Tyler, but I seriously doubt your judgment in this matter.'

'Okay Guv, even if I'm wrong about the size of his fist, Spider still doesn't have a motive for killing Denzil. Denzil and Spider were close. They were like brothers. Why would Spider betray Denzil like that?'

'*I* can't answer that question, Sammy boy,' said Gene, getting to his feet and jangling his car keys. 'But we both know who can.'

The Cortina screamed to a stop at the foot of an imposing concrete tower block.

'That's the place,' said Gene. 'That's the address Stella gave us.'

'I'm still not buying your theory, Guv,' said Sam. 'I

can't see Spider betraying Denzil like that, least of all to a monster like Patsy.'

'Perhaps Spider bought his life with that betrayal,' said Gene. 'After all, it's Denzil who wound up in the morgue, not Spider.'

'You might be right that Denzil was betrayed by *someone* he trusted – but who's to say it was Spider? What about Dermot, their trainer from the gym? What about Stella herself?'

'It weren't Stella,' Gene scowled.

'Why not?'

'Coz it weren't. I'd sense it otherwise.'

'That's no argument,' said Sam.

'I'm your DCI, I don't *need* to argue!'

Sam looked across at him: 'I hope you're not letting your feelings sway your judgment, Guv.'

'*Feelings?*' roared Gene. '*For what? That clapped-out slapper?!* I'll forget you spoke, Tyler.'

Feeling he had touched a raw nerve, Sam bit his tongue and fell silent as he followed Gene out of the Cortina and across to the tower block. The lifts were burnt-out wrecks so they were forced to take the stairs. The found themselves panting and grunting on an endless trudge up concrete stairwells that reeked of urine.

'Spider *would* have to live on the eighty-second millionth floor,' growled Gene.

'Hell of a view, though,' panted Sam, looking out

across Manchester as the sun struggled up. And then he felt a sudden sense of overpowering vertigo. For a moment, he was sure he was falling – falling – hurtling towards the hard concrete below. He gripped a metal railing and steadied himself.

A memory of the future, he told himself as he steadied his breathing and calmed his beating heart. *A flashback ... or a flash forward.*

Either way, it made his head spin to think about it. Time and Space, it all began to swirl like colours in a kaleidoscope.

'Move yourself, Tyler,' barked Gene, shoving past him as he strode along the balcony looking for Spider's front door.

'Right with you, Guv,' said Sam, forcing down the sense of disorientation that had overwhelmed him. And he thought: *you made the right decision to jump, to come back here ... don't let anything make you doubt that.*

He caught up with Gene and found him examining a black front door.

'Looks pretty solid,' he said.

'And the window's blocked up with plywood,' said Sam. 'Like a barricade.'

'He's expecting trouble,' said Gene. 'He'll be jumpy. We'd better tread carefully. Don't want to spook him.'

'Good idea, Guv.'

Gene hammered ferociously on the door and yelled

through the letterbox: 'Open up, Spider you slag, it's the law!'

'The gentle touch,' commented Sam.

They heard movement on the other side of the door.

'It's okay, Spider,' Sam called out. 'It's CID. We just want to talk to you about Denzil.'

'I bet he legs it out the back way,' snarled Gene, sizing up the door to smash it.

'We're eight storeys up, Guv – I don't think there *is* a back way.'

A voice called out from behind the door. 'Show me your badges.'

'Spider, it's me, the copper who spoke to you at the fair last night. Under the rollercoaster, remember?'

Gene gave Sam a sideways look: 'Oh aye? Under the rollercoaster? And what did you two get up to under the rollercoaster?'

Sam ignored him: 'Come on, Spider, don't muck us about.'

'I said show me your badges!'

Gene and Sam held their ID up to the spyhole.

'Let me see your faces,' the voice demanded.

'Just open this door,' Gene snapped.

'Your faces! Show 'em!'

Sam and Gene exchanged a look, then obligingly brought their faces to the spyhole. Sam imagined how they must look, distorted and bulbous in the fisheye lens.

There was a pause – and then, one by one, a series of heavy bolts were thrown back. The door inched open, and there was Spider. He stared at them warily; when he swallowed nervously, the spider tattoo on his neck seemed to flex its legs.

'Hey-ho, remember us?' said Gene, pushing Spider back into the hallway.

Sam followed them in. The flat was cramped and filthy. The windows were all blocked in with plywood; the only light came from a few bare bulbs dangling from the ceiling on frayed cables.

'Your cleaner phoned in sick, has she?' said Gene, shoving Spider into his one and only armchair. 'Sorry to come barging into your web like this, Spider, but you seem rather shy when it comes to talking to policemen.'

'I don't trust coppers,' Spider said, eyeing them both suspiciously. And to Sam he added: 'Bet you're saying I went for you, ain't 'cha.'

'No, Spider, I'm not saying that. You got a bit heated, but I can understand that. You're upset. You're stressed.'

Spider looked away, disgusted by this attempt to empathize.

'We just need to talk to you,' said Sam. 'It's like I said before, it's in your interests to cooperate. We're not here to fit you up. We want to get our hands on the man who killed Denzil as much as you do.'

'No you don't,' muttered Spider. 'Maybe you *do* want him … but nowhere near as much as I do.'

'You'd like us to think that,' said Gene.

'Guv, just give the fella some space,' protested Sam. 'Spider, why were you at Terry Barnard's Fairground last night?'

Spider shrugged: 'Free country.'

'What were you hoping to find there?'

'A decent toffee apple.'

'You were looking for Patsy O'Riordan, weren't you. Well? Weren't you? You wanted to size him up, see what state he's in – because he's after you, isn't he. He killed Denzil Obi, and now he's coming for you. Am I right?'

Spider said nothing. Sam heard Gene inhaling loudly through his nostrils – a sure sign his patience was rapidly running out – so before the guv could put his foot in, Sam said quickly: 'Spider, I'm going to level with you. Patsy O'Riordan is our prime suspect. We think he killed Denzil. And we think *you* think so too. Why did he do it? We don't care about whatever you and Denzil got up to in the past – we're not here for you, we're here to find Denzil's killer and bring him to justice. And to do that, we need your help. So please, just tell us what you know. Why would Patsy have a grudge? Spider? Please talk to us.'

'You're wasting your time, Sam,' piped up Gene. 'He won't say a word. And you know why? *Coz he's got blood on his hands.* Ain't that right, Spider?'

Spider said nothing. His eyes flashed menacingly at Gene. His tattoo flexed its spindly legs as he swallowed.

'I'm not just talking about your murky, mucky past,' said Gene, looming over Spider. 'You cut a deal with O'Riordan, didn't you! Eh? Speak up! It were *you* led O'Riordan to Denzil's flat, weren't it! It were *you* who betrayed your own best mate, just to save yourself, weren't it! *Weren't it!*'

Spider looked up at Gene, eyes filled with hate. Gene glowered back at him.

'That's my superior officer's theory, not mine,' Sam put in. 'If DCI Hunt's wrong, just say. Spider – staying silent won't help you and it won't help us nail O'Riordan.'

'I knew it ...' Spider murmured.

'What, Spider? What did you know?'

'I knew you'd point the finger at *me*.'

'Nobody's pointing the finger at you, Spider,' said Sam.

'*I* am,' intoned Gene, '*if* you hadn't noticed, Tyler.'

'For God's sake, Guv, this isn't helping!'

'He's a scumbag,' said Gene. 'Look at him. Look at that stupid tattoo. Look at his stinking rat hole. You don't negotiate with human crap like this, Tyler, you flush it down the khazi.' And turning to Spider he said: 'Consider yourself well and truly flushed, Spider. I'm nicking you. Obstruction. Withholding evidence. Being in possession of a criminally grubby flat that don't have no bleedin' lifts. I'll work out the details on the way to

131

the station, they don't matter much – what counts if that you'll be 'fessing up by the time I'm through with you.'

Sam expected Spider to react defensively, furiously – but instead, he seemed more resigned than anything else. Had he come to expect no more from life than injustice and rough treatment? Did he know nothing better than a world of threats and intimidations?

When I came face-to-face with him under the roller-coaster, he seemed like a man on the very brink of a breakdown. His nerves were shredded. Denzil's death had shattered him. And look at how he lives! Barricaded-in, paranoid, alone. What kind of existence is this? Is it as bleak and grey and cheerless on the inside of Spider's mind as it is in the walkways and stairwells of this awful estate? How can we expect a man as strung-out as this to work with us?

Damn it all, Gene's bloody gorilla routine is only going to make things worse. Spider needs empathy, not threats. He needs to know that when he speaks, he'll be listened to. Unless he trusts us, he'll clam up, go into himself, pursue whatever private plans for revenge he has.

I need to shut the guv up. I need to get him out of the way, and establish some sort of contact with Spider that will start to win his trust and–

At that instant, there was a sudden flash of light, and Sam found himself falling backwards, striking a wall, slithering to the floor.

A bomb … he thought, his head spinning, his vision full of popping lights.

Gene's voice was reaching him as if from the far end of a huge, echoing cavern: Tyler … get off your arse and help … Tyler!

The lights began to disperse. Sam saw the floor, the blocked-in window, the yellowed light bulbs – then he saw Gene and Spider locked together, grappling.

'Guv …' he said – or rather, he tried to, but his jaw was burning with pain.

What the hell happened? It was like a bomb went off …

His spinning brain was starting to put itself back together again. Here and there, normal service was resumed. Thoughts began to flow again.

He punched me. Spider bloody well punched me! A lightning blow, I never even saw it coming.

He wondered dimly if his jaw was really broken or if it just felt like it was.

Only feet away from him, the guv and Spider crashed to and fro, hurling each other against the walls, until suddenly Spider broke free and dashed from the flat. At once, Gene turned on Sam, looming over him like a very pissed off yeti in a camelhair coat.

'You're not dead yet, Tyler!' he boomed into Sam's face. 'So you got no excuses! On your feet and get *moving*!'

Tyler felt himself dragged up, and the next thing he knew he was running out of the flat and along the concrete balcony, following Gene's flapping coat tails. Up ahead, Spider dashed down a stairwell and vanished from sight.

Despite his spinning brain, and the pain throbbing through his jaw, Sam had enough wits to comprehend that Spider was fleeing the interview, that they were pursuing him, that this was a chase.

'Shift your lazy arse, Tyler!' Gene bellowed. 'The spider has legged it! The bastard's getting away!'

CHAPTER NINE

SPIDER

Sense and consciousness was still coming back to Sam's spinning head as he pounded down the stairwell after Spider. His jaw throbbed. It had been one hell of a punch – a real boxer's punch – a jaw-cracker of a blow.

Spider belted down the concrete steps, turned sharply and dashed away along one of the balconies.

'After him!' gasped Gene, doubling up and struggling for breath. His face was puce, his eyes bloodshot. His diet of eighty fags a day washed down with a bottle and a half of scotch was kicking in.

Sam belted along the balcony. Spider glanced round, came to a stop, and raised his fists, ready to fight.

'Don't be an idiot, Spider,' said Sam, edging closer. 'I need to talk to you, that's all.'

Spider tightened his stance. He was serious.

'Pack it in, Spider. We can't nail O'Riordan if you don't help us!'

'You don't want to nail O'Riordan, you want to nail *me*!'

'No we don't! Ignore my guv'nor, he's just trying to intimidate you.'

'I know what he's doing!'

'Spider, please, trust me – I know it's hard but *trust me*!'

A front door right next to him suddenly opened, and a bleary-eyed bloke in his vest and pants peered out. 'Do what?'

Spider shoved past him and dashed into the flat.

'Oi!'

Sam flashed his badge at the man in pants – 'Police!' – and raced in after Spider, crashing through a pyramid of empty Kestrel lager cans heaped in the hallway. He smashed through a door at the far end and saw clothes strewn on the floor, a bed, and a woman in the bed clutching the blankets to her breasts and screaming as Spider clambered across her, making for the window.

Sam hurled himself at Spider – but he was too late and Spider clambered out the window. The woman in the bed shrieked.

'Police,' said Sam, flashing his badge again, and he thrust his head out of the window to see Spider clinging from a tiny windowsill and searching with his foot for purchase further down.

'For God's sake, you'll get yourself killed!'

Spider slipped nimbly from one windowsill and caught hold of another. He was as agile as an insect. Was *this* why they called him Spider?

The woman in the bed was still screaming in Sam's ear. Angrily this time, Sam shoved his ID badge in front of her face – 'Police! I'm the ruddy police!' – then rushed from the room. The bloke in pants was shuffling back along the hallway; Sam went to rush past him, but the bloke grabbed him and began grappling ineptly.

'Gotcha!'

'Get it into your head, *I AM THE BLOODY POLICE*!' And he pressed his ID badge hard into the man's face until the bloke fell over, sprawled amid the Kestrel cans. 'And clean your bloody flat, you people!'

Sam burst out of the flat and tore back along the balcony. He almost slammed into Gene, who was lumbering down the stairwell, puffing like a steam train.

'Guv! Guv! He's round the back, scaling the wall!'

'Nick 'im, Tyler! I don't care how you do it! Just nick 'im!'

'There was no need for all this!' Sam called over his shoulder as he leapt and sprinted down the stairs. 'It's your fault he bolted, Guv!'

'He assaulted one of my officers!' Gene hollered wheezily.

'*You* made him!' Sam shouted back.

Reaching ground level, he tore round the back of the block. There were no balconies on this side, just row upon row of window ledges. And there was Spider, thirty feet from the ground, clambering nimbly down. He glanced at Sam, then tried to climb back upwards.

'Spider, this is pointless!' Sam called up to him. He rubbed his jaw – good God, it was on fire! 'Come down, before you break your neck.'

'You bastards want to stitch me up!' Spider called out, his fingers groping for a firm handhold on a crumbling sill above him.

'My guv'nor's full of bull, Spider, it's just his way. But I'm different.'

'You're a copper!'

'Yes! Yes I am! A decent copper!'

'That's a laugh!' Spider snorted. He slipped, groped about blindly for a moment, then regained his grip on the side of the building. 'It don't mean nothing to scum like you, but I'd die a hundred times over if it brought Denny back!'

He meant it. Stella hadn't exaggerated about Spider and Denzil; neither of them had anyone else in this world. With Denzil gone, Spider's life was broken; he could go after the man who killed him, he could take revenge

– and after that, what? He would still be alone. His world would still be shattered. Seeing him clinging to the side of that grim concrete tower block, it struck Sam how it summed up Spider's whole existence; precarious – joyless – hunted – hanging by his fingernails.

That's me, he thought suddenly. *I'm hanging on by my fingernails too. That damned Test Card Girl keeps telling me – my dreams keep telling me – my heart keeps telling me ...*

'There's a reason for that,' said the Test Card Girl softly, appearing out of nowhere and slipping her small, cold hand into Sam's. 'Shall I tell you what I know? Shall I tell you the secret about Annie?'

'I'm sick of this,' said Sam, pulling his hand free from the girl's icy grasp. He rubbed at his eyes. 'I'm sick of it! You hear me? *Sick of it! SICK OF IT!*'

'Yeah,' came Spider's voice from just above him. 'You and me both mate.'

Spider dropped lithely to the ground. His face was pale and his shoulders were slumped. His energies had drained away. He looked defeated.

'Sick of it,' he said. 'All of it.'

And with that, Spider slumped down and buried his face in his hands.

Sam looked about him, but he knew already that there would be no sign of the girl. She had vanished back to whatever dark recess she had so suddenly emerged from.

139

Sam crossed over to where Spider was collapsed against the foot of the tower block, crying silently, and sat down beside him. He sighed, exhausted.

'It's not easy, is it,' he said.

Without looking up, Spider shook his head.

'Sometimes you feel like ... just jumping off a roof.'

Without looking up, Spider nodded his head.

'I tell you, Spider – I don't know what I'd do if I lost the person I care most about.'

Spider said: 'I hope you never have to find out.'

He sobbed, just once, then swallowed it down; the tattoo on his neck flexed its inky legs, looking more vulnerable and pathetic than the mark of a hard man.

'My jaw hurts,' said Sam.

'Sorry,' snuffled Spider.

'That's okay. Not your fault.'

'Are you going to arrest me?'

'Nah.'

They sat together for a bit, each one lost in his own thoughts, until at last Gene Hunt appeared, swaggering up in his camelhair coat, issuing threats and smart-arse wisecracks.

'Wait for us in the car, Guv,' Sam said without getting up. His voice was tired. He was in no mood for Hunt right now. 'Just ... wait in the car.'

Gene fell silent, staring down at Sam and Spider, his expression unreadable, eyes narrowed. Then, without a word, he turned and marched away, aggressively firing up a Woodbine as he went.

'You're going to A&E!' Annie ordained. 'Right *now*!'

'Nothing's broken, I'll be okay,' said Sam, wincing as she touched his bruised and swollen jaw.

'Since when were *you* the expert, Sam? I'll take you to casualty myself.'

They were back at CID. After all the argie-bargie at the tower block, Spider had at last come along quietly. Sam had walked with him back to the Cortina, where Gene had been unusually quiet. Sam reiterated to Spider – and perhaps to Gene too – that nobody was being arrested and nobody was being accused, that Spider was expected to do nothing more than help them with their enquiries back at the station. Spider had shrugged and nodded, and without a word got meekly into the back of the Cortina. The three of them had driven back to CID without saying another word.

But by the time they had gotten back to the station, there was a huge and monstrous bruise burgeoning across Sam's jaw and cheek. The sight of it had shocked Annie, so much so that she seemed on the verge of battering Sam herself if he didn't go to A&E and get it checked out.

'Later,' he said.

'That means never.'

'No, Annie, it means later. We've got a witness to interview.'

'And you don't want to look like a sissy in front of the boys, is that it?'

Sam laughed, then winced. Laughing sent bolts of pain stabbing through his jaw.

'Don't think I'm being gung-ho,' he said. 'You know as well as I do that bumps and knocks are all part of this job.'

'"Bumps and knocks"?! Sam, you look like one of the Black and White Minstrels!'

'God, I hope not,' Sam muttered, wincing as much from the memory of white men grotesquely blacked up and singing *Old Man River* as from the pain in his jaw. 'Look, Annie, I can't stand here arguing. Spider's in a fragile mood; he lost everything he thinks of as family when Denzil died – he's a broken man. He'll talk to me, I know it. He'll talk to me *right now*. I can't delay. And God knows, I can't leave the interview to Gene.'

'But, Sam-'

'Trust me, Annie. It's important.'

Annie looked hard at him for a moment, then her face softened.

'I just worry sometimes,' she said. 'Seeing you come back all covered in bruises ...'

'I know. And I worry about you too.'

'I don't see why, Sam, it's not *me* getting into fights.'

'That's true,' said Sam. 'It just seemed like the right thing to say. But I meant it. I do worry. You can't help worrying about people that you …'

'People that you what, Sam?'

'People that you like. People you care about. Care about a lot.'

This was not the time, and it certainly wasn't the place, to follow this conversation where it wanted to go. Over Annie's shoulder he could see Ray talking on the phone; Ray tipped him a crude, blokey wink. Sam felt the urge to wrap that telephone cable round his neck and throttle him.

'I don't mean to sound like your mother, Sam, but you can't muck about when it comes to your health,' said Annie, looking at him with such seriousness that Sam wanted to laugh again. 'Don't you smirk! It's important to take care of yourself.'

'If I didn't hurt so much I'd kiss you right now!' said Sam.

'Lucky escape for me then, innit,' said Annie, and she headed back to her desk. 'And don't think I haven't got my eye on you, Boss. The minute you're done with your interview, I'm whisking you straight down the hozzy to be checked over. And that's final.'

'Nurse Cartwright knows best,' said Sam.

'Nurse Cartwright knows *everything*,' she replied, trying to sound more serious than she actually was.

But as Sam turned away and headed for the Lost & Found Room, he felt a sudden unease. Annie's silly remark echoed through his head.

'Nurse Cartwright knows everything.'

Everything, he thought. *She knows what it is, the secret that she carries, the secret that the Test Card Girl wants to tell me ... the deep, dark secret that will tear my world apart ...*

'Utter crap,' he muttered to himself as he strode purposefully along the corridor. 'There *is* no secret. Annie's Annie – and that's all there is to it. And we're going to be together. And we're going to be happy. And that's that.'

He willed the Test Card Girl to show up, with her mournful little face and intimations of a terrible revelation. But this time, for once, there was no sign of her.

It was just Sam and Spider, sitting across from each other in the Lost & Found Room. Gene was off sulking; just as Sam had felt excluded from the highly charged, sado-masochistic interview he had conducted with Stella, so Gene felt excluded from this. As Sam had told Annie, Spider was indeed in a fragile mood; he was willing to talk, but not to Gene. The overbearing, red-blooded, Woodbine-chewing technique of the mighty Hunt would not work here. What was called for was something altogether more low key, more one-to-one. It felt less like a police interview than a counseling session. And Gene Hunt didn't *do* counseling sessions.

'So,' said Sam, handing Spider a cup of revolting CID coffee. 'Are we right about Patsy O'Riordan? Did he kill Denzil?'

Spider nodded.

'And does he want to kill *you*?'

Spider nodded again.

'Why?' asked Sam in low voice. 'What's going on here, Spider?'

Spider cupped his coffee in both hands – Sam noticed the old scabs and bruises on his battered brawler's knuckles – and stared silently for a few moments, lost in himself. Then, in a voice so soft that it was almost a whisper, he began to speak.

'When we were kids,' he said. 'Denzil was the nig-nog. The coon. To the *white* kids, anyway. To the black kids he was the honky, the white-boy. *Everybody* took a crack at him, being half-caste an' all.'

'Mixed race,' said Sam.

'Don't matter what you call him, he still had the shit kicked out of him from all sides. But I could never get worked up about all that stuff – you know, the colour of a fella's skin. Maybe it's something your parents teach you. I dunno. *My* parents didn't teach me nothing, except how to take a punch. But then ...'

He waved away these useless old memories.

'Whatever. One day, when we were kids, Denzil was getting a pasting. There was a whole load of 'em piling into him, white kids and black kids, and I thought to myself: *stuff this, it ain't right.* So I waded in, helped him out. Me and Denzil really cracked a few faces. We were ... what? Ten? Eleven? I don't know how old we were. When I think back, I always imagine us as grown-ups. It's like we weren't *never* kids, not properly.

'Anyway. I waded in, and from then on we were mates. We looked after each other. Of course, I got a lot of stick for knocking about with a darkie, but I didn't care. Stuff 'em. Denzil was sound. He was always there for me. And after a bit, we got these done-' – he indicated the tattoo on his neck – '-the Spider, and the Black Widow. Two against 'em all – just me and him.'

'Two against them all,' said Sam, nodding. 'I can understand that.'

'Bollocks you can,' said Spider, without a scrap of anger. He wasn't insulting Sam; he was just stating a fact. 'You don't know it, not the way *we* knew it. Anyway. Time goes on, this happens, that happens, and we find ourselves in the boxing game, making a few quid, trying not get on the wrong side of ... certain gentlemen. But it don't work like that, coz it's them 'certain gentlemen' what run everything. You understand what I'm saying?'

'Yes. Go on.'

'Me and Denzil, we get a visit. We're told it's in our

146

interests to help out a certain gentleman with a problem he's got. We're told it wouldn't be polite to refuse. We're told the certain gentleman in question would take a refusal very personally.'

Sam nodded.

'So we had no choice but to do what we were told to do,' said Spider.

'And what *were* you told to do?'

'The certain gentleman in question had a grievance. Something to do with things being said that shouldn't have been said. Something to do with a ... I remember the phrase: *a distinct lack of respect*. Somebody had been speaking out of line.'

'Who had been speaking out of line? Was it Patsy O'Riordan?'

'Yes. O'Riordan was a boxing legend. A real hard bastard. Everybody went up against him – but nobody could crack him. Me and Denzil included. He flattened us both. Patsy was *hard*. And he knew it. He was full of himself. And when a bloke like that gets too full of himself, he starts saying things he shouldn't. He starts mouthing off when he should keep his trap shut. He stops showing respect to ... to certain gentlemen. And then he finds himself in trouble. It can all get pretty serious.'

'I see,' said Sam. 'So – you and Denzil were pressured into ... what? Punishing him? Disciplining him?'

'We had no choice, not if we didn't want our hands busted, or worse. We agreed to sort Patsy out, but secretly we were scared. We'd both been up against him – we knew what he was made of – and we reckoned he could have the two of us even if we came at him together.

'Then Denzil comes over to my place one night. He looks real scared. He's got this thing all wrapped up in a cloth, and I says to him: *what's that?* And he says: *we're gonna use this.* And he shows me. It's a gun. And I says: *Denny, we ain't cowards, and we ain't bloody cowboys – we can't use a shooter.* But Denny says: *we got no choice – think about it.* And he was right. Patsy'd make mincemeat of us any other way.

'So we set up a fight. Patsy versus me. We make him think it's the usual thing, an illegal bout, the sort of fight he wins without breaking into a sweat. He agrees to show – it's easy money – and he turns up to fight. It was round some old warehouse, out of the way. But when he gets there, he finds there's just me and Denny, and he knows at once that it's a set-up. It's an old trick, it's been done before, it's been done since – nobody likes falling for it – makes you look like a mug.

'Patsy clocks what we've done, and he goes mental. He comes right for us. And Denny shoots him, once, in the stomach. Patsy keeps on coming. Denzil shoots him again. And then again. Third time does it – Patsy goes down. He's lying with his face pressed on the floor. I can't see if he's breathing. Denny's shaking. I say: *stick another one in him – right in his head,* but Denny says he can't pull the trigger again, he just can't do it. I says: *don't think about it, Den, just do it!* But he won't. He just won't. So I says: *give it to me – I'll do it.* And I take the gun, and I stick it right next to Patsy's head. But I'm shaking, even worse than Denny, and I'm thinking to myself: *I can't do it – I can't do it.* But I tell myself *you gotta do this, Spider – you'll be in real trouble if you don't.* So I close my eyes, and I'm shaking, and I pull the trigger, and the gun goes off.'

'And?' Sam prompted gently.

'I bloody missed him!' said Spider. 'At point bloody blank! I'm shaking and I got my eyes closed and I miss him! All I do is catch his ear – blow it off. But even then, Patsy doesn't move. He doesn't say anything. He just lies there. He's dead. He's gotta be dead. He's not moving. And I say: *we've done it, Denny, let's get out of here.* But Denny's being sick. And I feel sick too. It's not ... it's not because we give a damn about Patsy, it's because ... well, it ain't right, what we done – tricking a bloke like that, then using a shooter when he ain't got nothing but his fists.'

'You had no choice,' said Sam.

'When do blokes like me and Denzil *ever* get a choice?' Spider suddenly spat out. 'In this world? You think, if we had any sort of choice, we'd *choose* to fight like bloody animals just to earn a few quid? Eh? You think living like that is a *choice?* It's not like joining the bloody police! It's not a *career.* It's either that, or you're dead. *That's* the nearest thing me and Denny ever got to 'making a choice' – do this, or end up dead!'

Sam shrugged. He didn't know what to say. Spider glared at him, then calmed himself down.

'Anyway,' he said. 'As far as we was concerned, Patsy was dead. So we ran off. And we told … we told a certain gentleman that we'd done what he asked, and we got our wages, and that was that. And if you want to nick me for what I done, I can't stop you.'

'It's okay,' said Sam. 'All this is just between you and me. I told you – it's Patsy we're after, not you. Go on with your story. You left Patsy for dead, you got your money – then what?'

'It was years ago,' he said at last. 'I thought … *we* thought, me and Denny … we thought Patsy O'Riordan was history. And then he turns up again. Out of the blue. Back from the grave.'

'Back from the grave …' muttered Sam. The phrase sent a chill running down his spine – a chill that had nothing to do with Patsy or Spider or Denzil. He forced himself to concentrate on the interview. He said: 'I'll tell you something, Spider – as a copper, I've met men like Patsy before. They get shot, stabbed, blown up, have bloody great anvils dropped on 'em – and they're so damn hard they just keep getting up again. They're like Terminators … what I mean is, it feels like they're indestructible.'

'Nobody's indestructible,' said Spider, and there was a hard glint in his eyes. 'Not even O'Riordan.'

'Spider, I understand how you feel about Denzil, but this isn't the Wild West. You can't go roaming the streets, a man alone, looking for revenge. It's a police matter now. I know you don't want to hear that, but that's the reality of it. If you really want to see justice done, you've got to work with us.'

'The police,' said Spider, smiling bitterly and shaking his head.

'We can help you.'

'How?'

'First up, we can keep you safe. Patsy can't hurt you if he can't find you. I know it's not the Ritz but we can put you up in one of the cells here. You won't be a prisoner, Spider, I promise you – you'll be out of harm's way, that's all.'

'For how long?' asked Spider. 'How long am I supposed to live in one of your cells?'

'Until we've got a case against O'Riordan strong enough to move in and nick him.'

Spider laughed bitterly and shook his head: 'You won't get your case. Patsy knows you're onto him. He'll disappear when the fair moves on; go to ground and bide his time, just like he did before. He waited nearly ten years before he took his revenge on Denzil. He'll wait again. He'll wait for you coppers to lose interest in this case, then he'll come after me. Or are you going to keep me locked up safe and sound in your cells for the rest of my life?'

'We *can* build a case, Spider – if you help us. Tell me something. Denzil had a spyhole fitted in the door of his flat. He could see who was there. And yet, he opened the door to his attacker. My guv'nor reckons it was *you* he saw, that you betrayed him to buy your life. He believes you led Patsy to Denzil's flat that night. But he's wrong, isn't he.'

'Who's going to take my word over your guv'nor's?'

'I am. Denzil saw *somebody* – somebody he trusted, somebody who in reality had led Patsy to his door – but that somebody wasn't you.'

'Of course it wasn't me.'

'Who, then?'

'I don't know. I've thought about it …'

'And?'

'I can't think of anyone.'

'What about Stella?' asked Sam, but Spider shook his head emphatically. 'If it wasn't her, what about your trainer, Dermot?'

'Why would any of these people have it in for Denzil? Stella's been good to us. So's Dermot.'

'But Spider, there must be somebody who connects Denzil to Patsy – somebody Denzil trusted – somebody willing to betray him.'

'If I knew who it was,' said Spider, 'they'd be suffering right now. Believe me.'

Sam sighed and sat back. There was a missing piece in this puzzle, something that was eluding them. Were they overlooking something? Were they wrong about Denzil opening the door to his attacker? Was Sam seeing all the evidence but from the wrong angle, trying to fit the different elements together in the wrong way?

'If Patsy can't find you,' said Sam, 'you think he'll disappear?'

'I know it,' said Spider. 'He'll wait until the heat's off, then come looking again.'

'I don't want him to do that. I want him to get impatient. I want him to do something that'll give himself away.'

'Don't underestimate him. He's smarter than he looks.'

'Then we'll just have to up our game,' said Sam. 'We'll keep you here in one of the cells, Spider. As a precaution. I'll see you get what you need. If Patsy can't find you, he'll get frustrated – he'll get impatient, no matter how smart he is – and the more frustrated and impatient he is, the greater the chance he'll make a mistake that gives himself away. We'll raise the pressure. We'll provoke him.'

'In other words, you'll use me as bait,' said Spider.

'No,' said Sam. And then, with a shrug: 'Yes. In a way. But what choice have we got?'

'All I want is revenge for Denny,' said Spider quietly. 'If that means using me as bait, *I* ain't got a problem.'

'We won't do anything that'll put you in danger,' said Sam. 'However we play this, you'll be safe. I promise.'

'You can't promise that,' said Spider. 'This is Patsy O'Riordan. *Nothing's* safe. *No one's* safe.'

'We'll see about that,' said Sam with resolve.

'Yes,' said Spider, almost inaudibly. 'We will.'

CHAPTER TEN

GENE PISSES ON A PLAN

As good as his word, Sam came looking for Annie so she could take him to casualty. But the figure who confronted him in the corridor, dressed in a camelhair coat with a cigarette smouldering in his gob, wasn't Annie.

'Your bird's busy on the phone,' Gene intoned. '*I'll* drive you. And on the way you can tell me all about your little chat with Spider.'

Sam followed him to the Cortina. Gene gunned the engine and roared off into the Manchester traffic.

'Spider didn't betray Denzil,' Sam said. 'I don't know who did, but it wasn't him.'

'Pity,' said Gene. 'That would have made our lives a lot easier. So what did you do with him – send him home?'

'I think home's the last place he should be. He's not safe there. I put him in one of the cells, out of harm's way. He's willing to cooperate with us, Guv.'

'Cooperate how? By acting as bait?'

'Spider's convinced that Patsy'll disappear when the fair moves on – he'll lie low, wait for us to shelve our investigation, and then come back for Spider when the heat's off. We need to somehow make it clear to Patsy that he can get his hands on Spider right now, that if he acts straight away he can have his revenge, that he'll never get his chance otherwise. We need to provoke him into doing something – *anything* – to give himself away.'

'Such as?' asked Gene. After a few wordless moments, he said: 'Your silence tells me you don't actually have a plan, Tyler.'

'I *do* have a plan, Guv. I'm just not sure how you're going to react to it.'

'I don't like being second guessed,' said Gene, scowling at the road ahead. 'Try me.'

'Okay, Guv. This is my suggestion. We go and see Patsy O'Riordan in person.'

'Undercover, I take it.'

'Yes,' said Sam. 'We'll pose as fight promoters.'

Gene barked out a single, contemptuous laugh.

'What was that for?' asked Sam, offended.

'I was trying to imagine *you* as a hard-as-nails under-world fight promoter, Sam.'

'Sporting this bruise I reckon I look the part, Guv.'

'No, Tyler, you just look like a weedy bloke with a big angry missus.'

'Hear me out, Guv. We go and see O'Riordan. We tell him we've got a score to settle with Spider, and we've heard that he has too. We tell him we'll set up a fight between them, but that the whole thing's a trap, that Spider'll get there, expecting a fight, and instead he'll find just us and Patsy. A trap – a chance for Patsy to really go to town on Spider.'

'But in reality we will have officers ready to swoop in and nick Patsy first,' put in Gene. 'Sounds like a right laff, Sammy, but your imagination's starting to run away with you in your old age. This plan's bollocks.'

'It's not bollocks, Guv, it's sound,' insisted Sam. 'It's exactly the same sort of trap Denzil and Spider tricked Patsy into all those years ago. It's the sort of trap Patsy'll understand. It's part of his world. And I'm betting on the fact that Patsy'll go for the chance to turn the tables on Spider, to trick him in the same way. The thought of it'll cloud his judgment, get him fired up and eager to take his revenge. He won't want to disappear and bide his time, not when he's got the chance to give Spider a taste of his own medicine right here and now.'

'And Spider's dopey enough to risk his neck going along with this scheme, is he?' asked Gene.

'Not dopey, Guv. *Brave.*'

'Dopey or brave, there *are* times when it's hard to tell the difference,' said Gene. 'But this isn't one of those times. I can sense a hundred and one things that could go wrong with this plan of yours, Sammy, and a *thousand* and one ways Spider and you and – worst of all – *me* could end up getting royally bashed in the process. One slip-up, and we could be in *serious* trouble.'

'There are risks, Guv, but we'll make sure we minimize them.'

Gene shook his head in incredulity.

'We'll wear wires, Guv,' Sam went on. 'We'll record everything Patsy says to us. We'll get him to admit he killed Denzil.'

'Which he's *bound* to do – sure he is – good as gold, bang on cue.'

'If we're smart, Guv, if we can entice him to give himself away, why not?' Sam pressed on. 'If we don't act now, Patsy'll slip through our fingers! This way, there's a damn good chance we'll have him bang to rights!'

Gene rolled his eyes silently.

'It's dangerous, I know,' said Sam. 'It's going to take bottle. Nerves of steel.'

Gene said nothing.

Sam tried a different tactic: 'Of course, Guv, if you don't feel you can handle it, I can always team up with Ray.'

'You won't convince me like that, Tyler.'

'Ray's up for undercover work, I'm sure he'll have the balls for it.'

'I said forget it, Tyler.'

'I'm just saying, Guv. It's going to be dangerous. I understand if you don't want to get too involved. You can stay out of the way, if you like ... monitoring the recording ... at a nice safe distance ...'

'You're wasting your time playing these games with me.'

'I'm not playing games with you, Guv. I'm just saying there's no pressure on you to take risks you don't feel comfortable with.'

Without warning, Gene hit the brake. The Cortina howled to a stop in the middle of the road. Sam damn near went through the windscreen. Behind them, car horns bleated and complained, but Gene ignored them.

Turning to Sam he glowered at him, his eyes narrow, and said: 'I'm not in this job to prove my manhood to twats like you. I'm here to bring justice to these mean streets. There ain't enough avenging angels in this world, Tyler, and there sure ain't enough in this city. But one good man in a Cortina can make a difference. *That's* why I'm here – to see the right thing gets done once in a bleedin' while – to see the scum of the earth get what's coming to 'em – not to swagger about comparing dicks with gormless berks in poncey leather jackets. You getting my drift, Tyler?'

Behind them, car horns were braying. But Gene's eyes remained fixed on Sam.

'Guv, I was just-'

'That poofy bruise on your gob might make you feel like the Man With No Name, Tyler, and it might very well get D.I. Crumpet dripping in her knickers, but it don't cut no ice with *me*. If I put a plan into action, it's not to prove the size of my John Thomas – it's because that plan's the *right* plan, the plan that'll get the job done, the plan that'll put some bastard behind bars and see this city one degree safer come nightfall.'

Honk! Parp parp! went the car horns.

'There's only one person I'm out to impress,' Gene growled. 'That bird you might have seen around – the one with the sword and the scales, and the hanky tied over her eyes. You know the one I mean, Tyler?'

'I know the one you mean, Guv.'

'Good. Keep her in mind. She wears a blindfold, Sam, but don't think she ain't got her eyes on you *and* me.'

Beep! Beeeeeep!

In his own time, Gene settled back in his seat, put the Cortina into gear, and calmly moved on. He turned right.

'You're going the wrong way,' said Sam.

'No I'm not.'

'The hospital's straight on the left.'

'Correct.'

'Then why aren't we going straight on and then left, guv?'

'Because we're not going to the hospital, you dollop. God, Tyler, for a professional copper you can be unnervingly slow on the uptake.'

'If we're not going to the hospital, where *are* we going?'

The Cortina nosed its way up a walled-in service road until it reached the grounds of a derelict factory. The sun was starting to set behind the rotting corrugated iron roofing.

'What the hell are we doing here, Guv? Are we carrying out an extreme makeover on this place?'

Without answering him, Gene cruised the car round the yard until he saw an open shed with dilapidated doors. He parked the car inside.

'This'll do,' he said.

'Guv, please, I'm not getting my head around this. What's going on? Why have we come here?'

Gene pointed. Sam looked through the windscreen of the Cortina and out through the doors of the warehouse. In the courtyard beyond, a rough-looking group of men appeared, hurrying through the evening shadows towards a large abandoned warehouse. As they disappeared inside, several more men appeared and went in after them.

'Who are they?' Sam asked.

'Punters,' said Gene.

'For what?'

'Well, Tyler, while you were having a tender heart-to-heart with Spider, me and the boys were getting on with some *real* policework. We were digging up some old contacts from the underworld, putting our ears to the grapevine, getting the word from the street, and all that bollocks. Looks like Patsy O'Riordan's still active as an illegal bare-knuckle fighter. He's something of a legend. Nobody's ever beaten him. And like the fastest gun in the west, whatever town he rolls into there's always somebody keen to take him on.'

Sam watched as more men arrived and headed inside the old workshop. Now that he thought about it, he saw that it was the perfect place to hold an illegal fight. It was enclosed, private, walled-off from prying eyes. A hundred men or more could gather in that workshop and the world outside would know nothing about it.

'Forget your poncey plan about posing as fight promoters,' said Gene. 'We'll just wait for O'Riordan to knacker himself out fighting, then nick him.'

'*Nick him*? Here?! In front of a crowd? Guv, we'll get ourselves lynched!'

Gene drew deeply on his cigarette, unconcerned.

But Sam was insistent. 'Think about it, Guv. We don't have enough evidence to put together a case.'

'And at this rate we never will. I want that bastard banged up and off the streets. If you're right and he's ready to do a disappearing act, then we can't afford to fanny about anymore. We'll nick him after the fight – it don't matter what the charge is – lock him in the cells so he can't go nowhere, put together the rest of the case, then charge him. No need for pricking about undercover, Tyler.'

'It won't work, Guv.'

'You're not the one to make that decision,' said Gene firmly. He fixed Sam with a granite stare.

Sam stared back, said: 'You're jeopardizing the case, Guv.'

'I'm your DCI, so lump it.'

'Sir, I will not.'

'*Sir*? You're calling me *sir* now? That sounds ominous.'

'I refuse to arrest Patsy O'Riordan before we've established a watertight case against him,' said Sam, his voice controlled but angry. 'It is reckless, unprofessional and counter-productive.'

'No, Sammy-boy, it's just good basic policing. And I won't argue about it.'

'Sir, I formally urge you to reconsider.'

'There's that word again! I could get used to it. *Sir Gene Hunt*.'

'If you're going to go ahead with arresting O'Riordan ...'

'Which I *am*.'

'Then you've left me no choice,' declared Sam. 'You're on your own here tonight.'

And with that, he flung open the door and clambered out.

At once, Gene popped up on the other side of the Cortina and glared fiercely across the car roof at him.

'Don't you walk out on me, Tyler!'

'You've given me no option!'

'I'm your superior officer, I don't have to give you ruddy options!'

'Is all this macho stuff going to your head, is that what's going on? I saw you in Stella's Gym, Gene, you were behaving like bloody Popeye Doyle, swaggering about, acting the big man. Why? *Why?* What the hell for?'

'Because I'd had me spinach.'

'Popeye *Doyle,* Gene! From the bloody *French Connection,* not the one with the anchors! Oh for God's sake! What is it that gets into you and makes you carry on like this? Does it make you feel good? Or are you such a bloody hairy-knuckled caveman that when you're around hard nuts and muscle men you just *have* to give 'em all the old Mike Tyson routine?'

'The whaty-who routine?'

'Is it Ray who's put this idea into your head about coming here and nicking Patsy?' barked Sam. 'I bet it is. I bet you and him were talking while I was interviewing Spider. *That poofy Tyler, all tea 'n sympathy, he don't have the balls for a case like this. Stuff 'im, Guv – nick*

O'Riordan, bring 'im in, put the squeeze on his ol' ball bearings and get him to fess up!'

Gene narrowed his eyes suspiciously: 'Have you been eavesdropping on us, Tyler?'

'No, Gene, I just know you and Ray too well. You want to play John Wayne out here with the tough guys? Fine. Do it. Do what the hell you want. *I* can't stop you. But I won't be part of you screwing up this case. I won't sink to your level. And I'll tell you why.'

'Oh, please do Tyler, I'm hangin' on every word.'

'Because *I'm* a man, not a little boy.'

Sam slammed the Cortina door and stomped furiously away. He could feel Gene's stare boring into the back of his head. As he reached the doors of the warehouse, Gene called after him:

'I accept your resignation, Tyler. Get your desk cleared by the time I bring O'Riordan in.'

Sam kept walking. He didn't turn and he didn't speak. If Gene wanted to interpret what he'd said as a resignation, then so be it. So be it. There was no reasoning with the man. In fact, there was no point trying to work with him at all. Macho, arrogant, conceited, knuckle-headed, backward ...

'Borderline alcoholic, homophobic, racist ...' Sam added under his breath as he stormed across the factory courtyard making for the street. '... Unprofessional, bigoted, unthinking, unfeeling ...'

'Wrong way, son,' growled a huge man with a bristling beard who suddenly blocked Sam's path. Laughing with his equally huge and hairy companions, he clamped his massive arm around Sam's shoulders and swept him along. 'The action's through here!'

Sam tried to unhook himself from the man's iron embrace, but the next thing he knew he was stumbling and tripping through a set of doors into a cavernous abandoned workshop. It was filling up with men – with *blokes* – unwashed, unshaven, reeking of cheap tobacco and booze and stinking breath. They were gathering around a cleared space, an arena, empty but expectant, the bear-pit where Patsy O'Riordan and his opponent would clash.

The workshop doors clanged shut. A bolt was thrown. Nobody was getting in or out. Sam glanced round. He caught a glimpse of a camelhair coat amid the eager press of bodies, then lost sight of it.

Damn it! he thought, feeling trapped and frustrated. And then: *Damn you, Hunt, for getting me stuck here! You stupid macho pig! Damn you!*

Okay, Sam told himself, getting his head together. *Since I'm stuck here, I can do something useful. I can make sure Gene doesn't arrest Patsy O'Riordan, because if he does – if he shoots his bolt too soon – I can see this whole case going right down the swanny.*

He looked around, trying to get a fix on where Gene was, but he couldn't see him. The place was a riot of excited men, shouting and clamouring and flapping wads of fivers and tenners at each other as they slapped on their bets for the fight to come. Billows of cigarette smoke fogged the workshop. Cans of lager cracked and frothed. There was pushing, shoving, sudden outbursts of temper – men squared up, flung a few punches, were dragged apart; there was braying laughter and phlegmy coughing, burps and belches and huge, ripping farts. Men stood against the wall and pissed openly.

I bet Gene feels completely at home here, thought Sam. *It's all blokes. Just blokes. Nothing but blokes. Blokes being blokes. Full-on blokeage. A bloke-fest. Wall-to-wall bloke-a-rama in widescreen with THX sound. A world of pure bloke.*

Streams of urine trickled from the makeshift latrines, flowed across the floor, and pooled round Sam's feet. Disgusted, he forced his way through the jostling crowd to escape a soaking. Heaps of fag ash fell across his jacket. Somebody pulled the ring on a can of lager and showered him in foam.

And still he couldn't locate Gene Hunt amid the scrum.

What's Gene's plan? He said he'd nick Patsy after the fight – presumably when he's exhausted. But would an ogre like Pasty ever go quietly? And what about everyone else in here – does Gene really think they'll stand by meekly and watch O'Riordan led off to the station? They'll lynch him!

The place was a powder keg, charged with testosterone and the thrill of imminent violence, ready to go up if Gene was stupid enough to start flashing his police badge and shouting the odds.

I need to stop him. He'll not only blow the whole case, he'll get himself killed into the bargain!

'You need me, Hunt,' he said to himself. 'You'll just have to delay my resignation for another day.'

All at once, the atmosphere in the room shifted. There were cheers, shouts, sporadic booing. Sam saw the monstrous figure of Patsy O'Riordan appear in the arena, the demon face inked onto his huge body glaring and snarling. Patsy postured, flexed his muscles, prowled about like an animal. It was the same sub-human display he had put on at Terry Barnard's Fairground, just before he had pasted that foolhardy kid who'd so rashly gone up against him.

But his opponent this time won't be a kid, Sam thought. *This is a serious fight. This is the real deal.*

The crowd parted, revealing the biggest, broadest, blackest man Sam had ever seen. He was a hulking mountain of muscle. His jet-black skin shone. His eyes blazed like points of cold, white light.

A chant went up from a section of the crowd: *Chalk-ee, Chalk-ee, Chalk-ee!*

Chalky. What else would he be called? This was the 70s.

Confidently, Chalky stepped into the arena and eyeballed his opponent. Patsy stared right back. The crowded bated and goaded them, but neither man moved. A man with combed-over hair and catastrophic teeth pushed himself between the two boxers, keeping them apart. This was the ref – or rather, the nearest thing a fight with no rules would get to having a ref.

No gloves, no rules, no mercy, thought Sam. *This is going to be a nasty fight – nasty and vicious and bloody and cruel.*

At that moment, he sensed something – a sharp, lemony fragrance that managed to cut through the stench of fag smoke and aftershave and body odour and piss. He knew it at once. And the moment he recognized it, a voice whispered in his ear – husky, hard, but definitely female.

'Didn't expect to see *you*, soft-boy. Is this business or pleasure?'

Sam turned, and there was Stella, all lipstick and eye shadow, winking at him. She drew regally on a cigarette held between her red-taloned fingers and blew the smoke into Sam's face.

'You want to know what *I'm* doing here?' coughed Sam. 'What are *you* doing here?'

'Getting my rocks off, what do you think?'

Her eyes glittered expectantly at the two men about to beat the living shite out of each other in the arena. A shiver of delight ran through her body.

'Have you got your beautiful guv'nor with you?' she asked. 'Don't tell me you left him at home.'

But Sam said nothing. He was thinking. Was Stella the one who had betrayed Denzil? Spider had said she had no motive, but here she was at a Patsy O'Riordan fight. It was surely no coincidence. Was there a connection between her and Patsy? And if there was, did she have a motive to betray Denzil, and Spider too?

Before he could think of something to say, he saw Stella's face tighten into a tense expression of sexual arousal – and at the same moment, there was a surge and roar from the crowd.

The fight was on.

The referee leapt clear from the arena, his comb-over flapping loose, as Patsy and Chalky slammed into each other like colliding freight trains. It was a far cry from the blind thrashing the boy at the fair had hurled at Patsy; these two huge men fired punches like artillery shells, pounding each other's faces with staggering force. They grappled together, rabbit punching, biting, kneeing each other in the balls – then broke apart, the sweat flying from them, and the blood too. Chalky hulked menacingly, his huge hands clenching. Patsy stared out through his tattooed flesh, eyes blazing, his tiny, compact fists raised and ready, the ridges of his knuckles hard as iron.

Seconds later, they were at each other again,

pummelling and pounding. The crowd went wild. The roar of men's voices was deafening. Stella shamelessly ran her hand down her body and between her legs, her eyes widening then narrowing but never wholly blinking as she followed the action in the arena.

Between the no-holds-barred fighting, and the wildness of the crowd, and the flagrant arousal of Stella, Sam felt he had materialized in some lawless, subhuman zone outside of civilized society, somewhere where all decency had broken down, where there was nothing but violence and lust and cruelty. He was amongst savages.

Perhaps Stella didn't need a motive to betray Denzil. Perhaps the pleasure of witnessing violence was motive enough.

As he looked at her, he tried to imagine her reacting in just this same way to Patsy beating Denzil to death in his bedsit. Had she licked her lips then as she was doing now? Had her breasts heaved in the same way? Had she rubbed her crotch so shamelessly as Denzil Obi was killed in front of her?

She's clearly a sadomasochist. But is she a monster? Would her depraved pleasures lead her to be complicit in murder?

He found it hard to believe – and yet, here she was, under the same roof as Patsy O'Riordan, lapping up the violence like it was quality erotica.

But this was no place for him to pursue a line of

enquiry. The clamour of the men was deafening. In the arena, Patsy was slugging away at Chalky like a man demolishing a wall. Blood was splattering and streaming down Chalky's face. Wet, red chunks were flying into the air. Blow after blow impacted against the man's jaw, lips, nose, eyes, until his face was so pulped that it looked as if it were melting. Patsy rammed a punch into his opponent's stomach, doubling him up. Chalky vomited. Patsy slammed him upright again with an uppercut, then battered his head this way and that with a rapid succession of left-right-left-right punches. Sam waited for the ref to intervene, for the bell to sound – and then realized that this fight would continue, unchecked, until only one man was standing.

Go down! Sam silently urged Chalky. *For God's sake, don't take any more of this! Go down! Go down!*

Incredibly, Chalky ducked Patsy's blows and staggered past him. There was still one last scrap of fight left in him. Blind and disoriented, he hurled drunken blows at Patsy, stepped into the pool of his own vomit, skidded, lost his footing, and fell. And as he did, Patsy got in one last blow – a crowd-pleaser, an act of pure theatrics on an already defeated opponent. It was a merciless left hook that caught Chalky full-on as he toppled, spinning him over in mid-air and sending him crashing into the ecstatic crowd.

Thank God it's over, thought Sam.

But it wasn't over. Pumped up and raging, Patsy waded into the crowd which parted before him like the Red Sea, revealing the crumpled, bleeding remnants of Chalky on the hard concrete floor – lying in a red sea of his own. Patsy leathered into him, kicking him like he was a football, stamping on his head, aiming blows into his neck, his kneecaps, his genitals.

It's Denzil Obi all over again ...

This couldn't go on. It wasn't *boxing*. It was obscene.

Sam shoved forward, roughly pushing his way through the howling men.

'Stop!' he bellowed. And then, his instincts taking over: 'Police! Stop!'

His voice was swallowed by the noise. He was an agent of the Law, but the Law had no place here amid these hollering, blood-crazed men. Struggling to reach O'Riordan, he found himself the target of blows and kicks from the crazed onlookers. He stumbled and went down, glimpsing Stella's glistening, wet-lipped face loving every second of it. Furiously, he fought his way back up. Somebody grabbed his shoulder and hauled him power-fully to his feet – and in the next moment, Sam was nose-to-nose with Gene Hunt.

'Tyler, you twonk!'

'Get your hands off me, Hunt! I'm nicking him!'

'You've changed your tune all of a sudden!'

'Somebody has to stop this! Now get off me!'

'You wade in now, Tyler, and O'Riordan will *kill* you! And I mean *kill* you!'

'*Now* look who's changed their tune!'

A few yards away from them, Patsy was picking up from the floor what was left of Chalky, holding his limp body with one hand so that he could pulverize it further with his other. Sam glimpsed Chalky's head lolling from side to side, his face a shapeless pudding of blood.

'Wait!' hissed Gene as Sam fought to get free of him. 'Wait till he's done!'

'That man will be dead!'

'For Christ's sake, Tyler, it's just a bit of fisticuffs!'

Patsy hurled Chalky's head down hard against the floor, then jumped on it with both feet. Blood snorted from Chalky's nostrils.

And that, it seemed, was that. Panting, heaving, the saliva swinging in gloopy ropes from his slack mouth, Patsy glared about at the cheering crowd, all humanity extinguished from his burning eyes. He raised his arms and began to parade around the workshop, exultant and victorious.

Gene kept his grip on Sam, snarled at him: 'Wait! We'll get him after. Not here. After.'

'I don't have to take your orders anymore, Hunt. I resigned, remember?'

'No. I don't remember. Must be getting older.'

As Patsy completed a triumphal circuit of the workshop, Sam looked across at the mushy heap that was

Chalky. It lay still for a while, then, at last, began to move. With heroic effort, the man dragged himself, dripping and bleeding, to his feet – then slithered back down to the floor, senseless and exhausted.

And then, to Sam's surprise, and to Gene's too, Stella appeared like an administering angel. She was still panting from the orgasmic pleasures of the fight, but now she crouched down beside Chalky and began attending to him, clearing the blood from his mouth and nose with a cloth, supporting his head with her hand, offering him sips of water from a bottle. She looked up at Sam, and then at Gene, and, raising her voice to be heard over the racket of cheering men, she said: 'Don't just stand there, gorgeous. Give us a hand.'

In a filthy, windowless room adjoining the workshop, beneath the hard light of a single naked bulb, Sam and Gene carried Chalky in and sat him in a chair. Stella gently cupped the man's swollen cheek with her hand.

'Still with us, Ben?' she asked.

Chalky – or rather, Ben – mumbled inaudibly. He could barely move his mouth, and he couldn't open his eyes at all.

'Good boy,' said Stella, and she stroked him tenderly. 'I'll see you're okay.'

From the workshop next door, the shouts and cries of the excited crowd echoed in.

'This here one of your boys is it?' asked Gene. 'You told me you were legit.'

'*I* am,' said Stella. 'But boys like Ben need to make money where they can. Or try to.'

'What's your connection to Patsy O'Riordan?' Sam asked.

'This isn't the most convenient time for an interview,' Stella replied. But then she sighed and said: 'There isn't *any* connection. I was here to keep an eye on my boy.'

'*And* to get your kinky kicks watching it,' put in Gene.

'A girl's business is her own.' Then Stella thought for a moment, and said in a low voice: 'Why are you asking about O'Riordan? Is he a suspect?'

'That's classified information,' said Gene, puffing out his chest self-importantly. 'And since *you're* still a suspect, luv, *and* a filthy mare, it's got chuff all to do with you.'

'Don't be like that, Hunt,' said Stella. 'We've had good times together.'

'Don't kid yourself, Grandma,' growled Gene. 'Stay here and play Florence Nightingale with what's left of your toyboy. Me and gormless here have got a murder enquiry to be getting on with.'

He went to the door and looked out into the workshop beyond. Men were sorting out their winnings, arguing over monies owed, finishing off their lager or else pissing it out against the walls. There was no sign of Patsy O'Riordan.

'I'm not bloody losing him!' intoned Gene urgently. 'Let's roll, Tyler. Come on, move yourself!'

'I've told you, Gene, I'm against nicking O'Riordan until we've got a case against him.'

'Five minutes ago you were shoving your way towards him shouting *Stop, police!*'

'Yes, I was. It was instinct, Gene. Seeing that lad getting a pasting, I couldn't help myself.'

'Tyler,' said Gene, looking seriously into Sam's eyes. 'Don't muck about. Trust me. I know what I'm doing.'

Sam stared back at him, narrowed his eyes, and at last said: 'I don't think you do.'

Gene raised himself to his full height, glared momentarily at Sam, then swept out through the door. Sam knew at once that he was going after O'Riordan, that he was mad enough to try and nick him all by himself, and that nothing – least of the protestations of Sam Tyler – would swerve him from his course of action.

'You gonna let your guv'nor go into battle all by himself?' asked Stella, looking up at him with glittering eyes.

'This place ...' growled Sam. 'Biggest open-air asylum in the world!'

Gritting his teeth with rage, he barged through the door in pursuit of Gene Hunt.

CHAPTER ELEVEN

CAN THE CAN

Sam strode briskly across the now-deserted workshop, stepping nimbly over the trails of drying urine staining the hard floor.

'Guv! Wait!'

Gene had already reached the far side of the workshop and was disappearing through a tall set of metal doors.

'Hold up, Guv! Think about what you're doing!'

As Sam rushed forward, his foot came down on a fat gobbet of blood still wet and glistening after the fight. He skidded, lost his balance, and went down hard on the concrete floor. The impact shot a bolt of pain up his spine and set his bruised jaw throbbing. For several moments, he sat there, one hand hovering over his jaw, his face set in a grimace of agony, unable to move.

Panting and groaning, Sam at last managed to haul himself laboriously back onto his feet. But by now Gene had disappeared. Cursing his guv'nor under his breath, he limped across the workshop to the metal doors and looked out into a gloomy courtyard littered with old packing crates and a crumpled heap of beige sacking. There was still no sign of Gene.

'Damn it, Hunt. Damn *you*!'

Sam headed out into the shadowy courtyard, making for a corrugated metal gate that was the only way Gene could have gone. It was just as he reached it that a huge figure loomed out of the darkness, grabbed hold of him and hurled him to the ground. A burst of shattering pain ripped through Sam's jaw. He cried out – but even as he did, a boot slammed into his stomach and knocked the air clear out of his lungs. Sam found himself writhing on the floor, doubled up and gasping hopelessly for breath.

'Who is it?' came a rough voice from across the yard.

'Dunno,' answered the slab-like man who now stood over Sam, pinning him to the ground beneath his boot. 'Just some fella.'

Heaving and moaning, Sam fought to draw scraps of oxygen into his collapsed lungs. His vision swam. He told himself: *you will not pass out – you will NOT pass out – damn it, damn it, you will not pass out!* With effort, he angled his head to look up at the man who had him trapped. He saw battered jeans, a checked shirt, massive forearms, an unruly black moustache, and a wild mop of shoulder length hair framing a hard, flat face.

'He don't look up to much,' Moustache-man grinned down at him.

'Check him for a shooter,' the other voice called across.

Moustache-man roughly shoved his hands inside Sam's jacket and fumbled about.

He'll find my police ID, Sam thought. *And then what? How will he react when he finds I'm a copper?*

Thrusting his hand into Sam's inside pocket, Moustache-man pulled out the ID in its leather case.

'What you got?' the other man called across to him.

'Nuffing,' Moustache-man announced. 'Just a wallet.'

'Leave it for Patsy,' ordered the other man. 'Just so long as this little runt ain't got no tricks up his sleeve, that's all that counts.'

He didn't even bother to look inside, Sam thought as the badge was shoved back inside his jacket. *They're not interested in my money. This isn't a mugging.*

Now Sam could see that at the far end of the courtyard was another figure, just as huge as Moustache-man, but sporting a ponytail tied with a grubby red ribbon. He took hold of the mound of beige coloured sacking and began hauling it up. It was then that Sam realized that it wasn't sacking at all – it was Gene. He caught a glimpse of Hunt's face, his eyes closed and his mouth slack, before

Ponytail threw him over his shoulder and strode across to the corrugated iron gate.

'Bring 'im,' he barked, and Moustache-man reached down and grabbed Sam in his iron-like grip.

Sam kicked out, aiming to drive his heel into Moustache-man's crotch, but missed, catching his muscle-packed thigh instead. Drawing on every ounce of strength, Sam tried to scramble away, reaching wildly for a heap of broken crates, hoping to grab some chunk of wood and fight his way out. But at once he felt those powerful hands slam down on him, dragging his arms behind his back and immobilizing him. Agonizingly, he was dragged to his feet. Sam felt the rough bristles of the man's moustache prickling against his cheek.

'You like that I break your arms, boy? Eh? You like that?'

Moustache-man increased the pressure. Sam felt his arms being forced remorselessly further and still further up his back. Bones strained. Tendons screamed.

'Don't say much, do ya. But you will. You and your mate, we'll get you talking. You'll tell us who sent ya and what you're after. And when we're done,' – he pressed his stinking mouth even closer to Sam's face like he was about to kiss him – 'I'll snap you in 'alf like a Twiglet, you slag.'

Never had Sam heard the word Twiglet used as a threat before.

181

The man wrenched Sam's arms viciously. Sam's eyes were screwed up with the pain, but he felt himself being frog-marched roughly across the yard, then across hard concrete. Forcing his eyes open, he glimpsed Patsy O'Riordan's monstrous, heavily inked face, with its glittering, wolf-like eyes. Patsy peered at him, scrutinizing Sam pitilessly.

'I know 'im,' he growled, still panting and snorting from the exertion of the fight. 'I've seen this twat before.'

He must have glimpsed me in the crowd when Chris ended up in the ring with him. He's smarter than he looks ... more alert ... quicker-witted ...

'What shall we do wivvum, Patsy?'

'Sling 'em both in the back.'

The next thing Sam knew, he was being thrown like a sack of potatoes into the back of the van. The only thing that cushioned the impact was Gene's motionless body. Landing on him like this, Sam found the guv was surprisingly soft.

The van door slammed and the bolt was thrown. More doors slammed, the engine growled into life, and the van roared off.

'Guv? Guv, can you hear me ...?'

Gene's eyes were still closed. The only movement he gave came from the rocking and bouncing of the van.

'Guv?'

A huge bruise, the colour of a ripe plum, was spreading slowly across Gene's temple. There was something particularly unnerving to see him in such a state, and Sam realized that he had unconsciously come to think of Gene as somehow indestructible.

He isn't indestructible. He's flesh and blood like the rest of us. Cut him, and he bleeds. Clobber him hard enough, and down he goes.

Sam felt for a pulse and found one. The guv's strong heart was still pounding away. But how long would he be out cold like this? And what the hell did O'Riordan and his two lackeys have in store for them?

They must have clocked Gene steaming after them and thought he was sent by some underworld rival. It's like Stella said, that's what their world is like – it's all violence, vengeance and betrayal. They expect trouble – anywhere, and at any time. What will they do when they discover we're coppers? Will that make things better … or worse?

The van accelerated, hurtled round corner after corner, then seemed to leave the road and go bouncing and dipping across rough ground. Sam heard distorted music blaring out over huge speakers. It was Suzi Quatro, belting out *Can the Can* over the screams of kids on the centrifuge and the waltzer. The van picked its way, slower now, around the outskirts of the fair, then came to a stop. Sam heard O'Riordan, Moustache-man and Ponytail bundle out of the front, head round the back, and throw open the bolt on the doors.

He shot a glance at Gene, lying there with his mouth slack and his eyes closed. For the first time since pitching up here in 1973, Sam saw the guv as helpless and vulnerable. He was as defenseless as a sleeping child. Whatever O'Riordan and his heavies had in store for them, it was up to Sam to see that Gene Hunt came to no harm.

I don't know what the hell I'm going to do to get us out of this ... but damn it all, Gene, I expect you to bloody well appreciate it!

The van doors clanged open and a trio of muscle-bound monsters filled the opening. They were silhouetted against the evening sky and the crazy kaleidoscope of the fairground lights.

'One of em's awake, at least.'

'He'll wish he weren't soon enough.'

'Get 'em both out. And if that streak of piss in the leather jacket makes a move, open 'im right up like a can of beans.'

The men bundled in and grabbed him, dragging him out and throwing him down into the cold, wet mud. Struggling up, Sam was gripped and hauled. He glimpsed Gene, hanging like a slab of beef over Ponytail's shoulder, being carried away. He opened his mouth to protest – *Hey you! Bring that man back here! He's my DCI!* – but a fist clouted the side of his head, shutting him up. As fresh waves of pain coursed through his body, Sam glared this way and that, trying to orient himself as to where the hell he was. The fairground was away to his right, all lights and music and excited screams. So – he had been brought to the very fringes of it and set down amid the power generators, snaking cables, parked vehicles and trucks and caravans, away from the eyes of the public, in the private domain of the fairground travellers themselves.

Sam caught one last glimpse of Gene being carried away like a dead deer, then he was shoved roughly forward. His hands and knees sank into the boggy ground. As he lifted his head, he heard a growl – a deep, dark, animal growl, horribly close to his face. He froze, not daring to move anything but his eyes. He saw a monstrous set of paws clawing at the wet mud, then a set of slavering jaws, then a pair of glowering, hungry eyes. The Rottweiler strained and snarled, held at bay by the heavy chain padlocked to its neck.

'Say hello to Princess,' intoned Patsy, hunkering down beside the ferocious animal and roughly slapping its taut haunches. He turned his inhuman, painted face towards Sam and bared his teeth in what might have been a grin, or a leer. He looked even more bestial and uncivilized than the Rottweiler. 'Princess don't like blokes who come rushing out of the shadows after me. And neither do I.'

Princess snapped and snarled. Sam flinched. Moustache-man laughed.

Sam glanced anxiously about, still on his hands and

knees. He could see now that Princess was tethered outside a caravan which was presumably what Patsy called home. It seemed barely big enough to contain such a huge, ogre-like man.

'On your feet, son,' Patsy ordered.

Slowly, Sam obeyed. Princess bayed and snapped until Patsy barked roughly at her to *shart arp!* The beast glowered, fell silent, but continued to bare her fangs.

'Right then,' said Patsy. 'I've seen your dopey face before, haven't I.'

'I came to the fair the other night,' Sam said. 'I saw you fight.'

'And now you've come to see me fight again. Who sent you?'

'Nobody sent us.'

'Bollocks. You and your oppo thought you could jump me after the fight – you thought I'd be shagged out and knackered, didn't you. *DIDN'T YOU!*'

Patsy roared these words. Rage coursed like lava through his bloodstream. His ugly face distorted demonically; he clenched his narrow, bony fists and fiercely pounded his chest like a gorilla, bellowing wordlessly, more like an animal than a human being. Then he fell silent, breathing hard through his flattened nose, and glared at Sam as if he was about to pounce on him and devour him. It was like being in the presence of a grizzly bear.

'Who are you?' Patsy growled.

Sam hesitated. Would admitting to being a copper make things better or worse for him and Gene? Maybe he had no choice; if they went through Gene's pockets, they'd soon find his police ID badge.

Fixing his gaze on Patsy, Sam drew up all his courage, stuck out his chest, and said: 'My name's DI Tyler – Sam Tyler – CID, A-Division. And that man you've just carried away is my DCI.'

O'Riordan laughed – a repellant, wheezy, gurgling sound, like the noise of gas bubbles bursting in a clogged sewer. 'Rozzers! They're rozzers!'

Moustache-man joined in the laughter, and this in turn set off Princess, who howled and yapped until Patsy clouted her round the head and silenced her.

'Yes, we're police officers,' Sam announced, determined to gain some degree of authority here amongst these men. 'And *you* lads are in serious trouble. Assaulting an officer – *two* officers – and obstructing them in the pursuit of their duty. Abduction. Unlawful imprisonment. And while we're at it, I've a mind to see your license for the possession of a domestic dog, Mr O'Riordan – *if* you have one.'

'You got a way with words, bud. That's good. A man *should* be able to express himself – one way or another.'

Patsy puffed himself up, straining the fabric of the white tee-shirt that encased his massive torso. Sam could make out the dark, vague forms of the many tattooed eyes and daggers and demons and houris beneath it.

'You thought we were going to attack you,' said Sam. 'You thought we were working for some underworld character with a grudge against you, didn't you.'

Amused at his language, Patsy slapped his massive thigh: '*Underworld character!* Yeah, you're a copper all right! But what *sort* of copper, I wonder?'

'I told you – I'm a Detective Inspector.'

'Yeah, yeah.'

Patsy stopped laughing, very suddenly, and loomed over Sam, peering at him intently, sniffing him slowly the way a lion would. Up close, his tattoos looked less like ink than rotten, gangrenous veins threading through his sandpaper skin. Sam could see the red welts left by Ben's knuckles around his eyes and mouth, crusts of dried blood lodged in the nostrils of the spongy mass of his broken nose, and – somehow, most horrible of all – the misshapen, featureless hole on the side of his head that bore witness to Spider's ineptitude as a hitman all those years ago. Patsy was a walking catalogue of violence and pain – and yet, burning out of the battered, painted face were the fiercest eyes Sam had ever seen, unbroken, undefeated, utterly defiant, and malignantly cunning.

'We're always getting coppers hanging round back-streets fights,' Patsy muttered, his voice low and dangerous. His breath reeked of sewage and rancid milk.

'They love a flutter on the ol' fisticuffs. For some reason, though, they always seem to bet on the wrong bloke. Is that what happened tonight, is it? Did you bet on the wrong bloke?'

'I don't know about my guv'nor, but I didn't bet a penny,' said Sam. 'I'm not a gambling man. Also, I wash behind my ears and I'm always in bed by eight.'

Patsy grinned, running his fat, pink tongue over his uneven yellow teeth: 'So what were you after, then? Eh? Or shall I guess? Did it have anything to do with that blackie Denzil Obi?'

'If you mean Mr Denzil Obi, the mixed race gentleman whose murder we're investigating, then yes it did.'

'Reckon it was me what done it?'

'Yes. I think it was you.'

'And why would I go and do a fing like that?'

'Revenge. He tried to kill you nearly ten years ago. He put three bullets in you.'

'And then blew my ear off,' said Patsy, nodding. He shrugged. 'Water under the bridge.'

'I don't believe that.'

'Listen, sonny – if I went after every bloke I had a grudge against, there'd be a heap of bodies higher than that Ferris wheel, you getting me? I'm a boxer, not a murderer. Denzil Obi, *he's* your murderer … leastways, he would have been if he'd had half a clue in his dopey black head. And that slag Spider, he's no better. Ask yourself – who shot who?

189

Eh? It was *them two* who came after *me* with a shooter, right? And who did *I* shoot? No one.'

Sam opened his mouth to speak, then shut it again. His brain was still reeling from all the blows and the screaming pain coursing through his battered jaw, but he couldn't afford to be woolly headed. He had to *think*. He had to play the next few moments very, very carefully.

Gene's out of the game, at least for the time being. How this situation plays out is entirely down to me, and there's nothing the guv can do. My plan was to draw Patsy into a trap, win his confidence, and somewhere along the way get him to admit that he killed Obi. Gene pissed on that plan – but now's my chance to put it into action! He'll kill me for it later – but let him. It'll be too late by then.

'Listen up, Patsy,' said Sam, and he shot a sideways glance at the menacing figure of Moustache-man looming over him. 'I want a word with you, in private. You can help us – and, in return, we can help you.'

Patsy ran his small, bony, breezeblock-breaking hand over Princess's back, smacked her meaty arse, then turned to Sam and said: 'You can talk in front of any one of my lads. They're sound.'

'I'm sure they are. But this is … a little delicate.'

Patsy chewed this over, then told Moustache-man to bugger off. Moustache-man glowered fearsomely at Sam for a moment, as if warning him not to try any funny business, then loped off in the direction Ponytail had carried Gene.

'Well then,' said Patsy, drawing closer to Sam and looming over him. His nightmarish, tattooed face was drawn into an unreadable expression. 'You got what you wanted. It's just me now.'

'Get your goons to bring my DCI back here and then we can start talking.'

Princess growled.

'She don't like hearin' you givin' me so many orders, son,' said Patsy. 'And neeva do I. Spit out what you want to say, or clear off.'

It was hopeless trying to argue. Sam had no choice but to leave Gene in the hands of fate.

'That dog's making me jumpy,' said Sam. 'Let's go inside.'

'Inside then.'

Sam turned towards the caravan, but Patsy stopped him with a hand on his shoulder. His touch, surprisingly, was light, his hand barely resting on Sam's jacket. But even so, Sam could sense the implacable strength that resided within it, like the silent, terrible potential poised within the heart of a primed warhead.

'You don't want to nick me for what happened to Obi,' he said, his voice low, his eyes glaring. 'You really don't, son.'

'We know you did it,' Sam replied, almost in a whisper.

'Can you prove it?'

'No. We can't get enough evidence together.'

'So what you gonna do then?'

'What we always do. Pin it on somebody else.'

'Wiv my help?'

'Yeah. With your help, Patsy.'

Sam paused. He thought, in his own opinion, that he sounded pretty convincing. But would Patsy buy it?

For several moments, Patsy did nothing. Then he frowned. Or at least, Sam assumed it was a frown; the man's face was so disfigured by ink that his expressions were hard to read. He watched Patsy's troll-like face, watched the eyes narrow, watched the tongue dart back and forth across the tombstone teeth.

'Bent coppers,' Patsy said at last. And then he grinned: 'You gotta luv 'em! You always know where you stand with a bent copper. They're the only sort you can trust. I tell you, boy, you should have been up front about this from the off and we'd never had clobbered ya! C'mon, son, we'll have a drink and hammer all this out.'

He turned and squeezed himself through the door of the caravan.

Alone for a moment, Sam exhaled, letting out the nervous tension that had been building in him until he thought he'd burst. He looked down at his hand and forced it to stop shaking. Princess snarled at him, and he backed away from the tethered beast to join the untethered one inside the caravan.

CHAPTER TWELVE

CHEZ PATSY

Lavender. The inside of the caravan smelt of lavender. Sam glanced around at immaculate net curtains bunched with white ribbons at the windows, a row of dusted and precisely arrayed china ornaments, a coloured vase of fresh flowers on a spotless Formica table. Patsy's caravan was a masterpiece of hygiene and domestic order.

'Very nice,' Sam said. 'If only my colleagues at CID were half as housetrained as you.'

'I don't like mess and I don't like filth,' Patsy grunted. 'Gets me in a temper. I like all me stuff to be just so.'

Sam had a glimpse of Patsy industriously pottering about the place in his pinny, flicking a feather duster over the black-and-white portable TV with its circular indoor aerial, neatly arranging the rows of C-45 music cassettes, beavering away with the dustpan and brush on the wood-effect floor.

No – not Patsy. Tracy Porter, she's *the domestic drudge round here.*

Sam recalled Tracy's battered, brutalized face, her refusal to speak up and name Patsy as that bastard who assaulted her.

Glancing around the caravan, Sam thought: *So – these are the high standards of housework she must maintain. What did she do to earn herself a beating? Forget to dust the back of the TV? Miss a speck of dirt on the floor?*

Where was Tracy now? She didn't seem to be at home – the caravan was hardly big enough to give her a room to hide herself in. Perhaps she was manning one of the concessions at the fair, selling candyfloss or taking the money for the ghost train.

And what happens if she suddenly turns up? Will she react when she sees me? Will she warn Patsy I'm after him? Will she betray me?

Patsy took down something box-like and stashed it under the table in the middle of the caravan. Then he fitted his massive, muscle-bound body into a plastic armchair, produced a bottle of scotch and poured a couple of shot glasses.

'Before we talk, I need to know what's happened to my guv'nor,' said Sam. 'What have you done with him?'

'He'll live,' intoned Patsy.

'That's not what I asked.'

'It's the only answer you're gonna get, son.' Patsy passed Sam a shot glass of whisky. 'You wanted to talk to me. So start talking.'

Act tough. This bastard won't respect weakness. Put up a front that'll impress him.

In the way he imagined bent coppers would do it, Sam knocked his scotch back in a single go. It was a rough brew, like drinking paint stripper, and the burn of the stuff brought tears to his eyes.

'You killed Denzil Obi,' Sam said. 'Didn't you.'

'Never touched him.'

'Fine by me,' shrugged Sam. 'I couldn't care less, and neither could my department. But we're getting squeezed by the Home Office to finger *somebody* for the Obi case, so we've set our sights on Spider. We're going to fit him up. That should please you, Patsy.'

Patsy shrugged, said: 'Why Spider?'

'He's an easy target. The man's an idiot, and now Denzil's dead he doesn't have a friend in the world. He's just the sort of loser who's perfect for fitting up like this. We'll pin Obi's murder on him, plus a whole backlog of cases that need clearing. The Home Office will give us all gold stars and everyone in CID will be very happy.'

Patsy refilled their glasses but said nothing.

Sam went on, thinking fast: 'The trouble is, Spider's disappeared. Gone to ground. He's frightened of *you*,

Patsy. He thinks he's in line for the same treatment Denzil got.'

'Which was nuffing to do with me, like I said.'

'Whatever. The point is, he's vanished. So, we need to draw him out. *You* can do that for us.'

'How? I don't know where Spider is. I haven't seen him for ten years – since him and Denzil tried to murder me.'

He patted his belly and lifted the hem of his tee-shirt, revealing the tattooed bullet-holes that bore witness to those violent events from the past. Grotesquely, he insinuated a finger into one of the holes and picked out a tufty ball of lint.

'Spider used to train at the same gym as Denzil,' said Sam. 'There's boxers there who know where he is, but they're not talking. They won't tell us where he's hiding, but what they *will* do is take messages to him.'

Patsy waited for Sam to keep talking. Sam paused for a moment, hoped that whatever came out of his mouth next would sound convincing, and said:

'Offer to fight him. Just you and Spider. We'll see that word reaches him. And I tell you now, he'll accept the offer. He'll break cover to face you – and when he does, we'll nick him.'

'He won't face me,' said Patsy. 'He's not man enough.'

'We'll tell him it's a trap, that it's a police set-up to lure *you* out of hiding. We'll tell him it's *you* we're going to nick, Patsy – and instead, we'll nick *him*.'

Sam accepted another refill and knocked it back. Had his convoluted plan sounded remotely convincing? Did Patsy even understand it? And if he did, would he swallow it?

It's vital that he starts to trust me. The more he trusts me, the more likely he is to let something slip – something important – something that betrays his guilt beyond question. But he's got to trust me first. He's got to let his guard down.

'So ...' said Patsy in a slow, thoughtful voice. 'You want to use me as bait to lure him out of hiding.'

'Yes.'

'But he'll think you're using *him* as bait to lure out *me*.'

'That's right.'

'And then – although you reckon, for some reason, that it's me what killed Obi, you're gonna nick Spider and fit him up for it.'

'You got it.'

Silence fell between them, broken only by the muffled racket of the fair outside. Patsy said nothing.

Has he smelt a rat? Have I over-reached myself here? Have I failed to win his confidence?

'Come on, Patsy, it'll be a cakewalk,' Sam said. 'All you have to do is stand there, let him see you. He won't be able to resist. And the moment he shows his face – blam! Me and my boys swoop in.'

'I understand all that, son. I'm pretty smart for a pikey.'

Patsy knocked back his drink, and Sam did likewise, forcing himself not to grimace at the hard bite of the scotch as it went down.

'Let's say I go along with this,' he said, fixing Sam with a piercing look. 'What's in it for me?'

'I thought that was obvious.'

'Spell it out.'

'Well, for starters, you'll be clear of Denzil Obi's murder.'

'Which was nothing to do with me anyway, son.'

'Patsy, we don't care if it was you, Cassius Clay or Ken bloody Dodd who killed Denzil Obi. We can't prove it was you, but we've got what we need to pin it on Spider, and that's all we give a damn about.'

'Speak up, old son,' said Patsy, and he indicated the tattered remains of his ear. 'I'm a bit mutton on this side.'

'I said we don't care who killed Denzil Obi,' said Sam, raising his voice. 'It's not in our interests for you to go down for this. It's Spider we want. He's nothing. Worthless. But *you*, Patsy – you've got connections.'

'Wiv what?'

'Come on, Patsy, don't play Snow White with me. There's a lot of villains you can get access to ... and help *us* get access to.'

'I don't have no criminal contacts,' said Patsy. 'I'm clean.'

Sam laughed, hopefully in a macho way, and said: 'Clean as a whistle, I'm sure. But just think about this, Patsy: we can make it worth your while to play along with us. *Very* worth your while. You can settle a few old scores, get rid of a few old enemies, and make your new buddies in CID a bunch of very happy bunnies.'

Sam held out his glass for another refill, downed it in one, forced himself not to choke on the vile acid, and said: 'So there you go, Patsy. You're more use to us on the outside than banged up. And Spider's more use to us as a fall guy than anything else. The whole situation's perfect.'

Patsy looked thoughtfully into his whisky glass, and still he did not speak.

'Well, Patsy? What do you say?'

'I say you're asking a lot,' Patsy growled in a low voice. 'I say you're asking me to be a nark.'

'Yes. That's exactly what we're asking. Or would you rather I went back to the Home Office, got them to lay off the pressure, and continued compiling a case against *you*, Patsy? Would you rather we set about putting you away for life for the murder of Denzil Obi?'

'But I didn't kill Obi.'

'For God's sake, Patsy, I haven't got all night. Make up your mind. This could be a sweet little deal for both of us … the start of a very productive working relationship … perhaps even a beautiful friendship.'

'I didn't do Denzil Obi,' Patsy said.

'No. Spider did.'

'I mean it, son.'

'So do I, Patsy. All you have to do is help us make that a reality.'

Sam thought of Spider, depressed and forlorn, sitting in one of the holding cells back at the station. Was it right to use him as a pawn in this violent and high-risk game? Sam was playing all sides off against each other, using both Spider and Patsy as a bait for one another. Was he overplaying his hand? Could he really control the outcome of the situation he was creating?

After a few moments of silent thought, Patsy turned and looked at a little clock on one of the immaculately dusted shelves. The second hand ticked round, counting away the last few seconds until it was seven-thirty.

'Five,' said Patsy. 'Four. Three. Two.'

He pointed a tattooed finger at the door of the caravan, and bang on cue it opened.

'One. Hiya, Trace.'

A nervous, mouse-like voice replied: 'Hiya, babes.'

Dressed in nylon tracksuit bottoms and a faded Steve McQueen tee-shirt, Tracy stepped gingerly into the caravan, laden down with carrier bags from the Co-op. Her face was still bruised and swollen, even worse than Gene's.

Sam's heart leapt into his mouth. He forced himself not to betray any outer reaction, but inwardly his nerve endings were jangling. What would Tracy say when she saw him? How would she react?

'Nice to see you bang on time,' Patsy said.

'Yes, babes,' said Tracy. She looked across at Sam, and her battered face registered not so much as a flicker of response. Then she turned back to Patsy: 'I got a move on. Didn't want to muck you about or nuffing.'

'Got everyfing?'

'Yes, babes, I got everyfing.' She carried the bags through to the tiny kitchen area and began putting things away – cornflakes, gold top milk, lime cordial, a plastic tub of Wall's ice cream. As she opened cupboards, Sam glimpsed perfectly arrayed tins and jars inside.

She's not going to give me away, he thought. *She's been smacked too many times for speaking out of line to say anything now. She knows how to keep quiet.*

'It's only right for a fella to know where his bird is,' Patsy said to Sam. 'Can't let 'em go wandering off at all hours, can you.' Then to Tracy: 'Ain't you gonna ask me how I got on?'

'Sure. How'd you get on, babes?'

'How'd you think, you dopey mare? His brains were 'anging out his arsehole by the time I walked away.'

'Nice one, babes.'

Tracy folded the Co-op bags and tucked them neatly in a drawer, then picked her way over to Patsy to kiss him. It struck Sam that barely half an hour before, Patsy

201

had been in the thick of the nastiest, filthiest, most ferocious hand-to-hand fighting he had ever witnessed. And
now here he was, taking his ease in his favourite chair,
knocking back the whisky, and casually cutting a deal
with what he took to be a thoroughly bent copper. The
amount of physical punishment this monstrous man had
absorbed this evening was staggering. And somewhere
out there lay Gene Hunt, unconscious, downed by a
single shattering blow to the skull, while Patsy snogged
and slobbered over Tracy after taking enough of a
pounding to sink a battleship. Where did such an appetite
for violence come from? Were creatures like Patsy
O'Riordan born that way? Did he emerge from a hard-
as-nails gene pool, inheriting this staggering capacity for
physical punishment from his father and grandfather and
so and so on, all the way back to the primeval caves?
Perhaps he wasn't so far removed from the Neanderthals
as all that.

Maybe not. And I thought Gene was a bloody
caveman! Compared to Patsy, he's Quentin Crisp!

Settling Tracy on his knee, Patsy ran his small, bruised
hands roughly over her breasts. Fixing Sam with an
intense look, he said: 'You know what I reckon?'

'No, what do you reckon, babes?' asked Tracy – and
then yelped when he pinched her.

'Not you, soppy tits. I'm talking to the gentleman,'
said Patsy. 'I repeat – you know what I reckon?'

'No, Patsy, what do you reckon?' said Sam.

'I reckon that what we need's a push-me-pull-you.'

'What's that?'

'It's a thing that makes blokes like you and me trust each other,' said Patsy. He gripped Tracy in a bear hug.

'You mean an insurance policy? Okay. What would put your mind at rest?'

'Sumfing ...' growled Patsy, '... Sumfing that makes sure that if you try and push me, I can pull you ...'

'Name it,' said Sam. 'What security can I give you?'

'Oh, I've got my security already,' he said.

'What are you talking about? Do you mean my DCI? Patsy, you can't keep him as a hostage!'

Patsy laughed, then bit Tracy's earlobe in a way that was more cannibalistic than amorous.

'I don't need no 'ostage,' he said. And then: 'Get a shower on the go, Trace. Get in and get yourself ready.'

'Sure, babes.'

As Tracy slid from his knee, Patsy whacked her on the backside. She flinched. It was a pathetic, grovelling gesture. Sam's heart broke for her. As she squirmed past, her eyes did not even flicker in Sam's direction.

Too scared. Too scared to so much as risk looking at me.

Tracy disappeared into the tiny shower cubicle.

Patsy got slowly to his feet and said: 'I want to make this very clear, son – I did not kill Denzil Obi.'

'We've been through all that.'

But Patsy drew closer, his face very intense, and said: 'Now I want you to say it.'

From next door came the sound of the shower starting up.

'Patsy, I don't know what you're-'

'I said I want you to say it. So say it.'

Sam frowned. What was going on here? Why was he asking for him to say this? It was like he wanted somebody to overhear. But who? Tracy?

In the next moment, the penny dropped.

'You put something under that table just as I was coming in here,' said Sam. 'It was a tape recorder, wasn't it.'

'Say it. Say I didn't kill Denzil.'

'This is your security, is it? This is your push-me-pullyou? Well, if it keeps you happy.' Sam cleared his throat and projected his voice clearly: 'I – DI Sam Tyler, am officially telling you, Patsy O'Riordan, that you are most definitely not a suspect in the murder of Denzil Obi. And what's more, both myself and DCI Gene Hunt are recruiting you to pin the blame for that murder on a man we both know is completely innocent.'

There! That implicates Gene, whether he likes it or not! We're both in this plan together.

Patsy swilled down his scotch, and then heaved himself to his feet. Crouching, he leant under the table and produced the tape recorder he had hidden there, a huge black model with clunky buttons. He clicked it off and removed the C-90 tape.

'Push-me-pull-you,' he said, holding it up.

Determined to win his trust to the maximum, Sam said: 'You've got more than enough on that tape to get me into some serious hot water with the Home Office. If that tape ever got out, I'd be for the high jump. Discredited. Indicted. But it won't get out. Will it.'

Patsy said nothing, but poured himself another scotch – a huge one. He didn't offer any to Sam.

'Now we've made our contract,' said Patsy, 'let's sign it.'

'I thought we already had.'

'No, no. Like gentlemen.'

Sam frowned, unsure and all at once unsettled. What was Patsy expecting him to do? Were they supposed to draw knives across their wrists and mingle their blood? Did he want them to fight? To wrestle? God almighty, he wasn't about to get all Women in Love on him, was he?!

'She's yours for ten minutes,' Patsy said, and he nodded his foul, bullet-shaped head in the direction of the shower.

'Patsy, I'm more interested in what's happened to my DCI.'

'Don't talk like that, son. I'm offering to lend you my most treasured possession. A refusal often offends.'

Holding the incriminating C-90 in his hard, boxer's hand, Patsy lumbered past Sam, filling the doorway that led outside and pausing there. Without turning, he said: 'Say fank you.'

From outside came the blaring music of the fairground; from within, the hissing of the shower in the cubicle.

Sam said nothing.

'I'll be with Princess when you're done,' Patsy said, and carefully shut the caravan door behind him.

CHAPTER THIRTEEN

A HOT SHOWER

Sam hesitated, thinking of Annie, thinking of Gene. He glanced out of the net-curtained windows at the dark sky overhead and the crazy whirl of the fairground lights beneath it. Over the sound of music pounding from the rides (Suzi Q had long since given way to *Crocodile Rock*) Sam caught the yap and snarl of Princess as Patsy teased her in his bullying way.

Through the frosted glass door of the shower cubicle, Sam could see water streaming, steam rising, and the hazy pink blur of Tracy Porter within. Her nylon tracksuit trousers and Steve McQueen tee-shirt lay on the floor outside the cubicle, perfectly folded, in keeping with Patsy's fetish for domestic order and tidiness.

Demurely, Sam tapped his knuckles against the glass door.

'Tracy. It's me. He wants me to … to come in there with you.'

At once, Tracy opened the door. Sam averted his eyes from her naked body.

'I'm not going to do anything,' he stammered.

'Well you'd better!' Tracy hissed. 'Coz else he'll know!'

Sam risked a glance at her. Her hair was streaming wet and plastered across her naked shoulders, but Sam's attention was caught by the array of bruises, bites, cigarette burns and red welts that adorned *her* body almost as totally as Patsy's tattoos adorned *his*. How many months or years of abuse did those marks bear witness to? How much pain and humiliation had they cost this poor slip of a girl?

'Come on, get on wiv it,' she said, her voice low and urgent. '*He* won't want to 'ang about, not more than ten minutes he won't, not after a fight.'

So, Sam was to use this girl's body, perfunctorily, without humanity, as a goodwill gift from Patsy. And then he was to hand that body back over to its rightful owner to do with as he pleased.

He looked at Tracy's face, still misshapen and discoloured, her eyes already lifeless and doll-like as she resigned herself to what was expected of her. She would give herself to him, because that's how Patsy sealed his deals, and then Patsy himself would be in here, demanding his due.

Sam could not dare to imagine the life she endured.

'Get *on* wiv it!' she urged, stepping naked from the shower.

Sam grabbed a towel and threw it over her. Tracy let it fall. Sam gathered it up and this time draped it around her brutalized body with care, bringing it together over her breasts to cover them. Tracy looked at him, frowning, uncomprehending, anxious.

'You gotta do it,' she insisted in a low voice. 'He'll know if you don't. He'll blame me.'

Did she recall that they had met before? Did she not remember him at all?

'Please, Tracy, listen.'

'He *wants* you to do it. You *gotta* do it.'

'I'm Sam. I'm the policeman you met at the hospital.'

'I'm not *stoopid*, mate. I know who you are. And you ain't my first copper, believe me, so just do it!'

Sam was dumbfounded: 'Tracy – I'm here to help you.'

'Just bleedin' *do* it!'

She grabbed at his belt buckle, but Sam took her by the wrist and gently moved her hand away.

'No.'

She pulled her hand free and grabbed at him again. This time, Sam grasped both her wrists and held them. He could feel old scars and raised welts on them. There was a brief, confused struggle that dislodged Tracy's towel and exposed her once again. Sam released her wrists and tried to grab the towel, but somehow ended up falling into the shower cubicle, with Tracy beneath him. Hot water rained down on his head and streamed along his jacket as Tracy hooked her legs around his body and tried to kiss him with her bruised lips. Sam struggled free, got to his feet and stumbled back, sopping wet. Tracy lay on her back looking up at him, half in the cubicle and half out of it. Sam switched off the hot water, gently helped her to stand, and patiently wrapped the towel around her once again.

'I'll tell him we did it,' he whispered, wiping hot water from his eyes. 'You won't get into trouble on my account.'

'Are you a pooftah, is that it?'

'No, it's nothing like that.'

'Then it's me. I ain't like one of them page 3 birds. But you can do anyfink you want wiv me, so that makes up, dunnit.'

'Tracy, please.'

'He wants blokes to be jealous. He wants blokes to want me.'

'Tracy – listen to me – not all men are like Patsy. Not all men treat women like he does.'

She glanced fearfully at the open windows of the caravan, terrified of seeing Patsy's face appear suddenly at one of them. With a stifled cry, she hustled Sam inside the shower cubicle and slammed the glass door shut. Sam – sopping wet and fully clothed – stood pressed up against Tracy in her wraparound towel; above them, the plastic shower head slowly drip- drip-dripped hot water.

Sam opened his mouth to speak, but Tracy cut across him, her voice low and urgent: 'You wanna help me, mate? Then *do it*, and tell *him* it was all right, then clear off. Coz if you don't, it's *me* what's gonna cop it, you understand?'

'Do you *want* to live like this, Tracy?'

'You ain't the Samaritans, you're just some fella, so get your kecks off and *do it*!'

'I can't believe you want to live like this.'

'I just want to *live,* mate – that's the best I can hope for – and them what upset Pats, they don't live so long, you know?'

'Like Denzil,' said Sam, throwing the name out to see if she would react.

And, to his surprise, she came straight back with: 'Yes! Just like Denzil!'

'So you *did* know him?!'

Tracy laughed – or rather, she snorted. It was a bitter, cynical sound.

'I knew him all right,' she said.

'Did you ... have sexual relations with him?'

Tracy peered up at him as if Sam had spoken in Norwegian.

'What I mean is, Tracy, were you ... were you and him *doing it*?'

'I see ...' she said quietly. Her bruised face grew hard. Lines appeared on her forehead. Her eyes narrowed. 'You *are* a copper, ain't 'cha.'

'What do you mean?'

'Pin it on the bird, that's your game, innit. It's Pats what clobbered him, but it's *me* what's gonna take the blame.'

'Why? Why would *you* take the blame? You didn't do anything. Unless ...'

Tracy scowled at him, full of hate, but she didn't need to say a word. Sam was filling in the gaps in his imagination.

'Patsy used you to get at Denzil – didn't he?' Sam whispered.

'No.'

'You were sent to seduce him, to win his trust.'

'No. Course not.'

'Where'd you meet him – at the gym?'

'I never met him. I don't know no Denzil.'

'You met him at the gym. You won him over. And he invited you back to his flat.'

'No.'

'That's how Patsy found out where Denzil lived. But he needed to get past all those locks and bolts on the front door. He needed a decoy to get inside ... a Trojan horse.'

212

'No. I don't even know what that is.'

'So you turned up at Denzil's place. You knocked on the door. And he looked through the spyhole. And what he saw was you ... *you,* but not Patsy, lurking round the corner.'

'This is all bollocks.'

'And so he opened the door. He pulled back all those locks and bolts, and he opened the door. And in steamed Patsy ...'

Tracy's face was just as hard, just as full of hate as before, but now her eyes were filling with tears.

'No,' she said, her voice cracking. 'No, it weren't nuffing like that. It weren't *nuffing* like that! No.'

'He used you. That bastard Patsy used you!'

'No. No!'

'You poor girl. You poor, poor girl.'

Sam put his arms round her – but she shoved him away.

'You got ev'ryfing wrong!' she grizzled. 'Ev'ryfing!'

'I don't think I have,' said Sam quietly. He knew, in that way only a copper can really know, that all the pieces were sliding into place. 'He used you. And you were there. You were there when Denzil died, weren't you.'

'No I wasn't!'

'And you tried to stop Patsy. He was beating Denzil Obi to a pulp and you couldn't bear it – so you intervened.'

'Just shuddup, will ya!'

'You intervened, tried to stop him, and he turned on you. And that's how you ended up in A&E that night.'

'I fell against the door!' Tracy howled. 'I walked into the cupboard! *Now just drop your pants and do it!*'

And then, in terror at the sound of her own raised voice, she clamped both hands over her mouth and stared at Sam with eyes that almost bugged out of her head. The towel fell from her. Sam left it; instead, he put his arms round her frail, fragile body and hugged her. And this time, she didn't push him away. She didn't push him away, nor did she return his embrace; she just stood there, crying silently.

'I'm going to help you,' he whispered in her ear. 'I'm going to *save* you.'

'You can't,' she muttered.

'You'll see.'

'You'll get us both killed.'

'You'll see.'

'Just go. It's better that way.'

'No. I told you. I'm going to save you.'

'Why?'

'Because …' He hesitated. After a few moments, he said: 'Just because.'

Snuffling noisily, Tracy said in a timid voice: 'I think you've had your ten minutes, mate.'

'Good shower?' asked Patsy, as Sam emerged from the caravan drying his hair with a towel.

Patsy was standing, smoking a fag, Princess on red alert beside him, prickly and defensive of her master. Behind them, the fairground glittered and sparkled beneath the black sky. What with the lights and the night sky and his disfiguring tattoos, Patsy looked like a malign alien monster just emerged from its spacecraft.

'Very good shower,' said Sam.

'Hot enough?'

'Plenty hot enough.'

Patsy flicked away the fag and roughly patted Princess. It was then that Sam saw that – theatrically, melodramatically – the incriminating C-90 cassette was hanging from the chain around the Rottweiler's throat. The implication was clear: *if you want it copper, then come and get it …*

Princess snarled and slavered.

'Well,' said Sam, folding the towel neatly, just the way Patsy liked it, 'seeing as I'm all freshened up …' – he passed the towel to Patsy – 'I take it we can declare our business satisfactorily concluded for the evening?'

'Looks like it.' Patsy refolded the towel. Sam's folding just wasn't up to snuff. 'Now – if you don't mind, I've had a busy day. I could do with a nice early night.'

Those words, and what they might entail for Tracy, brought a fierce burst of anger boiling through Sam's veins. He clenched his teeth and did his best to act casual.

'You've earned it,' he said. 'I'll see that Spider gets the message about the fight. Where'd you want to do it? Back at the old factory?'

'No. Here.'

'At the fairground? It's way too public.'

'Four caravans, parked to make a square,' said Patsy. 'We've done it before. No one can see. All very cosy. Believe me.'

'Very well then. We'll do it here.'

'Sunday night. We're off Monday morning, movin' on. So it's gotta be Sunday. Eight o'clock. *Sharp*.'

'I can't guarantee that,' said Sam. He could, of course, but it sounded more realistic to say otherwise. 'If there's a problem, I'll get word to you. Otherwise – eight o'clock, Sunday.'

Patsy nodded curtly, then, without a word, lumbered past Sam and disappeared back inside the caravan. With care – daintily, even – he pulled the doors shut behind him.

Princess growled, telling Sam to clear off.

Sam glanced back at the caravan, its homely lights and neat net curtains so at odds with the violence and pain contained within. He silently repeated his promise to Tracy: *I'll help you … I'll save you … I promise …*

Turning his back on the fearsome Rottweiler, Sam began to trudge across the boggy ground, the lights of the fair spinning and popping away to his left. He turned over in his mind images of Tracy appearing at Denzil's

216

flat ... Denzil throwing back the bolts ... Patsy bursting in ... Tracy screaming *stop it, Patsy, please, please, don't kill him!* ... Patsy's fists pounding Denzil to a pulp ... and then those same murderous fists turning on Tracy.

Gene had better appreciate just how much progress I've made with this case tonight, he thought. *Single-handed, too! Still, perhaps it was better he wasn't around. He'd only have made trouble. Perhaps it was better I was on my own and ...*

He stopped dead in his tracks. He looked to his right. Then to his left. Then both left and right. Then he turned a full 360, like an anxious parent suddenly finding their child was missing.

From between a rumbling power generator and lopsided caravan, two ominous figures emerged from the shadows. Sam knew them at once. Moustache-man hooked his thumbs into his belt; Ponytail cracked his knuckles.

Sam squared up to them, dead macho, and said: 'Me and Patsy are best mates now. That means you boys and me are all on the same side. So – if you'll just give me my guv'nor back, we'll be on our way.'

Ponytail exchanged a look with his equally bone-headed companion, then turned to Sam and said: 'We ain't got 'im no more.'

'What do you mean you haven't got him? What the hell have you done with him?'

'It's not *my* fault he's a pansy,' Ponytail said. 'If he can't take a punch he shouldn't've come steaming after us like that.'

Sam felt a cold shiver run down his spine. This all sounded horribly ominous.

'What's happened?' he asked. 'Hasn't he woken up yet?'

Ponytail shrugged. Moustache-man lit a cigarette and said nothing. The only sound was the cacophony of the fairground filling the cold night air.

'I won't ask you bozos another time,' Sam snapped. 'I want my DCI and I want him now. Where is he?'

With the lighted tip of cigarette, Moustache-man indicated vaguely in a direction behind Sam. Turning, Sam saw the lights of a St John's ambulance trundling across the open ground away from the fair.

'We don't want a dead copper on our hands,' Ponytail said. 'If he snuffs it, better it's in the back of a wagon. Nuffing to do with us, that way.'

The cold shiver along Sam's spine solidified into a column of ice.

Brain hemorrhage, he thought. *Those two brainless hulks have smashed his skull like it was a glass vase! My God, they've killed him ... They've bloody gone and killed him ... They've killed Gene Hunt!*

Sam turned and ran, racing across the churned-up ground in the direction of the clanging ambulance. He forgot Moustache-man and Ponytail, he forgot Patsy and Princess and the clamorous fairground – he even forgot Tracy and Annie and the boys at CID. All he could think of was the guv, lying there in the back of that meat wagon, the blood filling up inside his cracked skull, the life fading out of him.

As he ran through the night, he glimpsed the pale, wan face of the Test Card Girl as she stepped from the shadows, clutching a black helium balloon.

'You'll be so lost without him,' she said gently.

But Sam just tore straight past her and kept on running.

CHAPTER FOURTEEN

A FALLEN IDOL

It was gone ten o'clock when Sam at last tracked down Gene to an open ward that reeked of carbolic soap and floor polish. A prim, hatchet-faced nurse – who seemed also to reek of carbolic soap and floor polish – emerged from her station and blocked his way like it was Checkpoint Charlie. Sam's police ID only made her primmer and more hatchet-faced, but eventually she relented and escorted Sam between the identical rows of beds, ssh-ing him if he stepped too noisily on the gleaming floor. As he tip-toed along in the nurse's wake, Sam glanced at the faces in the beds that stared back at him; young men with heavy sideburns–middle-aged men with trimmed, bank manager-ish moustaches – elderly men with toothless mouths and sad white wisps scraped across their pates. Strangers every one of them, they sat sadly in their beds with their bowls of manky grapes and folded copies of *The Mirror,* looking for all the world like extras in *Carry On Doctor.*

And then he saw him – Gene Hunt, the guv'nor – propped up against a heap of starched pillows, his eyes closed, his face half black from bruising. His coat, clothes and patent leather loafers were neatly stacked in an open cupboard beside his bed, upon which stood a jug of water and a single plastic cup. The guv himself had been put into regulation NHS pyjamas with white and blue stripes that made him look unbearably frail and vulnerable. Sam felt his stomach lurch to see him like this, a fallen warrior, crushed and defeated, the fastest gun in the west outgunned – or worse, just another extra in *Carry On Doctor.* It was not the man he knew.

'Guv ...?' Sam asked softly. But Gene did not respond. 'Sister, how is he?'

The nurse checked the chart that hung on the foot of his bed.

'Stable,' she said without warmth or emotion. 'I'm assuming you want some time with him?'

'I know it's out of hours but this is important.'

'You can have five minutes.'

And with that, she was gone.

Sam edged closer to the bed.

'Guv ...? Are you ...?'

'*Wide* awake,' Gene suddenly growled, and his eyelids snapped open. He fixed Sam with a hard stare. 'Now pull that bloody curtain round, Tyler you twonk. There's too many nosy parkers in this joint.'

The eyes of the whole ward were on them. Sam tugged at a set of orange curtains and sealed himself and Gene off from the public gaze. He was surprised at how much relief he was feeling – to have the guv back, glaring at him and mouthing off and treating him like shit. Normality had been restored. The world was back on its axis once again. The Gene Genie had not been reduced to a non-speaking extra in a bad sex farce.

'Gene, you've had me worried this evening.'

Gene pulled an unimpressed face: 'Got a smoke on you, Tyler? I'm gasping!'

'I'll pour you a glass of water.'

'I need fags and booze, you womble, I can't survive on that lukewarm piss-in-a-pot. Christ, who'd you think I am – *you*?'

'This isn't the Railway Arms, Guv. You've got to rest up and eat lots of grapes and be a very good boy for the next few days.'

'I'm *always* a very a good boy, Tyler, *every* day. Top of the bleedin' class, me.'

He was already starting to clamber out of bed – and as he did, he looked down at his striped jim-jams and grimaced.

'Jackie H. Charlton! You'd think I had enough to put up with without *this*.'

He thrust a leg out from under his blankets.

'Guv, what the hell are you doing?'

'Discharging myself.'

'Oh no you're not,' said Sam. 'Gene, your face is right out here like a pumpkin. You've been unconscious for hours!'

'I have *not* been unconscious for hours, Tyler, so you take that right back!' Gene glowered at him, struggling to keep his voice down. 'You take that *right* back, my son! I have been *mildly stunned. Very* mildly stunned. It's on me chart so that's official.'

Sam glanced at the chart, said: 'I tell you what *is* on here, Guv. Your date of birth. Well, well, well ...'

'You look away, Tyler, that's classified information.'

'You should be looking after yourself at your age.'

'That date's wrong. I'm twenty-one and three quarters, give or take.'

He broke off, silenced by a sudden burst of nauseating pain exploding through his skull.

'Take it easy, Guv,' said Sam. 'You've been in the wars tonight.'

'Don't talk to me like that, Tyler, next thing you'll be calling me a brave little soldier.'

'You got clobbered, guv. Properly clobbered. You were out for the count. I thought you were dying from a brain hemorrhage.'

'I was playing possum, keeping my ears open. I was fully aware of what was happening at all times ... except for when them nurses managed to slip these bloody pyjamas on me. If I'd caught them at it you'd seen some bloody fists flying then, believe me.'

He ripped off his striped top and reached for his nylon shirt – and then stopped. He swayed. He put one hand gingerly to his battered face.

'Guv? What is it? Shall I get the nurse?'

Gene said nothing. For once, with an open goal to come straight back at Sam with a smart-arse comment, he said nothing. Instead, he sank back slowly against his mountain of pillows and sighed.

'I'm not gonna be sick,' he muttered, as much to himself as much to Sam.

'You sure, Guv? Shall a get a ... a pot or whatever?'

'I said I am *not* gonna be sick!'

Sam pulled the blankets back over him, tucking him in like Gene was a little boy.

'You took a pasting tonight, Guv,' said Sam, sitting beside him.

'You're telling me,' muttered Gene, taking a few steady breaths. 'I didn't even see it coming. God, Tyler, it's been a few years since a fella's put me down like that.'

'We're none of us getting any younger.'

'Speak for yourself. Eternal bloom of youth, that's me. Twenty-one and three quar- *Jeee*sus ...!' He waited for the waves of pain in his head to subside. As Sam watched, Gene's whole manner seemed to change. The fire went out of his eyes. His posture deflated. DCI Gene Hunt, the guv'nor, shrank down to just a battered, middle-aged man lying forlornly in a starched hospital bed.

'You get some rest, Gene,' said Sam. 'Don't worry, I'm taking care of everything.'

'Taking care of what, Sam?'

'The case. Remember? The Denzil Obi case.'

For a moment, Gene seemed not to comprehend. Then he caught Sam's expression and hissed: 'Don't you look at me like that, Tyler, I do *not* have bloody amnesia!'

'I've set up an illegal bare-knuckle fight. Spider against Patsy O'Riordan. I know you put the kibosh on that plan, Gene, but I had to think fast back there. I'm winning Patsy's trust. I'm going to lure him on, let him incriminate himself, and then put him away for good.'

Gene said nothing. He had closed his eyes and was breathing deeply and slowly in an attempt to ameliorate the pain.

'I've also found the connection between Patsy and Denzil,' Sam went on. 'It was Tracy. He used her as a sort of honey trap. That's how he got into Denzil's flat. The whole case is coming together, Guv – what matters is that we don't lose track of Patsy, that he doesn't go to ground and disappear. We need to keep him close and make him trust us. Now, I've persuaded him to fight

Spider. I've led him to believe it's all a stitch-up to pin the Obi killing on Spider, and ...'

'Tyler.'

'Guv?'

'Enough.'

Gene lay still, his eyes closed, silent but for his deep, regular breathing. Sam looked unhappily down at him, at his disfigured face with its grotesque purple bruise, and found he could stand it no more. He turned away, ducked through the curtains that surrounded the bed, and strode back along the ward, his boots tap-tap-tapping on the polished floor.

'Ssh!' hissed the staff nurse.

But this time, Sam just marched straight past her. He just wanted to get the hell out of that awful place.

Primitive-looking ambulances were congregated outside the hospital, their lights flickering and flashing as they set off through the night.

Sam found himself marching out into the darkness, his head spinning, feeling a deep need to just walk and walk. It had brought him no pleasure to see Gene lain low like that. There was no joke in it. It was a brutal, crashing reminder of the hard, violent world they were all struggling to survive in, where not even the mighty Hunt was invulnerable. Until tonight, Sam had not realized just how lost, how utterly bereft, he would feel without the guv. Gene drove him mad most days, infuriated him – at times appalled and repelled him – and yet, beneath all the prejudice and banter and bullshit there was a powerful strength, an innate decency, that he had come to rely on. He was the burning spirit at the heart of 1973. He *was* 1973. The only thing that would crush Sam more than losing the guv'nor would be losing Annie.

Bang on cue, a small, round, pale face appeared, complete with a teardrop painted on each cheek. The Test Card Girl was standing motionless ahead of him, her hands clasped gently in front of her, a single black helium balloon bobbing in the air three feet above her head.

Sam stopped.

'You heard me thinking about Annie,' he said. 'Didn't you.'

He stared at the girl, and she – smiling ever so slightly – stared back. On their right, the lights of the hospital burned brightly in the deep dark of the night; far away to their left, barely visible but most certainly there, the coloured lights of the fairground whirled and span and flashed; in the dark space between the two stood Sam and the girl, face to face.

'You saw the horrid man,' the Test Card Girl said softly.

'My guv'nor's not so horrid,' Sam replied.

'No, not him, Sam. *Him.* The other man. The painted man.'

'Patsy O'Riordan? Yes, I saw him. And I've seen him before. In nightmares. Haven't I.'

The Girl nodded, said: 'And he's seen you. He watches you.'

'Not here he doesn't.'

'Oh yes he does. He watches from the dark. And it's dark now … dark all around …'

Sam felt his stomach tighten as if in anticipation of a blow. He silently cursed this ghastly, wan-faced creature for always stepping from the shadows and spooking the hell out of him – but for once, he decided to keep her talking. She had something to say, and this time he was resolved to hear it in full.

'I've seen Patsy in dreams,' he said. 'I thought it was some sort of devil. Now I know it was just a bunch of tattoos. Nothing but a painted devil.'

'And it is the eye of childhood that fears a painted devil,' smirked the girl. 'So now you're not frightened? Now you think that devil in the dark was just a horrid fat man who lives at the fair? Is that what you're thinking, Sam?'

'Of course. And you won't change my mind on that. There's nothing in the dark out there. The only demons are *in here.*' And he tapped the side of his head. 'Don't bother trying to scare me anymore. I know that's all you're doing.'

'But no no no it's *not,*' the girl said in a childish, whining voice. 'Sam, I'm trying to *help* you. Don't shake your head, it's true. I want to save you the pain.'

'What pain?'

'That devil in the dark ... it's out there, Sam ... it really is. And it's getting closer. All the time, closer and closer.'

'I don't know what you're talking about.'

Sam felt a strong urge to start walking, to push past that revolting little brat and march away into the night – but for some reason, his legs wouldn't obey him.

The Test Card Girl tilted her head to the side, looking quizzically at him, and said: 'Have a think, Sam. There's you ... and Annie ... and that thing in the darkness ... Have a think about it. Like a proper policeman. Have a think about the *clues* – see if you can make them make sense ...'

An ambulance roared by, its lights raking the pavement as it went, and in that suddenly dazzling moment the Test Card Girl was gone. Sam glanced upwards and saw a jet black balloon sailing away into the jet black sky – until, seconds later, that too vanished.

The devil in the dark.

Sam strode through the city, his head down, his face set. He passed beneath the orange glow of one sodium street light after another, oblivious to them as he was oblivious to everything else except his own thoughts.

Patsy O'Riordan is the devil-thing that I saw in my nightmares. God knows how and why I had premonitions about him, but I did. And it means something. Something important.

His feet guided him – across a silent road, down a gloomy back alley, behind a row of shut-up shops.

There's a threat against Annie. That little brat with the balloon keeps on and on telling me that. There's a threat against Annie, and it's going to reach her through me. So ... what do I do? How do I identify that threat? And how do I stop it?

A cat hissed and darted under a parked car. From behind a boarded-up fence a dog barked.

Whatever is it, this 'devil' is just a front. A mask. It represents something dangerous, something very real, but it presents itself in a disguise. It hides behind the mask of a monster to frighten me ... to frighten me like I'm just some little kid. Well that ain't gonna work, buster.

'I don't scare so easily, you creep!' he said out loud into the darkness. Then he sank back into his thoughts once again.

Whatever the danger is, it's somehow realized in the form of Patsy O'Riordan. Why else would I dream of him, see his ghastly tattoos grinning at me out of the darkness? I don't understand what, or how, or why, but it's Patsy that's the threat. It's Patsy that's the devil in the dark. It's Patsy that needs to be put away – forever.

Sam felt his heart quicken at the thought. If the Test Card Girl's threats and insinuations had any truth to them, they found their embodiment in the brutish, ugly, dehumanized form of Patsy O'Riordan. Strange and unfathomable as these threats might be, they at least now had a face. A face, and a name.

A face, a name, and a body made of flesh and blood. A man. Just a man. Not a monster, not a devil.

He had seen tonight that even a goliath like Gene Hunt could be brought low. Just as the Test Card Girl had intimated, there was a clue there – a clue for Sam …

'All men are mortal,' he told the night. 'That goes for me, Gene, and even Patsy O'Riordan. And what's mortal can be defeated. Destroyed. What's mortal can be brought *down*. And that goes for me … Gene … and even Patsy O'Riordan.'

Quite suddenly, Sam found he had reached the entrance to his flat. He stopped, looked up and down the quiet, deserted street. The Test Card Girl did not smile at him from the shadows. A devil did not leer at him from the darkness.

'You're going down, O'Riordan,' Sam vowed. 'You're going *down*.'

There was half a bottle of whisky in his flat. Sam finished it off that night with a toast to Gene's health, another to his future with Annie, and a third to the destruction of whatever it was out there in the blackness that wished to do them such terrible harm.

That night, he dreamt of nothing.

CHAPTER FIFTEEN

THE MAN WHO WOULD BE KING

Sam stepped up to the frosted glass doors of Gene's office, went to push them open, then paused.

He's not on the other side of those doors. Just go straight in.

It didn't seem right, barging in without knocking. Although, in his head, he knew he'd find nothing but an empty desk, an empty chair, a few empty bottles of scotch, his heart still braced itself for a relentless Gene Hunt earful.

'Make a habit of bursting in on a lady when she's about to do her ablutions do you, Tyler? That might be how they carry on in Hyde, but in my manor you treat your guv'nor like you treat your old chap – with respect, consideration, a mind for his privacy. Comprendezvous?'

Sam pushed through the doors.

Gary Cooper stared grimly from the poster for *High Noon*. Three darts with cross of St George flights jutted from the bullseye of the battered dartboard. An array of trophies and engraved pewter trinkets gleamed dimly from the top of a rickety filing cabinet. An opened packet of fags lay invitingly on the desktop, and the stale smell of panatellas hung in the air.

The familiar props that Gene surrounded himself with now looked unbearably forlorn, like the pipe and the slippers and the half-finished book Sam remembered seeing the day his grandfather died.

'The old bugger's not dead yet,' Sam said out loud. But even so, he found it painful to look at Gene's empty chair, its backrest and seat molded to the contours of the guv's now absent torso and arse.

The doors clattered open, making Sam jump, and there stood Ray, chewing his gum and appraising Sam coldly with his pale blue eyes.

'Measurin' up?' he asked curtly.

'Ray, what are you talking about?'

'Working out your new colour scheme for when you move in? What'll it be – pooftah pink? Or back-stabbing yellow?'

'Don't be an idiot,' Sam countered. He grabbed a file from Gene's desk. 'I only came in here to get this.'

'Oh aye?'

'Yes, aye. This is the guv'nor's office and it's *staying* the guv'nor's office, so don't you go round this department spreading rumours that I've got ambitions. You hear me?'

Ray shrugged: 'I can't stop the rumours.'

'Well, don't add to them.'

'There's plenty flyin' about already.'

'Oh yes?' said Sam, planting himself firmly in front of Ray. 'Thrill me.'

'They're saying he won't be coming back.'

'And who's *they*?'

'Who'd you think? Folk.'

'And you listen to what 'folk' have to say? Coz these are the same 'folk' who'll tell you that black people have a natural sense of rhythm, and cheese gives you nightmares, and the Americans are doing autopsies on aliens out at Roswell. Grow up, Ray. The guv's on sick leave, he's not been pensioned off and he's not in the morgue.'

'*I* know that,' said Ray. 'Just so long as *you* remember that too. Boss.'

'For God's sake. I came in to get the file on Denzil Obi. We've got a murder investigation in full swing, guv or no guv – and CID don't grind to a halt just because Gene's laid up with a bandage round his head.'

Clutching the file, Sam pushed past Ray – but Ray blocked him. They glared at each other, nose to nose, eyeball to eyeball.

'Loyalty,' Ray intoned, under his breath. Sam tried to shoulder past him but Ray wouldn't budge. 'Loyalty before ambition.'

'What do you take me for?'

'Do you really want me to say it? Eh? *Boss?*'

Indignant, offended, Sam shoved Ray hard enough to send him falling backwards through the swing doors. All eyes in CID were instantly on them as Ray stumbled against a desk, spilling a full ashtray onto the floor. In the next moment, Ray was coming back at him, throwing a punch. Sam ducked it and drove his fist into Ray's stomach, angling the blow upwards into the underside of his ribcage. It was enough to knock the breath clear out of him. Ray doubled up, gasping, helpless, a sitting duck for a fist in the face or a boot right up his jacksie. Sam felt his blood hot in his veins, his temper boiling within him. He clenched his fist … then relaxed it.

Step back, he thought. *Step back from the brink.*

He looked up at Chris's worried face peering at him from behind a mountain of piled papers, and Annie staring shocked and wide-eyed from behind her typewriter. It was only then that he realized that his face was pulled into a snarl, and he was breathing hard through his nose like a baited bull.

Who do I look like, I wonder … he thought.

Without a word, he offered his hand to Ray. Red-faced and still struggling to breathe, Ray glared up at him.

'Shake my hand, Ray.'

Ray made no move. Did he see Sam self-consciously mirroring the guv'nor's behaviour? The argie-bargie, the shove through the doors, the blow to the guts – it was all such classic Gene Hunt. Would all this just strengthen his conviction that Sam was trying to step into the guv's off-white tasseled loafers?

'All I want is to keep the Obi case on track in Gene's absence,' Sam said. 'Let's fight the bad guys, eh, Ray? Not each other.'

Reluctantly, Ray took Sam's hand and grasped it.

'You okay, Ray?'

'... I'm okay, Boss.'

'Good man.'

'Little boys,' Annie muttered to herself, shaking her head.

'Can I have everyone's attention, please,' said Sam, addressing the team.

'You've already got it, Boss,' put in Chris, still looking nervous. He edged round from behind his desk and shuffled anxiously towards Sam, ready to run at the first sign of trouble. Ray heaved himself painfully into a wheelie chair, and Annie perched herself on the corner of a desk.

Sam looked round at them, very seriously, and held up the Denzil Obi file. 'As you all know, the guv's out of action for a few days. So, until he's back in the saddle, I'm assuming temporary – *temporary*, Ray – responsibility for the Obi case. We're at a crucial point. We can't afford to be delayed by being a man down – even if that man *is* the guv.'

'It feels like the guv's still here, they way you're carrying on, Boss,' piped up Chris.

'Leave it, Chris,' Ray wheezed. He looked hard at Sam, then seemed to soften. 'Every ship needs a skipper.'

'And every skipper needs a deputy,' added Sam. 'Which is what I am. A stop-gap. A caretaker in the guv's absence. So let's have no more of this rubbish about me gunning for the top job and get back to nicking villains, okay?'

Ray, Chris and Annie answered as one: 'Yes, Boss.'

'Right. Now, as you know, we're looking after Spider down in the cells. His life's in danger, and that's the safest place for him. But we're not a hotel, and the poor bugger can't stay there indefinitely. So, he's agreed to act as bait to lure Patsy O'Riordan into a trap. I've set up a fight between them – a bare-knuckle fight, a nasty one, a grudge match between the two of them to settle their feud once and for all. They both want the other one dead, and we're going to use that to our advantage.'

'I don't see how this fight is going to incriminate O'Riordan,' said Annie. 'It still doesn't prove a link between him and Denzil.'

'You're right,' said Sam. 'The fight itself won't prove anything at all. But how we use that fight could nail this case once and for all.'

Everybody seemed to be paying him attention. Even Ray.

Excellent. They've got their minds back on the job, not on Gene, not on me and Ray coming to blows. They're concentrating ... and they're accepting me as the guv'nor, at least for the time being.

'The fight is nothing but a means to an end, a distraction,' Sam explained. 'It gets me close to Patsy, and the closer I get to him, the more likely he is to talk. Now, if I'm wearing a wire, we can record everything he says. The man's got a certain degree of cunning, but he's not Magnus Magnusson. If I get him talking – and I play it right – I'll get him to say something to incriminate himself. It might just be a tiny detail, something he lets slip without even realizing it. If he thinks he's getting his chance to get his revenge on Spider, he'll be pumped and excited ... just the frame of mind where I'll be able to nudge him into a boast or a threat or *something* that betrays his guilt.

'But we need more than that. We need a witness who's prepared to testify. And I think I've found one. Tracy Porter, Patsy's girlfriend. He used her to get at Denzil. She was the one who made Denzil unbolt his door to let her in the night he died. She was there. She witnessed the whole thing. She could tell us everything that happened, but she's terrified – and with good reason. Patsy beats that poor girl black and blue, and she knows

238

only too well what she can expect if she grasses him up
to the police.

'So – while Patsy is distracted at the fight, I want you,
Annie, to get hold of Tracy. She knows you. You can
talk to her. With Patsy well out of the way, you can you
persuade her to give a statement, to name Patsy as the
killer and testify in court against him. You think you can
manage that, Annie?'

Annie looked straight back at him and said: 'No.'

'Is that 'no' as in 'no'?'

'That's no as in 'no way', Boss. She won't say a word.'

'Then you'll just have to try.'

'Of course I'll *try*, Boss. I tried before but couldn't get
a word out of her.'

'This time it'll be different.'

'Not in her head it won't,' said Annie. 'Just because
Patsy's off fighting somewhere won't make her feel safe.
You've seen her. She's nothing but a punchbag for that
bastard. If you think her body's a wreck, just imagine
what state her mind's in.'

'She's right, Boss,' said Ray. 'Lasses like that always
stick up for their fellas.'

Sam chewed his lip, thinking the problem through.
'Offer her anything. Offer her protection. We can take
here away, put her somewhere safe. Tell her it's what we
did with Spider, and he's been perfectly safe in our care.
Make her see that cooperating with us is her way out of

this awful life she's trapped in. We can help her, protect her, but only if she makes a statement. After that, we can put Patsy away for life. Make her understand that, Annie.'

'I'll do my best, Boss,' said Annie, shrugging.

Sam wanted to impress on her how vitally important it was that they secure that conviction against Patsy. Couldn't she see what was at stake here? Couldn't she see that this wasn't just about putting Patsy away, but about saving themselves – saving Annie herself – from whatever the hell it was that was out there that wanted to hurt them so badly?

No, she doesn't see it. How could she? She senses that something's wrong, but for her it's just a vague feeling of unease, half-remembered dreams, confused recollections of nightmares. She doesn't see things as clearly as me. She doesn't have that little girl haunting her and goading her – and she hasn't seen the devil in the dark.

'Well, folks,' he said. 'That's my plan. How's it sound to you guys?'

'Iffy,' put in Ray.

'And why's that?'

'Too complicate by 'alf. The guv'd never go for all that round-the-mulberry-bush bollocks.'

'Well, as it happens, he's already pissed on this plan from a great height,' Sam admitted. 'But not even Gene can piss on me all way from central hospital, so there's not a lot he can do.'

'Are we back onto loyalty?' Ray said, fixing him with that look again.

'For God's sake, Ray, I've told the guv how I intend to proceed with this operation and he voiced no objections – admittedly because he wasn't feeling too clever, but that's by the by. I'm not doing anything behind his back – and if we get the result we're after, he'll be the last one to complain about it when he returns. We're all on the same side. We all want the same thing. We have to work as a team, with the tools we've got available, and make the best of the situation. At the end of the day, that's all that matters ...'

And here he found himself looking at Annie. All at once she seemed to him unspeakably vulnerable. He could almost see that awful devil in the dark looming out of the shadows behind her, its eyes glowing, the venom dripping from its fangs, its taloned claws slipping round her throat.

'... All that matters is that we nail Patsy O'Riordan. Right to the wall, guys. Right to the bloody wall. Chris, are you up for this?'

Chris shrugged: 'If that's the orders, Boss. But what am I supposed to do?'

'I'll be with Patsy, wearing a wire. You and Ray will be nearby, picking up everything that's said and recording it. If he lets slip something really juicy – something we can use to nick him then and there – then I'll want you

241

both as back-up so we can arrest him. Failing that, you'll be able to warn Annie in advance of Patsy's return. We can make this work. We can do it – but we've got to be smart, and we've got to be careful, and we've got to work as a team. Well? Are you with me on this?'

There was a silent pause.

It was Chris who broke that silence: 'I'm with you, Boss. I've defeated Hammer Hands O'Riordan once before ... I can do it again.'

'I'm with you too,' added Ray. And then, with a grudging hint of respect: 'Boss.'

'Are you all waiting for me to join in with this boysy moment?' asked Annie, folding her arms. She sighed, rolled her eyes, and said: 'Yes, yes, *I'm* onside too. Stone me, it's the ruddy musketeers round here, ain't it.'

Chris suddenly burst out with: 'Athos! Bathos! Davros! And ...'

He searched frantically for the last one.

'We get the idea, thank you, Chris,' said Sam.

Chris cursed, clicking his fingers and trying to dredge his memory: 'The guv'd know the name of the fourth one!'

'Ask him when comes back,' Ray suggested.

'It's d'Artagnan,' said Sam. But when Ray shot him yet another hostile look, he realized that it would have been better not to have said anything at all.

Sam went down to the cells and found Spider powering his way through a series of rapid press-ups.

'How are you doing, Spider?'

His face red and streaming with sweat, Spider ignored him, until at last he spat out: *three hundred and fifty!* And with that, he was done. He sat himself on the cell's meager cot and towelled his head and neck.

'Keeping yourself in trim,' said Sam. 'Excellent. Well, it looks you'll be safe to leave here very, very soon. I met Patsy last night. I've persuaded him to fight you.'

Spider stopped dead and glared at Sam. His jaw muscles clenched, making the tattooed spider on his neck ripple and flex.

'The whole thing'll be a sting,' Sam went on, 'just like we talked about. All you have to do is be there. No fighting. No danger to you. Just be there; provoke him – make him say something that reveals his guilt. I'll be wearing a hidden microphone, I'll capture every word he says. We can nick him, Spider. We can have him. Thirty years to life, in the hardest bloody prison in the country. You with me on this?'

Still panting, Spider nodded curtly. He seemed sullen and unfriendly. Sam wondered if he was preparing himself, mentally as well as physically, for a showdown with Patsy. Did he not understand that the fight between them would all be for show, that no actual blows would be exchanged? If all went as Sam hoped, they'd have

Patsy in handcuffs long before him and Spider got the chance to clash.

'Remember, Spider, this whole thing is about arresting Patsy O'Riordan. If you can somehow goad him or provoke him into admitting his guilt, that's worth far more to you and me and all the rest of us than trying to batter his brains in. It's a fight, Spider, but one that won't be won with fists, but with *this*.'

Sam tapped the side of his head.

Spider stared hard at him for a few moments, then said at last: 'I'm not dumb. I know what's what.'

'Good. Then we're on the same side. Are you feeling ready for this?'

'I'm feeling ready.'

'Sunday night. Eight o'clock, just outside the fairground.'

'I'll be there,' said Spider, his voice emotionless.

'You're doing the right thing, Spider.' Sam turned to go, but paused in the cell doorway: 'You won't understand this, Spider, but I want to see Patsy O'Riordan put away as much as you do. I want it for ... for different reasons. It's important. It's really important.'

Spider said nothing. He was drawing into himself, focusing his energies, narrowing down his thoughts until nothing existed except the fight.

If it helps him to treat it like a real fight, then so be it, thought Sam, heading away from the cells and back to CID. *How will he react when we arrest Patsy before he can get a single blow in? Will he feel cheated? Will he turn all that channelled rage on me instead?*

'I'm in control of this operation,' he told himself firmly as he strode away from the cell. 'I'm in control. I'm totally in control.'

CHAPTER SIXTEEN

BRITT EKLAND'S NIGHTIE

Still tucked away in the derelict factory where Gene had left it, the Cortina sat waiting for its fallen master, as faithful and patient as a loyal wolfhound. Sam looked it over while Annie stood nearby.

'All in one piece,' he said. 'Tyres, hub caps, wing mirrors ... Just as we left it. No smashed windows, no bumps or scratches.'

'It's fared better than Gene has, then,' said Annie. 'That'll cheer him up, at any rate. But what are we going to do with it? Shall we call in and get it towed back to the station?'

Sam brandished a key: 'He entrusted me with this, just in case. I've never used it. He never lets me drive.'

'Well, now's your chance.'

Sam held the keys in the palm of his hand, suddenly unwilling to use it.

'What's the matter, Sam? You look guilty.'

'I'm *feeling* guilty. The Cortina's special to him.'

'Oh, get on with it. It's only a car.'

'No, Annie. It's not. It's more than that.' He looked at her and shrugged: 'You wouldn't understand.'

'No, I suppose not. I *am* only a bird.'

'Opening it up and driving it away when he's not here, it's like ... sleeping with his wife.'

'I can't even begin to *imagine* the guv's wife!' Annie exclaimed. 'Have you ever met her?'

'Nope. I don't know anyone who has, except Gene. And to be honest, I'm not even entirely sure she actually exists.'

Annie thought for a moment, then said: 'You know what? I can see a posh lass going for him, one who's excited by a bit of rough.'

'Stella from the gym's hardly posh.'

'There's nothing between them two. A hoity-toity type – educated ... I can see a lass like that going for the guv. And him going for her.'

'If you don't mind, Annie, I'd prefer to leave the curtain well and truly closed across the guv'nor's sex life.'

Sam straightened his back, pushed all hesitation aside, and slipped the key into the door lock. When he clambered behind the wheel, he could feel that the driving seat still bore Gene's heavy, rounded imprint.

He hit the ignition and the engine sprang into life.

'It sounds different when Gene does it,' he said. 'More … aggressive.'

'You're imagining it. It really is only a car, Sam.'

He nosed the motor out of the derelict factory, passed through a series of drab, rundown streets and began working his way through the city traffic. The Cortina had never been driven so carefully and considerately. It seemed to want to lurch forward, like a dog pulling at the lead – but Sam didn't say anything, because he knew exactly how Annie would respond.

'Are you still having bad dreams?' he asked as he drove.

'On and off. I try not to think about them. What about you?'

'All the time.'

'What's happening do you think, Sam? Are we going slowly potty together?'

'Not if I can help it, Annie.'

Sam pictured Patsy O'Riordan, bristling with his demonic, inhuman tattoos – and then he imagined a cell door clanging incontrovertibly shut, sealing that monstrous creature off for ever.

Nothing is going to happen to Annie. I won't allow it. Whatever the hell it is that's out there, I'm going to lock it away along with Patsy O'Riordan. They can rot together in a maximum security cell. Me and Annie, we're the future.

'I think we're both going to be sleeping a lot easier in the near future,' said Sam.

'What makes you say that?' asked Annie.

'Just a hunch – you know, the way coppers get hunches.'

'Don't be mysterious. What are you getting at?'

Sam looked for the Test Card Girl as he drove, expecting to see the little brat popping up on a pavement or sauntering by on a pelican crossing. But there was no sign of her.

'I'm not sure I can even put it into words,' he said. 'Just a ... a good feeling.'

Annie laughed. It wasn't a cruel or condescending laugh, or a mocking laugh, or a laugh of exasperation. It was just a laugh. An honest laugh. An Annie laugh. Sam could not have asked to hear a more heart-warming sound.

'Sam, I don't know what you're on about!' she smiled at him. 'I don't think I'll ever understand you lot.'

'What do you mean 'us lot'?'

'*You*! Men. Fellas. The way you talk and that. The way you *think* ... if you can call it thinking.'

'We think,' said Sam, a little defensively. 'We think more than *your* lot ever give us credit for.'

'And what is it you fellas think about, eh? Boobs and brmm-brmms and Brian flippin' Clough.'

'If I lumped all women together in a big cliché like

that, you'd be the first to protest,' said Sam. 'Men *talk* about boobs and brmm-brmms and football, Annie, but that's just the surface. You've got to look behind the words to catch the meanings. It's like poetry.'

'Now I've heard everything!' Annie hooted.

'Take Gene, for instance,' Sam went on. 'You think he's a caveman, don't you.'

'I'm not the only one. You think he is too.'

'Of course. On the surface. And, to be fair, quite a way *under* the surface too. But if you were to go down *really* deep, right to the core of the man-'

'Journey to the Centre of the Guv,' suggested Annie.

'-you'd be surprised at what you'd find. And don't look at me like that, Annie, I mean what I'm saying.'

'I'm sure you do. That's what makes men so funny. But tell me, Sam – if I dug deep and reached the secret core of Gene Hunt, which is a pretty horrible thought, what would I find there that would surprise me?'

Sam felt the wheel tug beneath his hands. The engine gave a fit and a start and a sudden angry cough – then continued to run smoothly. It was almost as if the Cortina was aware of them, was listening in, was ... No, no, he wasn't going to start thinking like that. Such thoughts were the first steps on the pathway to madness.

'If you dug deep into the guv'nor, I'll tell you what you'd find,' said Sam. 'Hope.'

'Ha!'

'And fear. And compassion. And rage and forgiveness and arrogance and respect. And everything else. But above all, *hope*, Annie. A boundless sense of hope.'

'For what? For Britt Ekland to shimmy into his bedroom and drop her nightie?'

'That's not fair, Annie, we're *all* hoping for that.'

'What then?'

'It's not a hope *for* something, but a hope *in* something. He has hope in us, Annie – in you and me, and the team at CID, and all those millions of people out here – he has hope in human beings. Because I tell you, he's not a DCI for the money. There's something else drives him, like it drives all good coppers if you look hard enough. Why does he tear round these streets, risking his neck day after day? Why does he nick villains? Why does he uphold the Law? It's because he has *hope* in this world, Annie. It means something to him. It means *everything* to him. He loves the world, Annie. He loves it.'

'Well!' said Annie, still smiling. '*That* was a speech. A typical *man* speech. And I'm not sure what to make of it all. Perhaps it holds true for Gene, but not for all fellas.'

'It might do, more than you'd ever believe,' said Sam. 'Even Patsy O'Riordan.'

'How can you say that, Sam? He's a thug! You've seen what he does to that poor lass Tracy. There's no love or hope inside of him!'

251

'Precious little, I agree. But there's holes in him, Annie. I'm not talking about the bullet-holes in his belly. I mean the holes where love and hope and decency and kindness ought to be. And those holes hurt him, Annie, far more than he would ever, *ever* let on. Maybe that's why he fights other men, and batters Tracy, and covers himself in tattoos. I don't know. But I *do* know he's desperately unhappy, and desperately afraid, like all macho man who carry on like he does.'

'I see,' said Annie, looking slyly at him. 'You're coming on all philosophical because I said all you boys ever think about is birds and motors and winning the World Cup. Okay, you've put me in my place. I was wrong. You're all highly complex and intellectually deep and emotionally complex, even knuckle-draggers like Patsy and the guv'nor. I'm impressed. I'm over-awed. I'm excited and attracted and can't wait to drop my nightie for you all. There – happy now?'

It was Sam's turn to laugh.

They reached the drab, grey block of the police HQ and tucked the Cortina safely in its accustomed parking spot to await the return of its fallen master.

'Look at us,' said Annie, smiling across at him as the engine fell silent. 'You and me, all alone the in the guv's favourite motor. Whatever would I do if you took advantage of me?'

'You'd scream, and run a mile.'

'Only if you started banging on again about the depths of the male psyche.'

'Maybe I should start banging on about something else, then.'

Annie shrugged, and waited. Sam leant across and kissed her – politely, on the cheek, as if testing the waters. It was very gentlemanly.

But suddenly, he felt her hands on him, grabbing the lapels of his jacket and pulling him roughly towards her.

'That,' she said, 'wasn't a kiss. *This,* on the other hand ...'

She showed him how it was *really* done.

When at last he was free to speak, Sam said to her: 'You said more just then, Annie, than I could ever express in mere words.'

'You fellas, you don't half talk some cobblers,' said Annie, and she clambered out of the Cortina.

In the privacy of the Lost & Found Room, Sam called Chris, Ray and Annie together. To have convened this meeting in Gene's office, with Sam installing himself behind the guv's desk, would have sent the inflammatory rumours flying, and the incident room was too noisy and full of distraction for a meeting of this kind. Lost & Found offered the perfect neutral space.

'You all know why I've called you here,' said Sam. 'We need to review our surveillance technology. I'm going to be wired for sound on Sunday night and I want absolute assurance that the equipment is reliable and discreet. We need the most up-to-date, state of the art gadgets we can lay out hands on. Ray – what can you give me?'

'I've brought me selection of hi-tech goodies,' Ray said, and plonked a tatty cardboard box on the table. He rummaged inside, the said proudly: 'Cop a gander at this beauty, boss! The Grundig!'

He produced a portable tape recorder the size of a mansize box of tissues. It had big red buttons sticking out the front of it.

Sam stared blankly at it.

'Well, don't look at it like it's just let off,' said Ray, defensively.

Sam sighed: 'We're conducting an undercover operation, Ray, not an interview. That thing's the size of a bloody house brick!'

'House brick?' retorted Ray. 'This baby's the smallest recorder on the market. Look, even the tapes are tiny.'

'*Dead* tiny!' Chris agreed, impressed. 'I never seen tapes so tiny! That is *tiny*!'

'See? Chris understands. Don't turn your nose up, boss, it's dead new.'

'And Grundig's a quality brand,' put in Chris.

'And how precisely am I going to conceal it?' Sam asked. 'Shove it in my pocket and hope no one notices?'

'Don't be daft,' said Ray. He stuck the Grundig under his jacket and then tried to act natural.

'I can see a bulge,' said Sam. He ignored Chris's sniggers and added: 'The Grundig's a real doozy, Ray, but we need undercover surveillance equipment that can't be seen from the moon. What else have you got?'

'Well, there's always the thingy,' said Ray, rummaging again in the box.

'The whaty?'

'The thingy.'

He pulled out a metal box, the size of a box of kitchen matches, with coloured wires sticking out of it every which way.

'There you go – the thingy,' declared Ray, holding it up like it was a dead insect. 'I thought we had a couple more of 'em.' He hunted about in the box, to no avail. 'Nope. Somebody must've buggered 'em and slung 'em out. They're a bit flimsy.'

'A bit flimsy?' said Sam. 'Ray, I've seen tougher cobwebs than this.'

'At least it's small,' volunteered Chris.

'That's right,' said Ray. 'You can hide it under your shirt. Pin it to your tit or whatever. Walk about all day with it on, no one'll clock it.'

'But does it actually work?'

'On and off,' Ray admitted with admirable honesty.

'Don't play with the wires, it breaks the solder. And don't shake it. Or get it wet.'

Ray fished about in the cardboard box again and this time produced a random assortment of Eveready batteries. He tested a 7 volt one with his tongue, then fitted it into the body of the bug.

'There you go,' he said. 'All juiced up.'

'Is it in full working order?' asked Sam.

'Dunno.'

'Well, can we test it? Where's the receiver?'

Ray hauled out a huge lump of metal and plastic strapped together with duct tape. He fiddled with the massive on-off knob, and static began to hiss from the round grill on the front.

'Go on Boss, give it a blast.'

Sam counted one, two, one, two into the thingy. His words emerged from the grill on the receiver – crackling and distorted, but just about audible.

Chris's eyes shone: 'Oh, yes! It's like James Bond, this!' And in the voice of Q he added: 'Pay attention, 007. There's a poison dart concealed in this wristwatch. Mind out that you don't shoot it up your jacksie when you're having a wipe. It nacks like a bitch, take it from me.'

Sam looked flatly at him: 'Thank you, Christopher. But if we can just momentarily return to the world of the grown-ups, I need to know if this tatty bit of fourth form electrics is the best equipment we've got.'

'We're CID, guv, not *Tomorrow's World*,' said Ray.

'Isn't that the truth,' Sam sighed. 'Well – we'll just have to work with what we've got.'

'Like the actress said to the bishop,' put in Chris. And grinning, he waited in vain for the laughter. The silence slowly wiped the grin from his face.

'Right then,' said Sam, ignoring him. 'I'll conceal this 'thingy' beneath my shirt. Ray – Chris – you two sit in the car nearby, recording everything on the Grundig. Make sure all the equipment works, boys. I don't want the electrics going phooey on us.'

'Yes, Guv. I mean Boss,' Ray and Chris said in perfect unison.

'And remember,' Sam went on, 'be on standby to either rush in and help me arrest Patsy, or else send a warning to Annie that O'Riordan's on his way back. It's vital, boys, it's *vital* that Annie can rely on you, absolutely, one hundred and fifty percent. Her life might depend on you getting word to her in time. Is that clear?'

'We should arrange for back-up,' put in Ray. 'Get some uniformed boys on standby in case things kick off.'

'We don't *want* things to kick off,' said Sam. 'We want to keep it as low key as possible. The more manpower we draft in, the more chance Patsy or one of his lads will get the wind up, and then this whole thing will have been for nothing. Let's just keep this operation stream-lined, yes? We're CID, we can handle this. Agreed?'

'Yes, boss.'

Sam turned to Annie: 'Are you happy with this arrangement?'

Annie looked down at the array of electrical rubbish scattered about on the table in front of her. The colour drained slightly from her cheeks. She said: 'It's not the equipment I'm putting my trust in – it's my colleagues.'

'Quite right. I hope you two boys are listening,' said Sam, looking across at them intently.

'We're listening, boss,' said Ray. He nudged Chris with his elbow.

'What? Oh, aye, yeah, me too,' piped up Chris. 'Listening like a hawk.'

CHAPTER SEVENTEEN

WIRED

Sunday evening. A wretched, grey evening was settling over the city, against which Terry Barnard's Fairground hurled out its lights and noise and music as if raging against the dying of the light.

From inside an unmarked car parked on the very edge of the open ground where the fairground was pitched, Sam peered through a rickety pair of police binoculars. Beside him, in the front passenger seat, sat Ray; squeezed together in the back were Chris, Annie, and Spider.

'Business as usual at the fair,' said Sam, surveying the scene. 'Looks like a few bits and pieces are already being packed up – the fair moves on tomorrow morning, first thing.' He scanned across. 'There it is! The arena for the fight.'

He passed the binoculars to Ray, who squinted through them, nervously chewing his gum.

'Away to the left – four caravans, parked up into a square,' said Sam.

'I see 'em, Boss.'

Ray offered the binoculars to Spider, but Spider made no move to take them; he was as silent and withdrawn as before, focused in on himself, utterly self-contained. In contrast, Chris was bouncing in his seat excitedly, his head full of 007 and daring commando raids. He grabbed the binoculars and mucked about with the focus.

'This is hopeless!' he whined. 'Why can I see *two* lots of everything?'

'Try it with one eye closed,' said Ray.

'I don't want to do it with one eye closed,' Chris complained. 'They're binocs. You do binocs with both eyes. You don't see James Bond doing binocs with one eye, do you? You think he'd pull all them birds doing binocs with one eye?'

Ignoring him, Sam turned to Ray: 'You've got the receiver ready to go?'

'Aye, boss.'

Ray produced the bulky receiver from beneath the passenger seat and twiddled the knobs. Feedback howled out of the loudspeaker grill, making everybody wince – even Spider – and Ray instantly switched it off.

'Well, at least that shows it's got batteries,' said Sam.

He fidgeted with the microphone taped uncomfortably to his chest. 'Are you *sure* it's not obvious I'm wired?'

'Dead sure, boss,' said Ray. 'Honest, you can't see a thing.'

'Annie? Tell me.'

'He's right, boss,' said Annie, leaning forward. 'You'd never know.'

'You guys had better be right,' said Sam, arranging his shirt over the mic. 'If Patsy spots this wire, I'm in trouble.'

'We'll be hanging on every word, boss,' Ray assured him. 'First hint of trouble, we'll be right there.'

'But that's just it, Ray, I don't *want* any trouble. We don't want any trouble. Let's get through this evening with as little violence as possible, okay? And that goes for you, Spider. This isn't a fight. It's a police operation. You're not going up against Patsy, you're there to provoke him into saying something incriminating. Right?'

Spider stared straight ahead.

'I said *right*, Spider?'

After a few moments, Spider nodded, very curtly, just once.

'Chris, give the binocs to Annie.'

'I'm still playing with them,' murmured Chris, holding down one eyelid with his finger.

'Chris!'

Reluctantly, Chris handed them over.

'Patsy's caravan is right over there,' said Sam,

261

indicating where Annie should look. 'It's easy to pick out because it's spotless. Little net curtains on the windows. Flowers in the vases.'

'I see it,' said Annie, and then to Chris: 'You've left these binocs all sweaty.'

'I'm excited!' Chris said, bouncing in his seat. 'Undercover operations, they get me going!'

'The distance between where I'll be in the arena and Patsy's caravan is no more than a hundred and fifty yards,' said Sam. 'I'll keep Patsy preoccupied for as long as possible – but if he decides to suddenly head home, you're not going to get much warning, Annie. You've got to be ready to get the hell out of there at the drop of a hat, with or without Tracy.'

'We'll be watching all the time,' said Ray, looking over his shoulder at Annie. 'Don't you fret, luv.'

'I'm not fretting,' said Annie, passing back the binocs. 'I'm just hoping Tracy's actually at home.'

'She will be,' said Sam. 'Patsy keeps her on a very tight leash. Speaking of which, mind out for the Rottweiler he's got chained up right outside his door. It'll have your hand off.'

'A Rottweiler? *Now* you tell me!'

'It's no worries dealing with a Rotty,' put in Ray. 'The secret is to grab its back legs.'

Sam pulled a face that said *you're talking bollocks, Ray,* but Ray ignored him and carried on.

'Grab the back legs and hoik 'em off the ground. Don't, whatever you do, go anywhere near the front end.'

'That's the end with teeth,' Chris added helpfully.

'Lift the rear legs and start walking backwards,' Ray went on. 'Your Rotty'll be too busy trying to keep balance on his front legs to bite you. I've seen it done. It's the biz.'

'Sounds like grabbing the tiger by the tail,' said Annie, looking anxious. 'You're okay until you let go. And sooner or later you've *got* to let go.'

'Not the tail, the legs,' Chris corrected her. 'Rotty's ain't got much of a tail. It's more like the last bit of a sausage. Ain't that right, Ray?'

'Don't sweat, luv,' said Ray, winking at Annie. 'You won't be on your own. Like I say, me and Chris'll be keeping a close on eye on you.' And quietly, to Sam, man-to-man, Ray added: 'We'll be keeping a close on eye on her, Guv.'

Sam glanced round at Annie. She gave him an expression that reassured him: *it's okay*, her face said. *I'll look after myself. Everything'll be fine.*

'I just want to say one more thing,' he said, looking from one face to another. 'We're dealing with a dangerous man here tonight. The safety of all of us rests on us working together as a team. Every single one of us must be constantly thinking of the others. Spider, are you listening?'

Spider nodded, but still said nothing.

'Pity the guv ain't here,' said Ray, feeding a stick of Juicy Fruit into his mouth.

'Yes, it's a pity,' said Sam. 'But he's *not* here, and we *are*. So stay alert, and stay vigilant, and between us we'll make the guv jealous he was loafing around in a hospital bed instead of on the front line with us guys. You with me?'

'With you, Boss.'

Only Spider didn't join in the chorus of support.

Sam checked his watch.

'Time for me to go. As soon as Patsy leaves the caravan, Annie moves in and starts on Tracy. Ray, you pay close attention to what's being said between me and Patsy; wait as long as you safely can before sending Spider over. We need to give Annie as much time with Tracy as we can.'

'Wilco, boss.'

Sam turned to Spider: 'I'll see you in the arena, then. Good luck, Spider.'

No response. Spider sat, unblinking, like a waxwork.

'Good luck everyone,' Sam added, glancing once more at Annie.

'Good luck, Boss.'

Sam clambered from the car, his heart starting to pound. Every beat seemed to hammer against the microphone taped to his chest, shoving it forward, betraying its presence. He resisted the urge to fidget with it. The secret was to forget about the damned thing's existence entirely and concentrate on the role he was here to play; he was a bent copper, out to nab an innocent man and frame him for murder.

Striding confidently across the open ground, Sam looked up at the lights of the fairground as they flashed against the darkening sky. Lit up and sparkling, the Ferris wheel was turning. Sparks flickered from the bumper cars (from which Gene was banned, for life). Music pounded out. People screamed excitedly as the roller-coaster rattled by.

And then he looked at the caravans parked front-to-tail just on the fringe of the fair. A stone's throw from the light and laughter and music and fun of the fair, violent men lurked in the shadows, preparing arenas of combat where they would clash and batter each other to pieces.

And here come two of those violent men now ...

From the direction of the arena, Ponytail and Moustache-man came sauntering towards him, their shoulders back, chests stuck out.

Sam decided to affect a Gene Huntian arrogance. He maintained his brisk pace, aiming to stroll straight past them.

'Evening, girls. You're both looking ravishing tonight.'

Moustache-man blocked him. Sam side-stepped – and so did Moustache-man.

Forced to stop, Sam sighed and rolled his eyes: 'All right, you fairies, what's got your goat, mmm?'

Ponytail walked a slow circle around Sam, looking him up and down.

'Checking me out for a bumming?' Sam sneered. It wasn't the best line in the world, but then again, he wasn't addressing the most sophisticated of audiences. 'Not my bag all that – but your friend with the tash looks up for it. Don't you, Mildred.'

Out in the darkness, Sam caught a glimpse of Annie, picking her way along the very edge of the open ground, taking the long route round towards Patsy's caravan. All at once, he felt an overwhelming sense of longing for her. Not a sexual longing, but a longing to be with her, just the two of them, somewhere safe and decent – a need to protect her against all the filth and hatred and violence of the world.

She's a serving officer, she can protect herself.

But can she? Sam knew – he *sensed*, deep in his nervous system – that there were worse things out there in the darkness than knuckle-heads and Rottweilers.

Whatever it is out there, it has found its form in Patsy O'Riordan. Put O'Riordan away, for ever, and you've defeated it, Sam.

He stoked that thought in himself like he was stoking the embers of a fire. Sparks flew up. Flames leapt.

Defeat Patsy, and you defeat that Devil in the Dark ... Defeat Patsy ... Defeat Patsy ...

And then, just as he felt his courage return and his resolve strengthen, he heard Ponytail say from directly behind him:

'Open your shirt.'

'I told, I'm not up for it.'

'I said open your shirt. Or we'll open it for you.'

Sam's heart was racing. But he affected total cool when he turned slowly and fixed Ponytail with a straight look.

'I came here in good faith,' he said.

'Then prove you're not wired.'

'And why the hell would I be wired? I'm not here for Patsy, I'm here for that freak Spider.'

'Then open your shirt.'

'You don't trust me? If you don't trust me, then I don't trust you. And if I don't trust you, then tonight's off. I'm out of here.'

'Open your shirt.'

Sam forced himself to laugh: 'You don't have much between your ears, do you! Either of you! *I'm a copper, you dopes!* You two turnips mess me about and I can have you both banged up and buggered from here till bloody doomsday. So – if you don't mind – I have business to attend to with Mr O'Riordan. So naff off, the pair off you.'

He turned and pushed past Moustache-man – and the moment he did, he felt strong hands clamping themselves on him. At once, Sam felt his police training kick in. It was instinctual, completely beneath the level of conscious thought. He struck hard at the edge of Ponytail's wrist, right on the bone, dislodging the hand from where it gripped his jacket. At the same time, he ducked back, giving himself space.

'If you can fight with only one hand, do so,' they had taught him, years ago (or rather, years from now). *'Always keep one hand free – across your chest, across your stomach, tensed and ready to fend off a blow or an incoming blade.'*

Ponytail had clutched his hand, indignant at the pain Sam had inflicted. Moustache-man came lumbering forward, both fists clenched, leaning forward like a silverback gorilla.

'Keep your feet planted wide – a good, solid stance – mind your balance – the last thing you want to do in a fight is find yourself flat on your face or flat on your arse ...'

Sam aimed a kick, driving the heel of his boot into Moustache-man's kneecap. The man howled and crashed forward, carried by his own suddenly shifted centre of gravity, and slammed face-first into the mud.

Without pausing, Sam span round to face Ponytail and instantly adopted a pose he recalled from the one and only Tai Chi class he had attended. Knees bent, left hand, claw-like, tucked against left shoulder; right hand outstretched in a fist, turning slowly on the axis of his arm. For good measure, he made a low, cat-like mewling in the back of throat:

'Hiyeeeeeeeeeeeeeeeeeeee – YAH!'

He thrust forward suddenly and inexpertly.

'Look out, Joey, he's Bruce bloody Lee!' Ponytail howled, stumbling backwards, his fist raised but his whole stance one of imminent flight.

Moustache-man – Joey – picked himself up from the soggy ground, his face caked in mud. He limped anxiously away for a few steps, one hand on his knee, the other raised vaguely to fend off an attack.

Glaring fiercely, Sam took a step forward, crouching low and thrusting out his left hand instead of his right.

'That's right,' he said, working hard to keep the fear out of his voice. 'I'm a double black-belt Jedi Knight, taught by the great Master Yoda himself ... and I can break every bone in your bodies just by *looking* at you ...'

He chopped at the air and made oriental noises. It did the trick. Neither Ponytail nor Moustache-man would approach him, let alone touch him.

Recalling episodes of *Kung Fu* he'd seen as a kid, Sam slowly relaxed his posture, straightened up, placed his palms together and bowed his head. Such pose, such self-assurance, was even more unsettling than the violence. Perhaps this little man in a leather jacket really *could* break every bone in their bodies ...

'Now that we all trust each other again,' said Sam, straightening his collar, 'I'll be on my way. I have business with Mr O'Riordan.'

He turned and started walking towards the arena of parked caravans. Behind him, at a safe distance, Patsy's henchmen followed him.

Brain over brawn, Sam wanted to whisper into the microphone for Ray to hear. But he had too much sense to do something so reckless.

CHAPTER EIGHTEEN

BIG MEN, BIG TROUBLE

The four caravans were parked in a square, bonnet to rear bumper, with no more than a couple of feet between them for access. They defined a scrap of boggy ground as the arena, a space that was cramped and hemmed in and smaller by far than a regular boxing ring. It was a tight corner, a bear pit, graceless, practical, and private – a walled-off enclave where two men could settle their personal scores like savages. It was a patch of barbarism amid a civilized society.

Sam clambered through the gap left between two of the vehicles and glanced with distaste around the arena. Behind him, lurking nervously in the gap, he saw Ponytail and Moustache-man.

I've earned their grudging respect – or at least their

fear. That's good. They'll keep their distance. I can forget about them for the time being and concentrate solely on Patsy ... But where IS Patsy?

As if in answer to his thoughts, a monstrous devil-face appeared in the space between two of the caravans. It grinned at him from the shadow, bearing its fangs. Sam felt his stomach muscles tighten, his blood congeal. He felt a sudden overpowering sense of self-consciousness, and – unconsciously – raised his hand to his chest in an attempt to cover and conceal the wire taped beneath his shirt. When he realised what he was doing, he turned the gesture into one of coat-straightening.

Patsy loomed into the arena, wearing nothing but corduroy trousers and a pair of battered, workman's boots. So worn were the boots that the metal of the steel toe-caps peeked through the leather. Sam had a mental image of those boots connecting with the side of Spider's head.

There will be no fighting here tonight. Arrests, yes – but no mayhem, no brawling, no repeat of the savagery I saw between Patsy and that black boxer, Ben.

'Your boys gave me a warm welcome,' Sam said, adopting a macho posture fitting for a bent copper. Taking a gamble, he added: 'The bastards wanted to frisk me for a wire.'

Patsy glowered across at him, his eyes bright and white like chips of ice. His face was so disfigured with wounds and tattoos that his expression was almost impossible to read. More expressive than his face was his general air of menace and violence; it told Sam everything he needed to know about what was going on inside Patsy's hairless, bullet-like head.

'We're going to have to learn to trust each other,' Sam went on. 'It's no good getting paranoid.'

Patsy said nothing, but slowly paced the arena, flexing his muscles. His tattoos rippled.

Why isn't he saying anything? What's the point in my going to all the risk of wearing a wire if the bastard won't speak?!

'Limbering up, Patsy? I wouldn't bother – I'll be nicking Spider before you get a chance to touch him.'

Patsy clamped his small, hard palms together and pressed, making his arm and chest muscles bulge.

Say something, you thug, damn well say something!

'You know Patsy, without our … little arrangement, me and my department would be up the creek. You covered your tracks so well at Denzil's place that we really couldn't mount a case against you.'

Go on, answer, stop posturing and ANSWER!

'Just out of interest, Patsy, how did you locate Denzil at the gym? Did you have an inside contact? Or did you go there to work out and just suddenly see him?'

Patsy was throwing punches at the air, snorting like a bull. He seemed to be no longer aware of Sam's presence. Sam glanced back at Moustache-man and Ponytail, peering in nervously through the gap between caravans.

What's happening here? They know there'll be no fight here this evening, that it's just a put-up job. Why's Patsy focussing himself like this? He's acting like Spider ...

Acting like Spider. Yes. Spider was psyching himself up for a fight too ... and yet neither of them was *supposed* to fight – both of them knew this whole thing was just a trap ...

Unless ...

Sam swallowed uneasily.

Unless they're both intending to fight for real.

As Patsy snorted and threw blank punches, Sam raised a hand to his mouth and thought hard.

Does Patsy intend to ignore the deal and kill Spider here tonight? And does Spider intend to forget the operation and go instead for revenge on Patsy? Have both these fighters decided, independently, to use me to get to the other?

That was madness, surely. It was in Patsy's interests to see Spider take the rap for the Denzil Obi murder, just as it was in Spider's interests to see Patsy arrested for the crime he had committed. What the hell would a fight between them achieve?

Maybe they don't think like that. Maybe all they think about is vengeance ... battering each other's heads in.

274

'Patsy,' Sam said carefully. 'You do remember the deal we made, don't you?'

'All deals are off.'

It wasn't Patsy who spoke. It was Spider. Without warning, Spider was stepping into the arena, stripped to the waist, revealing his lithe, tight musculature and pale skin, so blank and clean compared to Patsy's inked and elaborate palimpsest of flesh.

Sam's temper flared. What the hell was Ray playing at, sending Spider in so soon?! He needed time! He needed time to get Patsy to speak – and God knew he hadn't said a *word* so far – he needed time for the lumbering thug to incriminate himself ... and Annie needed time in the caravan alone with Tracy, persuading her, winning her trust, making her see sense.

Glaring around, Sam saw that in the gaps between the ring of parked vehicles there were faces – men's faces, peering in – the faces of fairground folk, travellers, luggers, grafters – the faces of Patsy O'Riordan's people, come to see the showdown, come to witness all the fun of the alternative fair. In that moment, Sam realised he'd been duped. Patsy had no intention of being part of some police scam to frame Spider. All he wanted was to be alone in the ring with the man who once tried to kill him.

And at the same time, Sam understood that Spider had used him too, that he had never intended to play along with the operation but instead wanted to get his revenge on the man who killed his blood brother – or die in the attempt.

Patsy and Spider stared silently at each other from opposite corners of the arena. Sam stood there, uncertain, dithering, feeling at once like the referee in a boxing match.

But this is no boxing match. And there's no call for a referee because there's no rules ...

'Ray!' Sam hissed into the hidden microphone beneath his shirt. 'It's all gone tits up! Get down here now! And call for back-up!'

Instinctively, he waited for an answer – and then had to remind himself this was not a police radio.

I'll just have to trust that he heard me.

But just as he thought that, he heard voices – Chris's voice, and Ray's – coming from just outside the arena.

Through one of the corner gaps, Sam saw them. They were being dragged roughly by large men. Ray was glowering fiercely, blood streaming from his nose where it drenched his moustache and dripped thickly from his chin. Chris was hollering and complaining, and as he turned his head from side to side Sam saw that one of his eyes was swollen shut from a huge, black bruise.

'Ray! Chris!' Sam called out instinctively. And at once he heard his own voice coming back to him from the radio receiver that was held aloft by one of the thugs.

The receiver was hurled roughly to the ground and trampled. It smashed.

'They sprang up outta nowhere, boss!' howled Chris. He was silenced by a clip round the ear. 'OI! Watch out!'

'The bastards rushed us,' Ray growled, trying to staunch the flow of blood down his face. 'They got us … *all* of us … *as you can see.*'

Sam caught his meaning at once – *they got all of us, as you can see …*

Annie's not here. He's telling me that they didn't get Annie. She's okay. She's clear.

That was something, at least.

Sam turned sharply on Patsy and bellowed: 'What the hell's going on here, you moron! These are my officers your thugs have assaulted! Let them go – right now! We had a deal, Patsy!'

And now, at last, Patsy became aware of him. He turned his nasty, misshapen, green-and-blue inked head, and bared his teeth in a vicious grin. His eyes flashed wickedly.

'Patsy! I *demand* your monkey crew get their mitts off my officers!'

'You're in the arena,' Patsy growled, his voice low and bestial. '*My* arena …'

'The deal, Patsy! Remember the deal!'

'No deals … Not here …'

Sam turned towards Spider: 'Back off, Spider! This isn't the way!'

But Spider couldn't hear him. His entire will was fixated upon his enemy. His eyes were blazing. Every muscle was pulled tight. He was locked on, like a missile – primed, ticking, seconds from detonation.

With his heart hammering and his mouth dry, Sam strode boldly towards the two men and planted himself between them.

'I'm arresting both of you,' he declared. 'I'm arresting *everybody*!'

Patsy held out his right hand and placed it on Sam's chest, right where the bug was taped. But it didn't matter about that anymore – the operation had gone to crock. Patsy's small, bruised, scabby, painted hand rested on Sam for a moment – lightly, as if he were checking his heartbeat – and then, with a sudden show of strength that seemed to come out of nowhere, he shoved Sam back. Sam stumbled and fell, landing heavily on his backside in the churned-up mud of the arena.

Looking up, he saw Patsy and Spider launch at each other like head-on express trains. They slammed together with a shocking impact, and then it was all fists, a firestorm of fists, so fast and frenzied that they became a blur of colour. Blood splattered against the side of one of the caravans.

Sam clambered to his feet and scrambled away, like he was avoiding the spinning blades of some murderous machine run amok. He saw the faces of men pressing in at every gap between the vehicles, their eyes wide, their lips drawn back, their teeth bared as they lapped up the ferocious violence exploding and thudding in the arena. He even saw Ray's face, streaming with blood, as he peered in. And for a moment he glimpsed Chris, trying to see what the hell was going on with just his one good eye.

Turning back to the fight, Sam saw Spider hurling a series of truly monumental blows against Patsy's face. His fists slammed into the bigger man like hurled mallets, flinging Patsy's head back and to the side, over and over. Patsy flailed blindly, trying to defend himself, but he was retreating blindly. He slammed against the side of one of the caravans, struggling to keep himself upright against it.

I don't believe it! Spider's battering him! He's winning!

As Patsy raised both arms to cover his face, Spider switched his attack, firing rapid blows one after the other into Patsy's stomach and ribs. As Patsy doubled up, Spider switched again, blazing away at his face and head once more.

Nobody can take much more of that – not even O'Riordan!

Sam felt a sudden elation, an exhilarating joy in seeing so much violence up close. Or was it that? No – it was something else – it was the deep, vicious pleasure of seeing the Devil in the Dark being battered to a pulp. That enigmatic and nightmarish force which had been reaching out with such malice towards Annie, and which had found its expression in the tattooed body of Patsy O'Riordan, was being beaten into submission, mashed, smashed, battered, broken.

Destroy him, Spider! Sam found himself thinking, his blood ablaze with fury. *Rip him to pieces! For Annie! Do it for Annie! And me! Do it for us!*

In that moment, Sam wanted nothing – could think of nothing – except the ecstasy of seeing the enemy of all his happiness being systematically punched to death. He was dimly aware that Spider must be feeling exactly the same thing.

Do it for Annie! Do it for Annie!

Annie.

Her name was like cold water dashed into his face, bringing him back to his sanity.

Murder, he thought. *I'm witnessing a murder.*

And then: *You're a copper, Sam. Act like one.*

And then: *Annie would be disgusted to see you revelling in this violence. Stop this fight, Sam. Do it for her – do it for Annie – be a man – be a real man, not a bloody caveman – stop it, stop it, stop the fighting – do it for Annie!*

He ran his hand over his face, shook his head to clear, and moved forward to stop the fight. It had gone on long enough.

But at that very moment, Patsy decided it had gone on long enough too.

CHAPTER NINETEEN

AN EVEN HOTTER SHOWER

Patsy was sagging, slumped up against the side of one of the caravans, his head lolling as he absorbed a ferocious pounding from Spider – and then, without warning, he was battering Spider with his small, hard fists, lunging powerfully forward, driving Spider backward with bone-breaking strength.

He was playing possum! Sam thought, aghast, keeping his distance. *Patsy was swallowing all those punches whole – he was just toying with Spider, lulling him into a false sense of superiority ... just like he lulled* me.

Spider was thrown hopelessly off-guard by Patsy's sudden revival. He took a terrifying cannonade of fast, shuddering punches to the side of his head, his chest, his stomach, his rib cage, which sent him staggering and veering wildly until he slammed against one of the caravans and slithered down it, half senseless. He left behind him a huge smear of blood shaped uncannily like Australia.

Patsy loomed over Spider and smothered him with his whole body, like he meant to absorb him; he clamped his arms around Spider's body and squeezed, throwing his head back and roaring as he did so. Spider made no sound; his mouth opened wide, the blood vessels in his face and neck swelled and stood out. Sam saw the spider tattoo along his neck rippling and bulging, saw the veins thrusting out from beneath it, but the only sound that came from Spider was a muffled, sickening crunch.

With a cry, Patsy hurled Spider to the ground, and at once he planted one of his heavy, steel-capped boots onto the back of Spider's neck and drove his face down into the mud.

Sam found he was frozen. An inner voice was screaming at him – *get in there, you're a copper, break that fight up, nick Patsy before he kills Spider, do something!* – but his body refused to react. The horror of what he had seen had locked his joints, stiffened his muscles, unmanned him.

All around, he could hear the bellowing of excited men as they jostled and clambered to get a better view of the action in the arena. They drummed their fists against the sides of the caravans, creating a deafening timpani in every direction.

His foot still planted on Spider's neck, Patsy flung his arms into the air and roared. The crowd of men roared back. The lights of the fairground flashed in the sky beyond the confines of the arena, but to Sam they seemed to be flames lashing and whipping against the night; the low clouds reflected the smouldering glow of great lava flows that spread sluggishly across the face of the planet; the city itself was on fire, the buildings falling, the pavements melting, the very ground itself erupting in shattering bursts of hot lava and fragmented clinker. A million black balloons bobbed against the sulphurous sky.

Sam covered his eyes with his hands, forced himself back from this hellish vision, forced himself to be sane. Furiously, he opened his eyes again and glared about. The lights of the fairground were just that – coloured lights – and the city was no longer burning and dying. It had been nothing; another of the Test Card Girl's phantom visions – indeed, would he now glimpse the brat's face staring sadly at him from the men in the crowd?

I don't give a damn if she's there or not. Spider's under my protection, and Patsy O'Riordan will not kill him. I will not permit it. I will stop it – NOW.

Before he had a chance to lose his nerve, Sam strode forward with the intention of – somehow – arresting Patsy and calling for police back-up.

But now Patsy was glaring right at him, his massive

torso rising and falling with every breath, his tattoos glistening beneath a sheen of sweat and blood. His eyes blazed. If he was still just Patsy O'Riordan, or if he had become some other creature, the Devil in the Dark itself, Sam could no longer tell. The two monsters had, in Sam's eyes at least, become one. His heart quailed. He thought of Annie, told himself that it was he and he alone who stood between her and the evil intentions of this ogre. He was the thin blue line that defied the advance of chaos.

'Patsy O'Riordan, I'm arresting you on suspicion of the murder of Denzil Obi. You do not have to say anything, but anything you do say may be taken down and used in evidence against you.'

The men whooped, jeered, brayed, hooted. Something was thrown into the arena, landing heavily next to Patsy, but Sam's attention remained on that inked and inhuman face.

'You're coming with me, O'Riordan. You're nicked.'

Patsy leant over and picked up the object that had been thrown at his feet. It was a white plastic carton containing a transparent liquid.

'Get your foot off Spider's head, O'Riordan. That man needs an ambulance.'

Patsy unscrewed the cap of the carton and started sloshing the liquid onto Spider's back and legs, dousing him.

284

'Don't make me use force with you, O'Riordan,' Sam heard himself say. 'Come quietly. I'm warning you.'

Emptying the carton, Patsy cast it carelessly aside. It was then that Sam was struck by the chemical stink of liquid paraffin. Pasty began groping in his trouser pocket for something. The men gawping into the arena from all sides had fallen silent. Nobody moved. Nobody blinked. Distant screams and laughs and music reached them from the fairground as Patsy produced a cigarette lighter.

'O'Riordan,' said Sam, his voice low and even, completely devoid of emotion. 'Patsy. Stop.'

'Ten years he 'ad this coming,' said Patsy, his voice husky. Still panting, he fixed Sam with his pale eyes. 'You know what 'im and Denzil did to me.'

'I know. But we don't discuss it here, like this. We discuss it back at the station, like men.'

Patsy shook his head slowly: 'I knew what you wanted, right from the start. I knew you wanted to bang me up for Denzil.'

'Of course I want to bang you up for Denzil. You killed him.'

'Right.'

Patsy was flicking the lighter, trying to get a flame, and Sam realized then that reasoning with him was hopeless. He didn't give a damn if it was one murder he went down for or two, or a hundred, or more – it was all the same to him. For ten years he had nursed his hatred of

Denzil and Spider; for ten years he had looked forward to his revenge; and not once in all that time had he given so much as a thought to the consequences of killing two men. No threat of prison would deter him, or even give him cause for second thoughts. Such thoughts failed to register on Patsy's inner radar. All he knew was that he wanted payback, and that he would get it.

'*It's what the underworld's like,*' Stella had said, back in the Lost & Found Room. '*Fights that get fixed, fellas making off with winnings what aren't theirs, blokes paid to bust other bloke's hands. It's the way it is. Betrayal and revenge.*'

Betrayal and revenge. That was it. Nothing else. In Patsy's simplistic world of men and violence, that's all there was: betrayal and revenge, turning forever on a wheel, over and over to the end of time.

As the flame sprang from the lighter and danced there, cupped by Patsy's small, narrow, iron-hard, murderous hand, Sam all at once found his thoughts flowing very clearly through his mind:

Nothing I can say will stop Patsy burning Spider in front of me. But my duty is to stop him. If words and reason mean nothing to him, then I will have to use force. Regardless of the odds ranged against me, I have no choice. I simply have no choice.

Sam aimed a swift kick. It struck Patsy's hand and sent the lighter flying. But at once Patsy lunged at him.

Sam flung himself away, landing in the mud and scrambling frantically to his feet – or *tried* to. He felt his boots skidding and sliding on the boggy ground. The wet ground swallowed his hands and held them like glue.

With incredible calm, Sam found himself thinking: *will he kick me to death or punch me to death?*

Glancing round, he caught a fleeting glimpse of Ray and Chris, peering in at him between two caravans. Chris's one good eye was wide and fearful. Ray spat out a mouthful of blood and bared his teeth, cursing his impotence to break free from the hands that held him and help his fellow officer.

Helpless, thought Sam. *We're all helpless.*

He felt Patsy's hands clamp like vices on his shoulders and haul him with terrible, inhuman strength up out of the mud.

Ah – he's going to punch me – over and over, like he did to Denzil.

Sam was turned roughly around, and he found himself nose to nose with Patsy. He could smell the man's breath, hot and cloying as it gushed over him. It reeked of excrement.

This close, he doesn't look like a human being at all. Every bit of him is disfigured – his nose is flat and broken – his mouth is misshapen and ragged – his ear's just a scrap of flesh hanging from the side of his head – and his skin ... it's green ... green and blue from all that ink

... Is this the last face I'll ever see? Will I manage to think, for one last time, clearly and precisely, of Annie, before this monster finishes me off entirely? And after that, what then? Will he go after Annie? Whatever that Devil is that has come out of the darkness for her, it has found its expression in the body of Patsy O'Riordan – and I cannot stop it. I cannot defeat it. It will kill me ... and then it will go after Annie ... and I cannot bring myself to imagine the hell it intends to drag her to ...

'I'm sorry, Annie,' he said, just as Patsy clamped his hands around Sam's throat. And as his windpipe was squeezed shut, and he felt the blood bulging in his tongue and bursting in his temples, he thought: *Maybe the guv can do what I can't ... maybe the guv can do what I can't ...*

There was a blur of movement, and the sense of heavy impact, and all at once Sam found himself sprawled on the mud, gasping air greedily into his lungs. Beside him, reeking of paraffin, lay Spider, leaking blood into the damp soil.

In the next moment, he was surrounded by shouting and rushing and violent action. Sam scrubbed at his eyes, tried to clear them of the swirling patterns that filled his vision, and blinked stupidly this way and that. He saw Patsy staggering strangely across the arena, lashing at something on his back. It took a moment for Sam to realise that the something was a man – very short, very stocky, with cropped grey hair and a fierce, lined face.

I've seen that face before ...

'Dermot,' he croaked out loud. 'Dermot ... from the gym!'

The short but hard-as-nails trainer from Stella's Gym battered Patsy's head with astonishing force, rattling his skull, sending him lurching and staggering until he crashed against one of the caravans and toppled over. Patsy smashed into the mud like a chunk of falling masonry – but Dermot clung on, firing his fists with precision into the bullet-like head as if he meant to crack it open like a monstrous, ink-stained egg.

And now Sam was aware of the arena shaking all about him. The caravans lurched and shuddered as men fought and struggled on every side. He saw Ray break free from the man who held him, turn sharply, and throw a punch. He saw Chris ducking behind Ray and defending himself from the flying elbows of fighting men. And then he saw the guv.

Sam's heart leapt. Gene strode magnificently into the arena, planting his patent leather loafers into the mud heedless of how it soiled them. He still looked like a circus clown, with half his face black from bruising – and yet to Sam he appeared as an avenging angel arrived in a cloud of wrath.

Moustache-man loomed up behind him, balled his fist – and then went down as Gene's elbow rammed into his solar plexus.

'No time for playing mud pies, Tyler. We got a shout. Ain't you noticed?'

CHAPTER TWENTY

PRINCESS

The caravans rocked on their suspensions as all around him big men clashed with other big men. Sam saw faces that he seemed to recognise.

'The lads from the gym!' Gene declared, reaching down and hauling Sam to his feet. 'Better than the Special Patrol Group.'

'The gym?'

'Stella's Gym, you dope. You didn't expect me to turn up here empty handed, did you?'

'I didn't expect you to turn up here at all, Guv. How the hell did you know?'

If Gene had felt inclined to respond to Sam's question, he got no chance as two huge fairground roustabouts burst out of the melee and hurled themselves at him.

Gene caught one with a bone-crunching haymaker, delivered square-on and pulping the brute's nose like a squashed tomato. It was enough to send him slithering into the mud, senseless – but his companion, a huge brawny bastard in jeans and scuffed cowboy boots, dropped his head and charged like a bull, ramming into Gene at full speed and lifting him clear off his feet. Cowboy locked his arms around Gene's body as the guv'nor, carried along, rained hopeless blows on his back. Together, the two men slammed into the side of one of the painted caravans. Gene's bruised face grimaced. Cowboy released him, but only long enough to jab two rapid blows into the guv's guts, knocking the breath clear out of his lungs. In the next moment, Cowboy clamped his hands around Gene's throat – but instead of throttling him, he began twisting and straining, trying to snap Gene's neck.

Seeing his guv in trouble all at once cleared Sam's head and renewed his energies. Up he jumped, springing forward and looping his arm around Cowboy's neck. He wrenched hard – and again – and then yet again, harder still, hard enough to force Cowboy to release Gene and deal with Sam instead. Sam found himself staring up into the broad, sweating face of this bear-like man, his bushy brows knotted, his uneven teeth bared, his small, narrowly spaced eyes glittering with a brutish, dangerous light.

He's going to rip me to pieces, Sam thought very

clearly, everything going into slow motion the way it does in those split seconds before a car crash.

Cowboy's face drew closer – and then changed. His eyes went round. So did his mouth. His nostrils flared wildly. The blood drained from his cheeks. And from his throat issued a strange, high-pitched, girlish sound that built to a cracked crescendo.

'OooiioiiiyeeeioooOOOOOOOOOYOI!'

For a moment, Sam could not make sense of what he was seeing. Cowboy's hands were thrust between his own legs, like he was desperate for a pee; his face was drawn into a ridiculous Larry Grayson-ish expression; he began hopping and jigging, stamping his leather boots into the mud like he was beating out a squelchy tattoo.

And then, Sam glimpsed the guv's hand thrust between Cowboy's legs and firmly clamped onto the crotch of his denims. It was a merciless hold. Cowboy danced and howled, but he could not free himself.

Gene twisted, wrenched, and then – with a final crushing clenching of his fist – delivered the agonizing *coup de grace*. Sam winced just to behold it. Cowboy went down, whimpering in the mud, nursing his crumpled manhood.

'Like two seedless grapes and a pickled gherkin,' sneered Gene, glancing at the palm of his hand before wiping it in disgust on his shirt.

All about them, the boxers were starting to overpower and subdue Patsy's beefcake heavies, grappling them to the ground, clamping them into painful arm-locks that squeezed the tears from their eyes. Ray, his moustache red with blood so that he resembled some kind of Viking, was blazing; enraged and indignant, he turned on Ponytail, launching a punch so hard that it flung Ponytail back like he'd been struck by a mortar shell. Sam saw Moustache-man being thrown down into the mud by a barrel-chested fighter, and one-eyed Chris leaping on him at once, sitting on Moustache-man's chest and pinning him there, triumphant. It was clearly payback time for the boys from CID.

Sam turned his attention back to the inside of the arena. Patsy was slumped in a battered heap against one of the caravans, blood streaming from his nostrils and even dripping from the tatty remains of his ear. Dermot had dished out a superhuman beating to him, and now stood panting and glowering beside his fallen foe.

Nearby, still wet with paraffin, Spider was blearily lifting his head from the mud and peering drunkenly about.

'You still with us, Spider?' Sam called to him.

Spider murmured something incoherent through swollen, bloodied lips.

'Spider's still breathing,' said Gene. 'Time to collar O'Riordan.'

'I sort of already have,' said Sam. 'I've cautioned him, so technically he's nicked.'

'Well that's just delightful!' Gene declared, rubbing his hands together like a hungry man in a carvery. 'We can have him for the attempted murder of Spider, and figure out how to pin the Obi evidence to him at our leisure. Plus, I've just gotten to crush a bloke's bollocks. Oh, I do so love my work, Samuel, some days I just *do*!'

Sam thought of Annie, who even now was over at Patsy's caravan, working on Tracy, persuading her to testify against the murderous brute who held her so ruthlessly in his power. He knew in his heart that she would manage it. The Denzil Obi case was as good as closed.

And Annie's away from all this trouble, he thought. *Thank God for that.*

Dermot wiped his hands together like a craftsman finishing up after a job. He strode over to Gene and planted himself squarely in front of him. The two men eyeballed each other, and Sam recalled the intense animosity – bordering on outright violence – that had flared up between them when they had first encountered each other in the gym.

Dermot glared. Gene narrowed his eyes. Sam willed his guv'nor to say something civil.

'Okay,' said Gene at last. 'You did a good job – for a Paddy midget.'

'If you want to learn how to take a punch like a man, pop by and see me at the gym,' said Dermot. And when he saw Gene's one unbruised cheek flush with anger, he allowed himself the flicker of a smile and sauntered off to check on his boys.

Gene glowered after Dermot, muttering: 'Legs like a bloody hamster ...'

'Show some manners, Guv,' put in Sam. 'We owe him one.'

But Gene was in no mood to get sentimental. He bellowed out: 'Raymond!'

Ray's face, bloodied but fierce, appeared.

'Right here, Guv!'

'Call in for some plod! Tell 'em to find a couple of paddy-wagons that actually work so we can start carting off this bunch of bozos.'

'Me radio's buggered, guv. Some pikey trod on it.'

'Then use Chris's.'

'Mine's buggered too, Guv!' Chris piped up, still sitting on Moustache-man like he was afraid he'd float away. 'Same pikey what did Ray's.'

'Then find a phone, Christopher, for God's sake!' Gene bellowed. 'We've got this monkey-crew locked down, we can spare you for twenty minutes while you find a phone box.'

As Chris reluctantly clambered off Moustache-man and went padding off into the night, Sam suddenly caught sight of Stella standing just beyond the confines of the arena. Wrapped in fake furs, her white stiletto heels sinking into the mud, she observed the last of the fighting with wide eyes and wet lips. She ran a leather gloved hand down over her belly towards her-

I do NOT want to witness this!

Sam looked away – and cried out at what he saw. Or rather, at what he *didn't* see.

'He's gone!' he gasped. And then: 'They've *both* bloody gone!'

Gene span round. A smear of blood against the side of a caravan was all that remained of Patsy; an imprint in the mud was all that was left of Spider.

'Where'd they go?!' Sam yelled out, but everybody had been too preoccupied fighting and battering and generally smashing the crap out of Patsy's boys to notice. Sam cursed and grabbed Gene's arm. 'Come on, Guv!'

'*Off* the camelhair, Tyler!'

'We've got to get to Patsy's caravan. Annie's there. If Patsy turns up there … Jesus, Guv, let's *go!*'

He clambered from the arena and began to run across the open ground, telling himself that Patsy had scarpered, that he'd clear off, disappear, that Annie was safe. Labouring through the soft, sticky mud, he became aware of Gene loping along beside him.

'Tell me, Guv,' he panted as they ran. 'What the hell happened back there?'

'What you *think* happened? Uncle Genie rode in with the cavalry.'

'Cavalry? You mean naughty Stella and her dodgy boxers? Guv, you're a DCI, you've got *proper* cavalry. We've got trained officers for this sort of thing.'

Gene snorted contemptuously as he jogged along: 'I crawled straight from my sickbed to save your scrawny arse, Sam. I was pushed for time. You know how chuffin' long it takes rustling up enough boys for a shout like this. You get 'em together and they all start squabbling over the truncheons. You pile 'em in the van and it don't bloody start. Then when you *do* finally get there, half of 'em turn out to be pink-bollocked pansies.'

'So you swung by Stella's Gym instead. That was crazy, Gene, even for you.'

'Any port in a storm, Sammy-boy,' Gene gasped back. All this running about was starting to take its toll on his nicotine-encrusted lungs. 'Stella was most obliging.'

'I'll bet she was.'

'Meaning?'

Sam didn't have the breath or the inclination to answer. Whatever chemistry there was between Gene and Stella, he wanted no part of it. Spider's life had been saved, Patsy's mob of heavies had been neutralized, and Sam and Gene were now free to concentrate on nailing Patsy. That, when all said and done, would have to count as *a result* – at least in this particular case it would. With Sam at the helm, the operation had proceeded to go monumentally awry. He had to admit that Gene had indeed saved the day.

Struggling for breath, Sam asked: 'How *did* you know to come here, Gene?'

'Tip off.'

'From who? It was Ray, wasn't it! I bloody knew it. He wasn't happy you being away, Guv – he was like a dog without its master.'

'I *am* the master, Tyler, but you're thinking of the wrong dog. It weren't Ray. It were DI Bristols.'

'Annie? It was *Annie* who spoke to you?!'

'Discussion for another time, Sammy-baby,' growled Gene, hawking up and gobbing out a huge pellet of discoloured phlegm.

Up ahead they could see the caravan. There were lights in the windows.

Panting and streaming with sweat, Sam and Gene lumbered up – and as they did, they were met with frenzied barking. Princess dashed at them, slobber frothing around her muzzle, her teeth bared and snapping, her eyes wild. She reached the limit of her chain and was brought to a sudden, clanking stop. Straining, she clawed at the ground and howled furiously. Sam noticed that the C-90 cassette was still dangling from her collar.

With Princess holding ground between them and the caravan, Sam and Gene hung back, keeping clear of the wild jaws.

'Annie!' Sam cried. 'Annie, are you okay in there?!'

'Nobody in there, you bastards ...'

It was Patsy. He appeared like a huge, blank patch of darkness, stepping out from behind the caravan and standing by the post to which Princess's chain was clamped. Blood flowed down his face. He wiped it away slowly with the back of hand.

'You still standing?' intoned Gene. 'You're like one of them elephants too thick to know when it's dead.'

'*I* don't go down so easy,' Patsy growled back.

Gene bristled. But Sam was in no mood for macho exchanges.

'Patsy, it's over,' he said. 'You're nicked. No point running. And no point hurting anyone else.'

Patsy eyes glinted in the darkness.

He's not complying, Sam thought. *He's going to fight it out to the bitter end.*

'You said there's nobody in that caravan,' he said. 'Where's Tracy? Patsy, where is she?'

'She's supposed to be 'ere,' Patsy breathed, his voice barely human now. He sounded like an ogre speaking from the shadows. 'She's supposed to be '*ERE!*'

Sam glanced about frantically.

Annie's got more sense than to stay put here. She's taken Tracy and cleared out. But where?

The fairground was flashing and roaring just beyond the parked trailers and caravans, brimming with the sound of people.

She's gone where it's crowded. Safer there. Easier to hide. More chance of help if Patsy turns up getting heavy.

Patsy bellowed wordlessly, the rage crackling about him like an electrical charge. He grabbed hold of the stake to which Princess was chain and wrenched it from the ground. As it became free, so did Princess.

'Look out, Guv!'

The Rottweiler sprang, dragging the chain and post with it. As Sam dived away, Gene threw a punch at the hound, catching it on the jaw and cracking its head to the side. Princess yelped, landed awkwardly, and then scrambled back up, more furious than before.

'Patsy, you bastard!' Sam yelled, but Patsy was already loping away towards the lights of the fairground, towards Tracy – and Annie. 'If you touch her ...! *If you damn well touch her*!'

He lunged forward, meaning to run after Patsy, but all at once Princess was on him, sinking her teeth into his arm. Sam screamed and battered at the beast's muzzle with his fist, wildly hollering *bastard, bastard!* as if it were Patsy himself he was fighting.

A white tasselled loafer – soiled, but operational – connected hard with Princess's arse, but the pain and rage just made her clamp her jaws all the tighter. Sam clawed at her frothy snout, but it was solid and implacable as a sprung bear-trap.

'Gene! It's chewing my bloody arm off! Gene!'

The pain was extraordinary. Blood was starting to run down the leather of his jacket. It felt as if the dog's fangs had pierced all the way down to the bone.

Gene loomed up out of nowhere. In his hands he held the post to which Princess was tethered. For a moment, Sam thought he would skewer the beast with the sharp end, transfixing it like it was a vampire – but instead, he thrust the point between Princess's jaws, working it in like it was a crowbar, and then, in a single movement, wrenched that terrible muzzle open.

Sam felt the fangs sliding out of his flash and scrambled backwards, clutching his arm to staunch the blood. He saw Gene advancing, jabbing at Princess with the pointed end of the post like it was a spear. Snarling and snapping, the beast retreated, backing up the steps that led into the caravan. Here it chose to stand its ground, its hackles bristling, its muzzle frothing, surrounded by the spotless furniture and immaculately arranged knick-knacks of its master. Without warning, the hound sprang forward, but Gene booted the caravan doors shut straight in its face. He plunged the spiked-end of the metal stake into the ground and thrust the top of it against the door, wedging it firmly shut. Still chained to the stake, Princess went crazy, slavering and clawing to get out, muzzle appearing frantically at the edge of the door, but she was well and truly trapped.

Gene glared and said: 'Sit. Stay.' Then he turned to

Sam and, without sympathy, growled: 'If you've gone and lost a bloody arm, Tyler ...'

'I'm okay,' grunted Sam, his teeth gritted against the pain. 'Never felt better. Now let's not waste any more bloody time!'

Together, they made off after Patsy O'Riordan, whilst behind them Patsy's neat, prim little caravan rocked and howled.

CHAPTER TWENTY-ONE

GHOST TRAIN

Sam and Gene went blundering into the crowds milling around at the fair. Heaving and shoving, they fought their way between shooting ranges and candyfloss stalls and fun houses.

'Where the hell is he?!' hissed Sam, glaring about him.

'Hey! Anyone seen a bastard?!' Gene cried out.

'Bald bastard?' a kid in a woolly hat piped up, chomping on his toffee apple. 'Looks like a monster?'

'Aye, that's him.'

'Went that way, mate.'

Gene flicked him a fifty pence piece and launched off in the direction the lad was pointing. Sam shoved past him and took the lead.

They saw Annie. She was looking about anxiously.

Then they saw Tracy, clinging tightly to Annie's hand like a frightened child. They were standing together outside the ghost train; above them, a huge painted steam locomotive was tearing through a deserted station, ghosts and ghouls and living skeletons pouring from its funnel, scaring the crap out of the poor station master and sending him running for his life.

Sam called out to Annie, but she didn't hear him. He roughly heaved a young family out of the way and struggled towards her.

Patsy's bald and ink-stained head gleamed amid the crowd. With both arms he was cleaving his way through the punters at the fair, recklessly, making straight for the ghost train.

He's after Tracy. And Annie too. He knows I set him up, that this whole thing was a sting – and all he can think of is revenge. He knows Tracy can testify against him, so he'll rip her limb from limb. And when Annie tries to stop him, he'll kill her too. He doesn't care about consequences or repercussions. All he wants is to kill them. Kill them both!

Was it this that the Test Card Girl had been hinting at all along? Was this the moment she had forecast, the unhappy ending to the Sam and Annie story? Would the Devil in the Dark lay its murderous hands on her, and throttle her, before Sam got anywhere close enough to stop it? Was tonight about to become the worst, the most evil, the most tragic night of his life?

'Gene!' Sam cried. 'Get to them! Get to Annie and Tracy before *it* does!'

He didn't notice that he had referred to Patsy O'Riordan as *it*. In his exhaustion and pain and fear, he was thinking of that lumbering, painted monstrosity not as a man, but as the Devil in the Dark.

At that moment, there was a shriek and a commotion. Princess burst into the crowd, gnashing and snapping crazily left and right, froth flying from her wild muzzle. People screamed. The crowd rushed chaotically outwards in every direction, like waves radiating across violently disturbed water. Princess bounded about, insane in her fury, the chain clanking and clanging behind her, the stake she was tethered to gouging furrows in the mud.

A terrified surge of people threw Sam off balance and hurled him down into the mud. At the same time, it drove Gene backwards, slamming him against the wooden wall of an amusement arcade that bore the huge, lascivious face of an airbrushed babe in heart-shaped sunglasses. Sam struggled to right himself, but the panicking crowd buffeted and battered him.

And then, without warning, he glimpsed a flash of white between the running legs and flying mud. It was the glimmer of a patent leather stiletto. Above it swung a hem of fake fur, and a flash of leopard print.

Like a cheap and slaggy Angel of Mercy, Stella stood

motionless and serene amid the confusion. Princess went raging past her, and as the beast bounded by, Stella crouched down and took hold of something. In the next moment, Sam saw Princess racing towards him, her jaws savaging the air, her eyes rolling insanely – and then, as if hit by a magic spell, the hound shot backwards, her paws lifted off the ground, and away she sailed into the night sky.

Stella smiled a slow, sly, lipsticked smile as she gazed up at her handiwork. She had wedged the post into one of the struts of the Ferris wheel. As the wheel went up, so did Princess, dangling from the chain around her neck that had suddenly tightened like a garrotte. Princess gave a wild, pitiful, strangled cry, twitched, then went limp. The C-90 cassette at her throat snapped under the pressure and the magnetic tape spooled away on the breeze, like the hound's black soul leaving its body.

The crowd had formed a clearing, with Stella in the middle of it. She turned and observed Gene, her eyes glittering.

'Set a bitch to catch a bitch,' she observed.

'Remind me to punch your lights out later for that, luv,' said Gene, straightening his collar. 'I owe you one.'

Stella's cheeks flushed and her eyes glistened. She ran her tongue across her upper lip like she was licking off cream.

But Sam had no inclination – no inclination and no time – to witness this mating ritual. He was already racing towards the ghost train, hollering at Gene to move it, move it, *move his arse*.

Annie had pulled Tracy up the steps that led to the ghost train. The little carts were bumping and rolling along on the tracks, through the swing doors and into the ride. At the sight of Patsy, Annie yanked Tracy by the hand, dragging her between two of the carts and then through the swing doors. They vanished inside the ghost train.

Moments later, Patsy bounded up the steps, hurled two carts aside, and disappeared inside after them.

Now it was Sam and Gene's turn. They raced up the steps, shoving the last few frightened punters aside, and made for the swing doors. The painted Mouth of Hell greeted them – and together, they barged through it into the pitch blackness beyond.

Sirens howled, klaxons blared. A flash of light revealed a mummy in ragged bandages. An axe swung. Spiders dangled from above. A coffin lid creaked open and, bathed in sickly green light, a rotting hand emerged.

'Annie!' Sam yelled.

'Don't be a prat, Tyler!' Gene hissed in his ear. 'She's bloody hiding!'

In the eerie, ever changing lights of the ghost train, Sam saw him – saw *it*. Perhaps the pain from his mangled arm had clouded his brain; perhaps all this running and fighting and shouting had stressed him into a state of hallucination; perhaps he was mad ... or perhaps he was seeing more clearly than he ever had before, seeing past the veils and illusions of daily life and glimpsing something deeper, something darker, some terrible vision of ultimate reality. Whatever the hell was happening, what he saw was not Patsy O'Riordan, but a man in a black Nehru suit.

At the sight of that familiar apparition, Sam's heart froze. A sense of mindless panic threatened to overtake him and send him running crazily out of the ghost train and away through the fairground. The terror was irrational, instinctive, overpowering.

I will not run! I will be a man! I will NOT run!

Coloured light bulbs flashed and fizzed, revealing the Nehru man's monstrous head in shifting hues of red and green and purple; for a moment, it seemed as if the man in the suit was even more covered in tattoos than Patsy – but then Sam saw hints of movement, the squirming of maggots nestled in the rotten flesh, and he realised what he was seeing was a mouldering cadaver.

That's not part of the ride, he thought to himself with shocking clarity. *I don't know what that is ... but it's real. Whatever it is, it's real!*

The festering corpse turned slowly. It was aware of Sam. It wanted to see him, even though a flashing yellow bulb threw its sickly light into empty eye-sockets busy with earthworms.

In the next moment, the light shifted once more, and the scream of a siren split the air, and the corpse in the Nehru suit was Patsy O'Riordan, glowering furiously about, his narrow hands flexing as if he were about to smash the entire ghost train to splinters.

'Patsy!' Gene barked. If he too had seen that ghastly, mouldering horror, he certainly didn't *act* like he had. 'Pack it in! You're nicked!'

Patsy grabbed one of the empty carts and wrenched it clear off the tracks. He hurled it at Sam and Gene, who threw themselves out of the way as it crashed past them.

The noise and violence brought out a scream of terror from Tracy, who suddenly broke cover from behind a skeleton in a gibbet and made a break for it. Annie popped up, reaching hopelessly for her, trying to drag her back.

Patsy wheeled round, glaring at Tracy.

'Stop,' he intoned, his voice shockingly calm and level.

At once, in spite of herself, Tracy stopped. Coloured light bulbs flickered and flashed about her.

'Come 'ere,' said Patsy.

Tracy's eyes were two round circles of terror.

'Tracy, run!' Annie cried.

'I said come 'ere,' Patsy repeated.

Years of brutal conditioning took over. She could not resist. Tracy began shuffling towards Patsy.

'Okay, babes,' she muttered. 'I'm coming, babes.'

Annie flung herself between the two of them: 'Tracy, I said *run!*'

With terrible speed, Patsy lunged forward. Something snapped in Tracy, and she bolted, shrieking and howling. Patsy clamped his hands around Annie's throat and lifted her clear off the floor.

Sam and Gene kicked into action together. They powered forward and flung themselves at Patsy, launching themselves against his back like two men trying to bring down a tree. Sam battered at the rough, hard back, hurling punches at the rock-like head. He felt an elbow slam into him and send him crashing into a row of skulls that clattered about him in chaos. Leaping to his feet, he saw Gene being flung back and falling amid a confusion of bloodied metal spikes. Patsy was still holding Annie by the neck, letting her feet kick wildly in the air. Her face was bright red – but then, as the coloured bulbs went through their cycles, her face became pink, then green, then yellow, then blue. Patsy shook her. Annie clawed desperately at his hands, then her arms began to go limp and her eyes rolled upwards behind the fluttering lids.

One of the skulls Sam was lying amongst turned towards him. In the sad, frail voice of the Test Card Girl, it said: 'This isn't a ghost train, Sam. It really is Hell.'

Sam kicked the skull away. With a barbaric, inhuman cry, he jumped to his feet. Something rushed past him in the darkness. He ignored it and lunged at Patsy – and instead found Annie lying sprawled across the little railway tracks, unmoving. Instinctively, he flung his arms about her, not thinking of Patsy or why he had dropped her, not thinking of the thing that had raced past him in the dark, not thinking of the Test Card Girl, or Gene, or the crazy crashing and bellowing that was suddenly going on only a few feet away from him, or anything except *her,* his Annie, his love.

A pulse! She's got a pulse!

Placing his cheek to her mouth, he sensed a faint flicker of breath.

It was only then that he looked up. Patsy was lumbering and veering about madly, striking blows at a man who had leapt up and was clinging to him like a monkey. Sam glimpsed a spider tattoo on the man's neck; it stood out with sudden lividness in the garish red glare of an electric light bulb. The sharp stink of paraffin reached Sam's nostrils.

Spider hooked his legs around Patsy's knees. It was enough to topple him, bringing him crashing down into a mass of coloured light bulbs which at once popped and shattered. Electricity crackled. Sparks flashed. The paraffin ignited. The two men, locked together in their death struggle, went up like torches.

The sudden flames illuminated the interior of the ghost train, revealed the wires, the pulleys, the shoddy props, the cut-price sceneries. It was all cardboard, plastic, and fake cobwebs.

It's not Hell at all. It's just a ride.

Gene fought his way out from a tangle of papier maché dungeon, took one look at Spider and Patsy burning together, then turned sharply to Sam. He reacted to Annie's limp body in Sam's arms.

'Tell me she ain't snuffed it!' he barked.

Sam looked down. Annie's eyes struggled open. She coughed feebly. It was enough. It was more than enough.

'Let's get her out of here!' Sam cried, and Gene was right there, hoiking Annie up and, without grace or ceremony, throwing her over his shoulder. He loped between the little carts and burst back out through the Mouth of Hell, back into the open air, back into *life*.

Sam raced after him – then paused. He glanced back. Patsy was back up on his feet, burning. Spider was still clinging to him.

Spider knew what he was doing. He didn't want make it through this ... all he wanted was to take that bastard with him.

Ablaze, Patsy flailed about blindly, slowed, then sank to his knees and toppled over. Spider clung to him for several more seconds, then went limp, like a puppet suddenly losing its strings.

CHAPTER TWENTY-TWO

THE DEVIL IN THE DARK

They sat together in A&E. Sam cradled his mangled arm and winced; from time to time, he remembered the bruise along his jaw where Spider had punched him, and he winced at that too. Annie sat beside him, her eyes blood-shot, her hands gingerly cupping her darkening neck. Across from them, the stretched, blackened skin of Chris's massive black eye glistened painfully; and beside *him* sat Ray, picking crusts of dried blood from his moustache and from time to time testing his swollen nose to check if it was broken.

Standing looking down at them at all, his hands clasped behind his back like a stern teacher with his class, Gene glowered slowly from face to face, narrowing his eyes and tightening his jaw. His own face was still half-and-half, purpled all down one side so that he resembled some sort of carnival performer.

'Well, playmates,' he said at last. Stiffly, painfully, everybody turned their heads to look at him. 'Let's just hope the Queen don't swing by for a how'd-ya-do, us lot look like shite.'

Nobody said anything. One or two of them *couldn't*. But they knew that, in his way, Gene was expressing his relief that all his officers were, if not in one piece, then still alive and repairable. It was the nearest thing to sympathy any of them could expect from the guv. But it was enough.

Gene peered sceptically about at A&E.

'I've seen more than enough of the inside of this place already,' he muttered. 'All the medicine *I* need's down at the Arms. I'll be with Dr Nelson if any of you feel like joining me later.'

He swept his gaze over his battered team one last team, less out of expectation of a reply than from a grudging admission that he was proud of them. And then, without further ado, he turned on his heel and strode swiftly away.

'Know what?' said Chris suddenly, getting to his feet. 'I think I'll join him. Just a shiner, nothing life-threatening. Anyone else comin'?'

Ray flicked away a crust of dry blood and rose from his seat. He pinched his nose and gave it a tug: 'Nah, it ain't busted. A couple of stiff ones, that'll put us right. What about you two?'

Sam's arm was a mess and needed dressing. Annie could barely make a sound and was awaiting a neck X-ray.

'Stupid bloody question, really,' Ray admitted. 'Still – we'll keep a couple of places reserved for you. If you feel up to it.'

Together, Chris and Ray limped out.

Sam and Annie sat together, alone now except for the bustling nurses, the porters, the patients and their relatives going in and out of the waiting room. They didn't say anything, nor did they have to. They each knew what the other was thinking.

From across the other side of the waiting room there was sudden shouting. A large man was throwing his arms around, bellowing aggressively at the nurses who were trying to help him into a wheelchair. He was clearly drunk. He raised his fists, his thumbs tucked pathetically inside his clenched fingers.

'Get your 'ands off me, you dopey mares! I'll twat you right out, ya 'ear me? I'll smack the lot o' ya into next bloody week!'

Watching him, Sam felt nothing but a dull sense of boredom. He had had a bellyful of machismo. He could not even summon the interest to be appalled.

As the loudmouth threatened the nurses, he slowly

became aware of the three men who had come back in from outside, drawn to him by his raised voice. The three men stood over him, very close; one with a huge black eye, the second with a swollen nose and a moustache all crusted with congealed blood, the third sporting a bruise that covered half his face. In that moment the loudmouth, pissed as he was, sensed something, some power in these men that it was beyond him. He knew that he was on the very cusp of an unpleasantly physical encounter. He was out of his depth.

The fight draining out of him, he sat meekly in the chair.

'Thank you!' snapped a nurse at him, angrily throwing a blanket across his knees. And then, to the three men, she said warmly: 'Thank *you*.'

Without smiling, the man with the bruised face winked, tugged the lapels of his camelhair coat to straighten them, then turned on his heel and strode out into the night, his two loyal companions flanking him. Three men, in a man's world.

'I've brought you some grapes,' said Sam, setting them down by Annie's bedside.

They were in a side ward, nurses and medical staff bustling along the corridor just outside the door. It was mid-morning of the day after the showdown in the fair. Sam's arm was neatly bandaged and still reeked of TCP. Annie was propped up in bed, kept in for a day or so purely for observation, her neck a mass of deep purple bruises, but otherwise unharmed.

'Can you eat?'

'Very slowly,' Annie breathed, her voice hoarse and rasping. 'And only mushy stuff.'

'God, you sound sexy.'

Sam couldn't help himself. Annie rebuked him by threatening to punch his bad arm.

'Okay okay! Truce!' He smiled at her. 'For a moment last night, I thought I'd lost you.'

'What happened to Spider?'

'He's dead. So's Patsy.'

'And Tracy?'

'Don't try and speak, Annie. Rest your voice. Tracy's fine. Upset, but okay. She's been crying over Patsy all night apparently, saying she loved him. To be honest, I don't know if she means it or not. The girl's a mess. She needs help.'

Annie nodded, then winced.

'You tried to save her,' Sam said. 'You put yourself between her and Patsy. That was brave, Annie. I'm proud of you. It's the sort of thing that-'

Gently, she laid a finger on his lips to silence him. He took her hand, kissed it, and cupped it in his own.

'Let me say just one thing,' he said quietly. 'I think you'll sleep easier from now on ... now that Patsy's gone. I ... can't explain it. But I think I'm right.'

She waited for an explanation, but when it became obvious she wasn't going to get one Annie settled back against her pillows and closed her eyes, letting her body get on undisturbed with the task of repairing itself.

Sam was tempted to ask her about her sneaky manoeuvre behind his back, speaking to the guv about Sam's undercover operation and getting him involved. Why hadn't she confided in Sam about it? Had she thought he'd react badly, that his manly pride would be wounded at the thought he couldn't manage the operation without Gene?

What does it matter what her motives were? She did the right thing. God alone knows what would have happened if Gene hadn't turned up with reinforcements. She did the right thing to speak to him. She showed good sense. She acted like a good copper. What else matters?

He tucked her hand under the starched bed sheet, kissed her forehead, told her to get plenty of rest, and, with reluctance, left.

The fair was gone. The rides had been dismantled and hauled away. The common ground upon which they had stood was now just an empty patch of mud – except for the remains of the ghost train. What was left of it stood alone and forlorn, a burnt-out metal skeleton surrounded by flapping police tape and guarded by a single uniformed bobby.

Sam momentarily imagined Patsy's charred remains still smouldering inside.

No. What's left of Patsy's now in the morgue. There's no trace of him here – except ashes, perhaps, and some lingering stink of burning.

So. Was that it, then? Had the Devil in the Dark been destroyed?

'Well? Has it?' he asked out loud, waiting for a reply from the Test Card Girl. But no reply came.

I don't know what that Devil was, or where it came from ... and I don't know what the hell I saw last in the ghost train. A corpse ... a rotting corpse dressed up in a Nehru suit ... a festering body, and yet somehow alive and conscious. I'd seen that damned thing before, lurking about in the shadows, hovering on the edges of nightmares ... And Annie knew it too, had sensed it in dark dreams of her own. What the hell was it? Is it truly dead now? Was it destroyed in the fire? Gene didn't seem to notice it all. Perhaps it was just some sort of delusion. Perhaps it wasn't real.

He tried to believe that, but couldn't. He knew what he had seen. Like the Test Card Girl herself, that rotting, maggot-infested horror had been some manifestation from deep down within him, the product of some foul sewer of the subconscious where all the darkest parts of his psyche lurked and brooded. Did the Devil in the Dark represent some part of him that wanted to hurt Annie?

Is that what it all meant? Had he transferred that subconscious violence onto the form of Patsy O'Riordan, seen in him the embodiment of that barbaric, murderous fraction of himself?

Who knows what goes on the deep cellars of our minds, he thought.

Letting his mind be still for a moment, Sam tried to detect some hint of that demonic creature's presence – a tingle of fear, an icy sensation of dread, the suspicion that he was being watched by malevolent eyes. But he felt nothing.

Whatever the Devil in the Dark was, it's gone now. When Patsy burned, it burned too. I've purged myself of it. Exorcised it. I'm free. We are free, me and Annie. We are free.

He turned his back on the blackened remains of the ghost train, pulled his collar up to fend off a sudden chill wind, and began heading home. Up ahead, a group of lads were hanging about on the verge of the open ground, sharing cigarettes. As Sam passed them, one of them stepped out in front of him, blocking his way.

'Give us a light,' he said, his face and voice unfriendly.

'Sorry, don't smoke,' said Sam. As he tried to go by, the rest of the lads clustered around him, hemming him in. Sam sighed. 'Use your noodles, there's a copper just over there.'

'I said give us a light.'

'How old are you, son? You boys shouldn't be smoking.'

'And since when were you the boss of *me*?'

The boy jabbed at him, shoving Sam's chest.

He's testing me, seeing what I'm made of.

'Get on back to your mammies, lads, before I nick the lot of you,' said Sam gently. He made his way forward, found his path blocked again, but this time fixed the boy in front of him with a level, eye-to-eye stare. He didn't blink. The boy did. Moments later, the lads shuffled back. They were just a gaggle of bored kids, playing at being men.

Kids playing at being men …

Unhurried and unconcerned, he headed off along the street. What stopped him was the voice that suddenly called out to him. It was the same boy who had challenged him, but somehow his intonation had changed.

'That's the last time you turn your back on *me*, Sam Tyler.'

In that moment, the blood froze in Sam's veins. He felt that same panicked compulsion to run, run for his life, that he had felt in the gloom of the ghost train last night.

He span round. The boys were all standing in a loose group, staring at him, their leader casually lighting a cigarette.

'Who told you my name?' Sam asked. His heart was pounding. 'Who the hell told you my name?'

321

The boy drew on his cigarette, exhaled luxuriously, and said: 'I make it my business to know my rivals.'

'What do you mean, "rivals"?'

'You and my wife,' the boy said, his young eyes suddenly glinting with a very mature malice. 'You, Tyler ... and *my* wife.'

'Wh ... What the hell are you-'

'You think you got rid of me?' the boy hissed. 'Oh no. I'll keep coming at you, you cheating bastard. I'll keep coming at you until I've got my wife back ... *my* wife ... *mine.*'

The boy flicked his cigarette at Sam. It bounced off his chest in a shower of sparks.

His rage overcoming his terror, Sam lunged forward, heedless of the pain that at once shot through his bandaged arm.

The boys tore off, whooping and laughing, spreading out across the open ground, heading off in every direction – just a noisy group of scallies once more. They called back mockingly as they ran: *up yours, mistah! Come on then, nick us! Oooh, I'm brickin' meself!*

But the rage had gone out of Sam. In its place, he felt nothing but a cold, congealed dread. He looked back at the remains of the ghost train, and knew that whatever evil thing he had witnessed in there, he would witness again.

When the Test Card Girl appeared, stepping out from

behind the burnt ruins and standing innocently beside the bobby on sentry duty, Sam turned away in disgust and began walking. If she called to him, he didn't hear.

THE END
Gene Hunt will return in
BORSTAL SLAGS